DEATH BEFORE DR

SECRETS
OF THE
SWORD II

LINDSAY BUROKER

ACKNOWLEDGMENTS

Thank you for following along with Val and Zav's adventure. If you're eager to learn more about Chopper, and to see how humans and dragons plan differently for weddings, this is the book you've been waiting for. I hope you enjoy it.

Before you start, please let me thank my beta readers—Cindy Wilkinson, Rue Silver, and Sarah Engelke—and my editor Shelley Holloway. Also thank you to Luisa Pressler for the illustrations for this trilogy and Deranged Doctor Design for turning them into covers. Last, but definitely not least, thank you to Vivienne Leheny for narrating the audiobooks.

CHAPTER 1

T HE BOXING GLOVE POUNDED TOWARD my face like a jackhammer.
I dodged, the whisper of its passing whooshing in my ear, then slid in to throw two punches at Colonel Willard's side. She sprang back, my gloves only brushing her gi top, and turned her failed punch into an elbow strike. I dropped under it, rolled away, and sprang to my feet to face her again before she could rush in.

"That move gets Corporal Clarke every time," she grumbled her disappointment as we squared off again. "He claims to have the speed and agility of Baryshnikov."

"Baryshnikov fifty years ago or Baryshnikov now?" I asked.

"He didn't specify."

"Convenient."

Willard waved a glove to signal a break and headed to the benches and punching bags for her towel and water bottle. I followed, glad for a breather, though I would never admit it. Willard was a couple of years older than I and didn't have any elven blood to give her an advantage, so it battered my ego every time she outlasted me at some athletic endeavor. Never mind that she competed in triathlons and power lifting events in her free time.

"Are you ready for your trip to Dun Kroth?" Willard tossed me an ugly olive-green army towel.

We were training in the small gym in her unit's office in Seattle, where army decor and accoutrements seemed a requirement, despite the civilian setting. From the outside, the building claimed to be occupied by the IRS and appeared distinctly unmilitary. One had to step inside to notice the lack of beleaguered government clerks and stacks of tax forms. Not that many people bothered.

"Almost." I wiped sweat from my face. "I have to go shopping for a few more supplies."

"We've got MREs you can buy at cost."

"I was thinking more like chocolate and salami." Since I'd used my stash of apple-cider caramels to bribe the powerful fae queen to fix the magic tainting my sword, I was out of delicious rations.

"I see you stick to your health-food diet when you travel."

"Don't try to tell me MREs are health food. I well remember pounding people with the pound cake when I was in the army. They weren't just calorically dense. They were dense."

"True. I used to take my own food to the field."

"Organic wheatgrass smoothies travel well, do they?"

"You can get organic wheatgrass juice powder."

"How can you powder *juice*? Or make juice from *grass*?"

"The miracle of science."

I imagined Zoltan in the basement with fistfuls of grass and a mortar and pestle, then shook my head. Health food was scary. "In addition to shopping for snacks, I have to wait for Zav to get back to Earth. He's my ride, but he's off telling his family about the wedding."

"They care? I thought he'd claimed you as his *mate*—" Willard's dark eyes always twinkled when she used Zav's word for our relationship, "—months ago and that most dragons wouldn't recognize a human wedding as having any significance."

"Oh, they don't think it's significant, but he believes it will be a fun and festive event that they might want to attend."

"Uh huh. I've been meaning to talk to you about that." Willard propped a fist on her hip and gave me a frank expression. "When you asked me to help plan your wedding, I didn't think it would be... *atypical*."

"You didn't?" I touched my chest.

Even if she didn't agree with my daughter's assessment that I was weird, surely, she thought *Zav* was weird. He wasn't even from Earth.

"I knew *you two* were atypical, but I assumed you wanted a normal wedding. Church, priest, reception, rice, flower bouquets, etc."

"I was thinking outdoors instead of in a church, but the rest sounds fine." My first wedding had been when I was in the military, so it was very brief and very inexpensive. Thad and I hadn't been near our families and hadn't had much money. Even if I wasn't a girlie girl, I wouldn't mind a few frills this time around.

"An outdoor wedding in winter in Seattle. Sounds reasonable."

"Maybe under a pavilion. You know the ogres and goblins from the coffee shop think they're coming, right? Zav promised them meat carcasses from some animal that's a delicacy on another planet."

"That's not the only thing he's promising people," Willard said, her eyebrows drawing together. "Since he learned that I agreed to help you—don't forget you're supposed to catch that thief for me in exchange for this—he's been bringing me some odd requests. You need to talk to him. We're not going to have a *hunt* in the middle of the ceremony, nor will there be flying races. As fun as that sounds, your non-winged competitors would be at a disadvantage. He also seems to have attended a carnival at some point, because he believes there should be rides."

"Rides are fun," came a familiar voice from the doorway. Gondo, Willard's goblin assistant, walked in carrying a toolbox. "And goblins are resourceful, so don't think we can't compete. I could build a gyrocopter to race against a dragon."

"No rides and no races," Willard said firmly. "Thorvald's wedding will be right and proper. Or at least not embarrassing to her mother."

"Does that mean I can't have the DJ play Right Said Fred's 'I'm Too Sexy' when Zav walks down the aisle?" I asked.

"A *DJ?*" Willard looked scandalized, more at that than at the song choice. "I was thinking you'd want to hire musicians. A pianist at least."

"Can you play 'I'm Too Sexy' on the piano?"

"Why do I have a feeling that Zav's vision of a wedding might be in line with yours?"

"It's a mystery."

"I may have to sit you both down to watch wedding videos so you can see what's expected. My niece just got married and sent me a few hours of the footage."

"If you want to torture me, just punch me with your gloves."

"I would if you didn't skitter around so much. You're hard to hit."

"To the vexation of my many enemies."

Gondo waved a wrench. "I'm supposed to tell you that Captain Brisco wants to see you, boss. Something about the artifacts storage room."

Willard frowned. "We'll continue this discussion later, Thorvald." She headed for the door but paused to point at Gondo's wrench. "You're not planning to use that on something in my *gym*, are you?" She looked back at the racks of weights, kettlebells, punching bags, and mats.

Gondo looked thoughtfully toward one of the punching bags but smiled and shook his head. "Nope. Lieutenant Reed asked me to use my goblin ingenuity to fix a toilet that keeps running in the male locker room. Goblins don't use toilets, but I have downloaded schematics from the internet." He nodded, confident of his skills.

"Remind me to pick up an out-of-order sign from the supply room on the way," Willard muttered and headed out.

"Oh, the captain also asked to see the Ruin Bringer," Gondo called after her.

Willard paused and frowned back. "Why? Is one of the artifacts she brought in smoking ominously or throbbing with magical power?" Something about the look she gave me suggested this had happened before.

I held my hands up innocently. "I only kill the bad guys and bring their stuff for your people to examine. It's not my fault if you put it in the basement and strange things happen."

Gondo shrugged. "He didn't give me the details. He said I don't have a top-secret security clearance."

"That doesn't keep you from knowing about everything that happens." Willard waved for me to follow her.

"Goblins are resourceful."

"Goblins are snoops." Willard strode off down the hallway.

I grabbed my duster, weapons, and gym bag, though I wouldn't need the latter. It wouldn't be safe to take a shower in the women's locker room, not when it was located adjacent to the men's locker room Gondo would be working in.

"If goblins don't use toilets," I asked, jogging to catch up with Willard, "where does he go when he's working here? I've seen how much coffee he drinks. There's no way he holds it all day."

"I see you haven't come in the back way lately."

"I don't have a key for that door."

"There are two bushes that are dying by the steps. I suspect the soil grew too acidic."

"Ew."

Willard knocked and entered an office I hadn't been in before. Chunky, glasses-wearing Captain Brisco looked like someone who had to slide a five-dollar bribe to whoever ran the PT tests for the unit to ensure passing marks. But with three monitors competing for space on his desk and two wall-mounted televisions running news behind him, I trusted he made up for any physical lack with his intelligence-gathering abilities.

"Colonel." Brisco grabbed a remote and flicked one of the TVs from CNN to the view from a security camera. It displayed a couple of the wide aisles in the basement artifacts room, a place that reminded me of a cross between a library and a Costco, except that instead of giant tubs of pickles and mayo, the shelves held magical doohickeys, weapons, and massive handwritten tomes in other languages. "We have a problem."

"We heard about your toilet," I offered, "and that your repairman lacks experience with them. My condolences."

They both shot me humorless looks.

"One of the alarms went off in the artifacts room, and I got to the camera in time to see this." Brisco clicked his remote to rewind until the display showed a stocky woman in a dark-blue parka with the hood pulled up, a cheek and a hint of short black hair just visible in the profile shot.

"Is that the thief we've been trying to catch for two weeks?" Willard demanded. "And that Thorvald is supposed to hunt down for us?"

"I believe so, ma'am."

"I thought I'd be hunting her down on the dwarven home world," I said. "Didn't you say she's got a portal generator and was last seen disappearing through it?"

"Apparently, she's back," Willard said.

Our intruder reached for a shelf full of books but paused and glanced toward the camera long enough for me to make out dark almond-shaped eyes in a face broader than typical of Asian ancestry. Willard had mentioned that the thief might be part dwarf. She appeared to be in her twenties, but if she was part dwarf, she might be like me and older than she looked. Dwarves, like elves, lived longer than humans.

The woman threw powder toward the camera, and a yellowish cloud filled the air for a couple of seconds before the monitor went dark.

"It came back online five minutes later," the captain said, "but she was gone by then."

"It was annoying enough when she was stealing from *other* people," Willard said. "What did she take? And how did she get in? We have locks on the doors in addition to the alarms, magical and mundane, that should have gone off before she could get in. Did this just happen? I assume she didn't waltz in the front door."

"Maybe she came in the back," I said, "undeterred by the forbidding dead bushes."

"Will you be serious?"

"Is that a requirement of the job?"

"It should be." Willard turned her glower from me to the captain.

"We don't yet know how she got in or what she took." Brisco waved at the monitor, which was back to showing the artifacts room, the aisle now empty of visitors. "From the camera, it looks like the books were moved around, but I can't tell if she removed one or more."

"Have you got someone running an inventory to check?"

"Not yet. We can't get in. The door is locked and won't *unlock*. The keypad is working—it thunks, as if the deadbolt is turning—but the door won't budge. I thought someone with special blood could detect if something magical had been done to the door." Brisco looked at me.

"Special blood. I guess that's me."

"You're all kinds of special," Willard muttered.

"Maybe she just braced a chair against the doorknob."

"There aren't any chairs in there."

"Maybe she braced a sword against it."

"How would she have gotten out if she did that?" Brisco asked.

I shrugged. "How did she get in? Her portal generator?"

"Maybe. We don't know how to track her down and ask her." Willard's lips twisted in a sour expression. "That's why I'm putting *you* on the job. You have a dragon who can make portals and chase people to other worlds." Her lips shifted into a slightly different sour expression. "Assuming you can call him home, and he's done telling people about the races and hunts he thinks will happen at your wedding."

Captain Brisco raised his eyebrows at that.

"I can't call him home, but I'm sure he'll be back soon. We're mates, after all."

"Yes, I've heard how he enjoys spending time in the nest with you."

Brisco's eyebrows climbed even higher.

"Naturally. I'm amazing."

"Uh huh. Go take your special blood and check the door." Willard pointed at the video of the artifacts room.

Despite giving the order, she led the way out into the hallway, pausing to grab her pistol and holster from her office. I let her lead the way, but I would go first if we went inside. Fezzik, the magical, compact submachine pistol in my thigh holster, and Chopper, the even more magical sword in my back scabbard, were much better for dealing with otherworldly intruders than typical weapons.

Brisco joined us at the top of the stairs. He'd also armed himself.

When we descended to the basement and walked down the windowless cement-block hallway toward the artifacts room, the sturdy metal door started glowing a sickly green.

Willard swore, halted, and took several steps back, her hand dropping to her firearm.

"You needed me to let you know if there's something magic here, Captain?" I asked dryly.

"It wasn't doing that before." Brisco also took several steps back. "It looks radioactive."

"Don't worry. Thorvald will check it." Willard thumped me on the back. "She's already got a kid, and I don't think her dragon cares if she's fertile."

"Hilarious." It was my turn to shoot dirty looks. "He might object if I glow in the dark in bed."

"His *eyes* glow. He can't possibly be against photoluminescence."

Sighing, I walked forward, reminding myself that Willard was calling florists, ordering invitations, arranging seating charts, and essentially taking care of all the wedding minutiae that sounded like torture to me. I could check her glowing door for her.

I drew Chopper and, with the magic I'd been learning to use, formed a protective barrier around myself. Maybe it was overkill, but better safe than self-luminous.

I was three steps from the door when a female voice emanated from it.

"The Ruin Bringer carries the stolen sword of the Orehammer Clan. As a rightful descendant of the original crafter of the blade, I have come to reclaim it."

Chapter 2

"H ELL." I STARED AT THE door, though the voice didn't speak again.

A feeling of dread clunked into the bottom of my gut like a bowling ball. It was probably a scam—what were the odds that some Earth-born half-dwarf, or whatever that woman was, could be the descendant of the dwarven master enchanter, Dondethor, who'd made Chopper thousands of years ago? But I had claimed the sword after defeating its last owner in battle, not purchased it legitimately from some dwarf weapons dealer, so it was very possible—even likely—that my enemy had stolen it. As Zav himself had pointed out, that meant it wasn't rightfully mine.

Captain Brisco cleared his throat diffidently. "The door also didn't speak before."

"No shit," Willard said without diffidence. "Go poke it, Thorvald. See what happens."

"The last time I poked something magical, I ended up with a cut that wouldn't heal and a beacon on my sword that drew magical beings from a thousand miles."

"Your report said you struck the artifact with the intent of breaking it. That's not the same as poking it."

"I'm positive I didn't put that much detail in my report."

"I know you, and I read between the lines. Am I wrong?"

"I refuse to answer that question."

"I'm not wrong," Willard told Brisco.

Even as I argued, I walked forward with Chopper extended, not sure what else to do. The sword should protect me rather than acting as a conduit. It had before.

When its point touched the door, the blade flared a brighter blue, but nothing else happened. I didn't sense an increase in the amount of magic or any change from the door itself. The keypad on the wall wasn't glowing, so I risked stepping close enough to touch my finger to it. I didn't get zapped, but the door did radiate heat that was noticeable now that I was closer.

"What's the code?" I asked over my shoulder.

"Only two people in this building are authorized to know it, people with the highest-level security clearances." Brisco pointed to himself and to Willard.

I stepped aside and gestured for him to come forward and enter the code.

"3-6-3-2-9-9-8-7-2," he said.

"Way to defend national security," Willard told him.

"We can change it later. After we're sure the DNA in my balls doesn't get bent out of shape."

"It's magic, not radiation." I asked him to repeat the code and punched it in.

As he'd described earlier, a thunk sounded, as if the code had been accepted, but when I used Chopper to try to open the lever, the door didn't budge. I risked touching a finger to the metal surface. I didn't get zapped with magical energy, but it was hot enough that I jerked my hand back.

"It's toasty warm," I said. "Hopefully, that's a byproduct of the magic, not an indication that the artifacts room is on fire."

"There's not much in there that could burn," Brisco said. "Aside from the artifacts and weapons, it's all metal and cement."

I covered my hand with my sleeve and tried pulling on the latch. Nothing. Not the slightest bit of give.

"Not the byproduct," Willard said. "The magic must be intentionally heating the door."

I released the latch, the heat unpleasant even through my sleeve. "Why?"

"Go get a fire extinguisher, Captain," Willard said.

"Uh, all right. But if there was a fire inside, we would have seen flames or smoke on the camera."

"Not to put out a fire, to cool off the door with the carbon dioxide. It's probably not opening because it's heated enough to have expanded against the jamb."

"Ah, right." Brisco jogged for the stairs.

"Nobody reads science books anymore," Willard lamented.

"Not even your intel agents?"

"They're all about cryptanalysis and linguistics."

"I might be able to cool off the door. Chopper has three magical powers that I know how to access. And probably a lot more that I don't." I rested the flat of the blade against the door and whispered, "*Keyk.*"

The blade's blue glow shifted to an icy white. It might not be as effective as spraying the whole door down, but I tried to use my magic to will the sword to radiate its chill into the metal. Whether that would work or not, I didn't know. Magic was still new to me, and my half-sister Freysha had mostly taught me things that fell under her specialty of forest magic. Still, I'd managed to do a few other things by simply willing the magic in my blood to work. From what I'd seen, most magic was done by learning mental tricks to harness the magic in one's blood.

Footsteps sounded as Brisco tramped back down the stairs. The metal didn't seem to be radiating heat anymore, so I lowered Chopper and tried the lever again. This time, the door opened.

Brisco snorted and hefted a fire extinguisher the size of a SCUBA tank. "I'll just keep this in case we need to club someone."

"We might." My senses crawled as I peered inside, the interior hazy with something that looked like smoke but didn't smell like it. Fog? Mist? It didn't have a smell, at least nothing that I could distinguish from the mingling scents of bleach and musty books. "There's magic in there."

"There's a *lot* of magic in there," Willard said, "unless she stole *all* of our artifacts."

"It's something in addition to them." I could feel the cacophony of magical auras from hundreds of artifacts clashing against each other, as I always did when I walked into this room, but there was something else, something emanating from the back corner.

And had that fog grown denser since I'd opened the door? Shouldn't it have been the other way around? Whatever it was didn't flow out into the hallway like smoke would have.

Something about the fog or the magic made my chest tighten. I grimaced. My asthma had been better lately, since Zav irradiated the mold in our house, but it still reared its head when I got tense or emotional—or walked into a place with noxious air. My attempts to learn to meditate properly and ease my tension had not been successful.

Keeping my back to the others, I slipped my inhaler out and took a puff. Even though I hated using it in front of others—having anyone see that annoying weakness that I'd only developed in the last year—I'd learned not to put it off.

My skin tingled as I stepped into the doorway and the hazy air touched my skin. A strange feeling came over me, as if someone dangerous waited inside, and my heart rate quickened, pulse beating in my ears. It had grown so quiet that I had no trouble hearing its rapid thumps. The magic permeating the big storage room made me want to step back and close and lock the door.

"Hold on." I lifted a hand, aware of Willard a step behind me, her pistol drawn and pointed toward the ceiling, ready to bring to bear if we ran into the thief—or, more likely, a booby trap she'd left. If she'd been there, I would have sensed her. Unless she had a camouflaging charm similar to mine. That was possible, I realized. Even likely. The doors to the building were monitored, so the thief shouldn't have been able to saunter in during broad daylight. "I'm calling for back up."

"Zav?" Willard asked.

"He's still not on Earth." I touched the feline-shaped charm on the leather thong around my neck and summoned Sindari. "Think furrier."

The great silver tiger formed beside me in the doorway, a tight fit since he was over seven hundred pounds and his head came up to my shoulder. His green eyes closed to thoughtful slits, and he sniffed.

Where are we? He'd been in the building before but not in the windowless basement.

"Willard's office," I responded aloud.

It feels like a cursed shaman burial ground on the haunted world of Nagnortha.

"Sindari likes what you've done with the place," I told Willard, who knew Sindari could communicate telepathically with me.

"I bet. Are we going in?" Since Willard was mundane, she couldn't sense magic, but she ought to be able to see the fog and wonder what it meant.

"Is closing the door and forgetting this room exists an option?" I wasn't one to shirk from duty or hide from bad guys, but the thief had clearly set this up for me—how she'd known I was here, I didn't know—and it seemed dumb to stroll into a trap.

Maybe Willard thought so, too, for she considered her answer for a few seconds before replying. "We need to know what she took, and if she's still around, we need to capture her. She's been stealing a lot of priceless artifacts, magical and mundane, and she broke into a government facility and got a bunch of sensitive data off the hard drives there. Since she's believed to be from a rival nation, that's got my higher-ups twitchy. I can go in first." She tapped my shoulder. "If you think there's a trap set specifically for you."

I grimaced at the idea of a trap set for me going off and killing Willard. "Sindari and I will check it out. You and Brisco stay in the hallway."

I sense entities inside, Sindari told me.

Living beings? I stepped in and flicked the light switch. The fluorescents mounted on the ceiling remained dark. Naturally. I thought about activating my night-vision charm, but with the light flowing in from the hallway behind me, it would be too bright and hurt my eyes. Chopper's glow would guide me.

No, he said. *Malevolent entities.*

Like what? I remembered his comment about a haunted world. *Ghosts?*

Your language may not have an exact term, but along those lines, yes.

As I walked down the first aisle, Willard and Brisco stepped into the room behind me, both with weapons pointed into the darkness to the sides. So much for my suggestion that they stay in the hallway. Willard also wasn't the type to hide from bad guys. I trusted they were professionals and wouldn't shoot me.

Something brushed my cheek, and I swatted at it. Nothing was there. I kept walking, wanting to check out the strange magic coming from the back corner of the room. Thanks to the floor-to-ceiling shelving units, most full of items of all sizes, I couldn't see over there yet.

Another something brushed my forehead. Again, I found nothing when I probed my face with my fingers.

Sindari shook his head, as if a bug had flown in his ear.

Feels like cobwebs, I observed silently.

Yes. He sounded annoyed and prowled ahead of me, turning toward the corner when he reached the aisle running parallel to the back wall.

"That's the spot where she was standing when the video went out." Brisco pointed toward the shelves beside me while looking at a camera mounted on the back wall. Its power indicator light was on, and it appeared normal.

Though I wanted to stick with Sindari, I paused to examine the nearby shelves. They were stacked with old books written in languages like elven, gnomish, and dwarven.

"You'll have to come see if any are missing. I can't tell."

Trouble! Sindari barked into my mind. A growl emanated from the corner.

I hurried to the back wall, but something much stronger than the earlier cobwebs clawed at my torso. An image flashed in my mind of skeletal fingers trying to pull me into a grave.

Instinctively, I spun and slashed at them with Chopper. I didn't expect to hit anything, but the blade flared bright and met with resistance as it cut through something. Whatever it was, I still couldn't see it, but the fact that something was there had my heart racing. A *lot* of somethings. I whipped my arms about as fast as I could in an effort to break all the holds on my body.

Again and again, Chopper's blade met resistance. A faint clatter sounded as something I'd cut hit the cement floor. But as soon as I broke one hold, two more latched on to me, invisible grasping fingers seeming to grow out of the shelves.

More clatters sounded as a half-dozen more of whatever I was slashing at hit the floor. I spun, tearing free from their grips as I sliced at the threats all about me. Finally, the air around me was empty, and nothing more clawed at me.

I'd turned around several times and ended up facing Willard and Brisco with my sword aloft. They were staring at me as if I had gone crazy.

"You heard them hit the ground, right?" I asked.

They exchanged long looks. That meant no. All they'd seen was me fencing with an enemy they couldn't see.

Another growl floated back from Sindari, then escalated into a snarl. Something crashed to the floor.

"I heard *that*," Willard said. "Is your tiger *breaking* artifacts?"

Shaking my head, I ran around the corner at the end of the aisle and charged into the darkness to help Sindari. More invisible fingers grasped at me, almost tugging my duster off my shoulders as they strove to keep me from reaching my ally.

I wanted to ignore them and rush through—up ahead, Sindari's silver tail stuck out from an aisle along the far wall, swishing as he faced something—but the fingers clamped down even harder. Once again, I slashed all around myself, slicing rapidly to break the invisible grips.

Something grabbed my braid and yanked backward, jerking my neck painfully. Roaring with anger and frustration, I whirled and swung. For an instant, as Chopper's tip scraped the wall and tore out a chunk of cement, I saw something. A dark wraith-like figure in the hazy air. Then my blade bit into its torso, and a scream filled my ears. The figure disappeared, and so did the grip on my braid.

A crash came from the aisle where Sindari was fighting. One of the shelving units toppled toward him.

"Look out!" I yelled, running to help.

The unit slammed into the wall, clanks and shattering noises echoing through the room. Sindari roared and lunged, his tail disappearing from sight.

I intended to join him against whatever foe he fought, but a black box with its lid open came into view ahead of me, a purple glow emanating from within. It sat on the floor in the corner of the chamber. A second ago, it hadn't been there—or I hadn't been able to see it.

Barely visible shadows wafted out of it, and I halted several feet away. The impulse to slam Chopper into it flooded me, but I resisted, memories of my face-off with the fae artifact in the bog still fresh in my mind. Instead, I crept closer, thinking to kick the lid shut.

When I was a few feet away, fingers wrapped around my neck and squeezed. Pain shot down my spine, and as I whirled once again, with Chopper raised to slash, the fingers tightened instead of letting go.

Fear flooded me. I kicked and swung with Chopper at the same time, guessing at where the body and the arms attached to those invisible fingers would be.

Again, my blade sliced through something, but there were too damn many of those *somethings*. Even as I severed one of two grips on my neck, more fingers wrapped around my ankle. With a swift, powerful tug, they pulled me off my feet.

I braced myself to land on my back, but I never hit the floor. Instead, my momentum halted two feet above it, and the fingers pulled me toward the box. The purple light brightened, and I envisioned some creature waiting to eat me if I was sucked into it.

Now horizontal in the air, I kept swinging. The positioning was awkward, but desperation gave me extra strength. Chopper sliced through the entity that still had a grip on my neck. I gasped in air and lunged into a sitting position so I could swing toward the thing pulling me by the ankle. My toes were inches from the box now.

"Thorvald!" Willard barked from behind me. "What do I shoot at? I can't see what has you."

"The box!" I slashed at the air an inch from my boot but didn't connect with anything. The fingers had me from underneath. I twisted and stabbed.

My thrust drove Chopper's tip into the side of the box, and purple sparks flew. The blade didn't dig in or otherwise damage it.

"I can't see a box." Willard sounded like she was only a few feet away.

I had no idea how to ask her to help. Then Sindari charged in from the side, roaring as he swiped at the box. Claws screeched against metal. He rammed the box with his shoulder, and the lid fell shut. The purple light disappeared.

Finally, I slashed through what held me, and I crashed to the floor. I sprang to my feet, whipping my blade through the air around me, certain more fingers would grab me. This time, I connected with nothing, but nothing else grabbed me either. Dare I hope that Sindari closing the lid had been all it took?

Willard stood a few feet away, a hand up, as if she'd wanted to grab me but couldn't with me swinging Chopper around like a loon.

Sindari growled, and I turned to find purple mist forming all around the box. I leaped back, almost crashing into Willard, and pointed Chopper at it. For the encore, the cursed thing might explode.

Sindari lifted a paw, ready to take another swipe at it, though all his first attack had done was close the lid. The box faded before my eyes, much as Sindari did when he disappeared from this realm, and then it was gone.

CHAPTER 3

"WHAT THE HELL IS GOING on?" I demanded to the empty air where the box had been. The shadows had also disappeared, and the sensation of magic crawling over my skin slowly faded.

Sindari shook his head, as if driving out the memories of his battle. I assumed he'd also been dealing with invisible hands grabbing him. Had they knocked over the shelving unit, or had he backed into it?

As I said, this place reminds me of the haunted world. Sindari sat on his haunches, eyeing the corner where the box had been.

"You tell me," Willard said. "It looked like you were shadow boxing. If we hadn't seen something yank you into the air and pull you toward the corner, we would have thought you'd gone crazy."

"I suppose I should be reassured you don't already think I'm crazy." As the fog disappeared, I lowered Chopper.

"I do have questions about that, but you're already seeing a therapist, so she can work on your issues and medicate you as needed."

"Ha ha. We talk about my relationships with people and dragons, not my sanity." I poked the air where the box had been.

"I'm surprised that doesn't come up."

The lights flickered, then came back on. The artifacts room once again looked and felt like the normal basement storage area that I remembered.

"I'll get the inventory list and see what's missing," Brisco said.

"Wait." Willard gripped his arm, then pointed toward a spot where the ceiling met another corner. A camera was pointed in our direction. "Is that one of ours?"

Brisco eyed the compact black unit. Two other cameras were visible, larger cameras with wiring that disappeared into conduits running along the wall and up through the ceiling. This one didn't match those.

"No." He strode toward it.

"You're going to have to tell me more about this haunted world," I told Sindari.

"Haunted world?" Willard asked. "Nagnortha? The burial realm?"

That is its name, Sindari told me.

"Or *you're* going to have to tell me more about it." I pointed at Willard.

"It's referenced in a lot of books and scrolls we've gained access to over the years," she said. "The dragons found it first but decided that the underworld taint—as the scrolls called it—made it an unappealing place to hunt. Eventually, trolls, ogres, and orcs learned to make portals to Nagnortha and used it as a burial ground. They believed the magic of the place granted power to those interred there, so they could survive the dangers of the afterworld. Some say that the dead exist close to reality there and that deals may be struck with them. If you would like to be turned into a zombie lord, that's the place to go."

"I bet that's a big selling point in the tourism brochures."

I have been to Nagnortha, Sindari told me as Brisco found a crate to stand on so he could reach the camera. *It is a wild world with much to hunt, but it is also very strange. Some say that its dimensional anchor is weak and that it slips in and out of its place in time and space. If you are there when that happens, you might be lost forever.*

"Lost *and* zombified. There's no end to the possible bullet points that can be put on those brochures."

Willard, who hadn't heard Sindari's telepathic comment, raised her eyebrows.

"Never mind. Is there any chance that box came from this Nagnortha?" I asked, the question for either of them.

"I never did see a box." Willard looked around, gaze lingering on the upended shelving unit and the artifacts and books on the floor. "All I see is a mess."

"I think it was trying to suck me into it... or into *somewhere.*" Somehow, I suspected the box had wanted to do more than shut me inside and close the lid.

It is possible that it came from Nagnortha, Sindari said, *but as you know from my charm, there are many races with magic that can make artifacts that allow travel between realms and dimensions.*

You think that's what it was trying to do? Take me to another realm or dimension?

It seemed that way.

Willard walked toward the mess on the floor, bent, and picked up a couple of pieces of something.

"How would a thief that we believe is from our world get a magical artifact like that box?" I wondered. And had she deliberately placed it there to trap me? To drag me off to… where? That haunted world? Another dimension? A place where I would land in a cage and she would be waiting to take Chopper from me?

Willard returned and held open her hand. Two finger bones—they appeared too long to belong to a human—lay on her palm, the ends sliced off on one side. Where Chopper had cut through them?

Uneasy at this proof that something beyond mere magic had been gripping me, I touched my throat.

Willard squinted at the spot. "You've got red marks all around your neck. Like someone was trying to strangle you."

"Yeah. Enemies do that to me a lot."

"Have you talked to your therapist about it?"

"She would probably recommend more meditation and yoga to calm my inner self when the world is raging against me."

"That helps with strangulation?"

"Not that I've noticed."

The whisper of tape ripping free sounded in the quiet room, and Brisco returned to us with the camera.

"Nothing magical about this, I don't think." He held it up to me for a second opinion.

"Toshiba," I read off the side. "As far as I know, they don't mass produce magical cameras."

"Funny. I was wondering if something had been added to it." He wriggled his fingers and wrinkled his nose in an approximation of a television witch casting a spell.

"I don't sense anything weird about it."

"It's wireless?" Willard asked. "See if you can figure out where it's transmitting to. I can't imagine its range is that great. There might be a van parked outside."

He swore and ran for the exit.

I raised my eyebrows. "You think our thief used her portal generator to travel to a van parked around the block?"

"We don't know she used the portal generator at all. It wouldn't be that hard for someone with a cloaking charm—" Willard waved to my leather thong, "—to sneak in and out, though I don't know how she would have gotten past the door lock or the special alarms that are supposed to warn us of intruders using magic."

"Maybe you need better alarms. And a dragon door knocker to put on the door that flambés intruders who don't know the secret password."

"I'm not buying one of Dimitri's tchotchkes."

"I'm sure he would give you the friends-and-family rate."

Willard closed her hand around the bones. "I'll have my agents analyze these and try to figure out what species they come from."

"Can I have one? It's been a couple of weeks since I had any work for Zoltan to charge me an obscene amount of money for. He's probably feeling impoverished."

"He doesn't pay you rent, and he doesn't pay for what he eats. What does he need money for?"

"Alchemical ingredients are expensive. He also has an extensive bow-tie collection that he needs to add to periodically." I reached for one of the bones.

"My people will analyze them for free. And we've got someone at the university who will let us use the DNA sequencer."

"I like second opinions."

"And being overcharged, apparently." Despite her words, Willard dropped one of the bones in my hand.

It was cool, dry, and slightly porous. I didn't sense any magic in it, but that might change once I was out of the artifacts room and away from so many other magical artifacts filling the air with their emanations.

As we headed for the door, my phone buzzed with a text from my daughter.

What up, Val? Sword practice this afternoon?

I eyed the phone suspiciously. "What day is it, Willard?"

"Wednesday."

"Amber wants to practice today after school. We usually only meet on Sundays, and she complains the whole way through our session, assuming she doesn't try to get out of it altogether."

Amber hadn't canceled any practices since our run-in with the fae males in Magnuson Park, but she also hadn't asked for extra training.

"Maybe she's realized the value of having a caring mother in her life and wants to spend more time with you."

"You've met Amber. I'm amazed you can say that with a straight face."

"I'm working on my deadpan delivery to enhance comedic effect."

If nothing else tries to kill me today, I should be available, I texted back.

Great. Meet you at Crown Hill Park on Holman Rd.

Why that spot? We usually worked out in her backyard.

More space! I've got some new moves to show you. See you at 3.

"Is Crown Hill Park as small and devoid of anything interesting as I think it is?" If I remembered the spot correctly, a place I'd only driven past without stopping, it had a baseball field, some playground equipment, and a skate ramp.

"I don't even know where that is," Willard said. "You're the Seattle native."

I typed it into my map, frowned at the park's tiny size, and eyed the phone suspiciously again. "Either there's a cute boy who skates there, or I'm being set up."

Admiral Ackbar's famous "It's a trap" line floated through my mind.

"Set up? By your teenage daughter?"

"Uh huh." I zoomed in on the map until the establishments around the park popped up, then groaned.

Willard leaned in for a look. "Oh, there's a bridal shop."

I groaned again. Amber loved dresses and shopping and trying things on. I did not.

"You'll need a dress for your wedding. She's being thoughtful and helping you out." Willard grinned wickedly and not at all deadpan. "Send some photos of you trying on dresses. That should be entertaining. When was the last time you wore a dress?"

"In the army."

"Your Class-A uniform doesn't count as a dress."

"Thad said the same thing." I snapped my fingers. "Wait, I forgot. I wore a dress to my last bodyguard gig. Zav liked it."

"Sexy, huh?"

"It had a leg slit so I could reach my gun."

"Leg slits aren't allowed on wedding dresses."

"I'm positive there's no rule about that."

"I'm positive there is. No leg slits and no weapons as you walk down the aisle."

"What kind of wedding are you planning for me?"

"A right and proper one. Your mom will thank me."

"Mom thinks we should elope to Vegas and forget the wedding."

"Then your daughter will thank me." Willard pointed me toward the stairs. "Go meet her. I'll call you with any information we can dig up on the thief and the bone."

I cast a longing look back toward the artifacts room as I walked out. I would rather face wraiths and risk being pulled into a portal to a haunted world than try on dresses.

CHAPTER 4

BEFORE HEADING TO THE PARK to meet Amber, I stopped by the house to drop off the finger bone. Since it was daylight—Zoltan's sleeping-in-a-coffin hours—that had involved taping it to the basement door with a note. I would text him about it after dark.

Amber was already at the park when I arrived, sitting on a picnic table while two guys in baggy jeans with skateboards under their arms talked to her. Maybe I had guessed wrong, and she knew someone who went to school in the area who she'd wanted to see, but she hadn't mentioned any interest in boys—or posted about them on her social media pages.

Her shoulders were hunched as she sat fiddling with a cardboard coffee cup. I couldn't tell if the body language meant she was cold or she didn't want to talk to them, but I parked quickly and walked toward her.

One pointed at her and then at a beat-up truck in the parking lot. What did *that* mean? That he wanted to take her somewhere?

I quickened my pace, ready to rush in and beat the crap out of them—though I'd seen her fight and knew she was capable of doing it herself.

Amber glanced in the direction the guy was pointing and saw me. She waved at me with way more enthusiasm than usual, and I knew I was right, that she didn't want the company.

"Hey, Mom!"

Mom? Even more of a clanging alarm bell. She'd only called me *Mom* once in the last fifteen years, and that had been when that assassin had been about to kill me.

The guys turned to look at me. From the back, I'd assumed they were teenagers, but they both had scraggly beards and looked like they were in their twenties. A flood of rage at the idea of them hitting on my fifteen-year-old daughter almost had me reaching for Chopper. But the police only looked the other way when I killed criminal trolls and orcs. Murdering humans was frowned upon. Unfortunately.

"Mom?" one mouthed, checking me out instead of scampering off as he would have if he could see my weapons—and knew how well I could use them.

His buddy elbowed him. "Talk about a MILF."

"I have to go." Amber turned and scrambled off the back of the picnic table. Avoiding them, she grabbed a bag and strode toward me. "Hey, Val. This park is lame. We should go somewhere else."

The guys must have decided they wouldn't have any luck here, because they slouched off toward the skateboard area.

"Imagine both of them at once," one muttered to the other.

"Oh, I will be tonight."

Sometimes, having superior hearing wasn't a blessing. I hoped Amber's wasn't as good as mine and that she didn't catch that. But the crimson color to her cheeks suggested she'd heard enough. My rage returned, making my fingers snap into fists. A sound pummeling would be good for those guys. But that was illegal, too, damn it.

Ah, wait. Magic wasn't. The laws said very little about magic.

I eyed their backs, wondering if my root spell would work as well here as it had in the fae realm. Probably not, but I didn't need anything quite so epic.

I concentrated, and before they stepped off the grass and onto cement, roots grew up out of the ground and wrapped around their ankles, tightening like vises. One squawked and pitched forward onto the cement, cracking his elbow. The other crumpled where he was, dropping his skateboard in a puddle.

Laughter came from a couple of guys waiting their turn on the ramp. Humiliation wasn't as satisfying as a pummeling, but it would do.

"You okay?" I asked.

"Did you do that?" Amber was watching them try to scramble to their feet.

"Do what?" I let the magic go before anyone could investigate too closely, and the roots disappeared back into the ground. That spell hadn't impressed me much when Freysha had taught it to me, but it was turning out to be handy.

"Make them fall."

"I think they just tripped. Kind of clumsy. They probably shouldn't do a sport that requires balance."

Amber didn't respond right away. Her face showed a mixture of emotions, and I waited to see if she'd tell me to butt out of her problems or settle on the preferred reaction of finding my antics appropriate, appreciated, and delightful.

"I hope they landed on their dicks," she finally said, going back to the table to retrieve her coffee cup.

I groped for something useful to say. Something wise and motherly that wouldn't cause her to roll her eyes.

"You don't have to talk to people who are bothering you," I tried. "You can just walk away."

"Thanks for the after-school-special talk."

"You're welcome. You should also say no to drugs. And sugar-drenched vats of caffeine." I pointed at the cup.

"How do you know it's sugar-drenched?"

"Because no teenager likes black coffee."

"Did you really come here to lecture me?"

"No. I'd rather lecture those idiots." I jerked a thumb toward the guys. They'd recovered and joined their buddies in the skate park, where they were, I hoped, being soundly mocked.

"Let's take a walk, okay?" She hefted her gym bag over her shoulder, her practice swords sticking out of the end. "I don't want to work out where they're going to ogle us."

"No problem. I'm surprised you actually brought your stuff."

She glanced at me as we headed toward the sidewalk.

"I assumed this was a ruse." I decided not to mention Admiral Ackbar, though if Thad was the father I thought he was, he'd made her watch the original *Star Wars* trilogy at some point.

"It kind of was, but we can practice afterward."

"After going to the bridal shop?"

She smiled slightly for the first time. "You're not as dumb as you look."

"Thanks so much."

"They won't let you in if you're all sweaty and gross."

No? I supposed flinging myself on the ground like Rocket and rolling in a mud puddle wouldn't get me out of this. Such tactics worked for my mother's dog, but I wasn't a golden retriever.

"It's early for dress shopping, don't you think?" I asked. "We haven't set a date yet. Zav wants to get married as soon as possible, but fall and winter aren't good times for outdoor weddings in Seattle."

It was sunny today, a rare break from the November gloom, but that sun was wan and to the south this time of year, and it would be getting dark in a couple of hours. If dress shopping took more than the five minutes I hoped it would, we would have to find a lit place for our sword practice.

"It takes three to four months to get a custom dress," Amber said.

"Do I *need* a custom dress?"

She gave me that familiar look that managed to be scathing and pitying all at the same time. "You're six feet *tall*, Val. Don't you need custom everything?"

"Not everything." I *had* been fantasizing about a larger bathtub lately, but only because I liked to lounge in the bubbles with a book. I doubted Amber was referring to home fixtures. "You're six feet tall, too, you know."

It would probably horrify her if I suggested we could wear the same clothes. Besides, I doubted she had a wedding dress I could borrow. At least I *hoped* not.

"Don't remind me."

"You don't appreciate being tall? Longer arms give you more reach when you're sword fighting."

"My primary passion in life." Amber waved away the comment. "I just don't like that people always notice me."

"Like random guys at the park?" I guessed.

"Randos everywhere. Thanks for the blonde hair too." She waved at her beautiful locks that *most* girls would die for. "That makes it even worse."

"Has someone been bothering you? Besides those guys?" My hackles rose again.

"No. Never mind."

I wanted badly to pry, but I knew from past experience that she would only clam up further. Maybe Thad would know something and could fill me in. Even if I was only a part-time mom, I cared what happened to her and wanted her to be okay.

As we reached the intersection and headed in the direction of the bridal shop, Amber glanced at me. "I'll probably have more time to practice sword stuff this winter."

"Oh?"

She'd informed me numerous times that she had a ton of homework this year.

"I'm thinking of quitting swim team."

I halted ten feet from the door of the bridal shop. "What? Why? I thought you loved it. And you're really good. Those long levers are good for butterflying, too, right?"

That earned me the much-anticipated eye roll. "Butter*fly*, Val."

My phone buzzed. I checked the caller, intending to ignore it unless it might be an emergency, but it was Thad.

"Ugh." Amber saw his name on the screen. "Don't answer that."

"You're not in trouble, are you?"

"No." That *no* came out surly.

"Did you have another fight? About Nin?" I'd thought Amber was getting along better with Nin now that they'd thrown magical grenades together in another realm.

"*No*. He just doesn't know I'm here."

Not wanting him to worry, I answered before it could drop to voice mail. "Hey, Tha—"

"Do you know where Amber is?" he asked tensely.

"Yeah, with me."

Amber sighed and slumped against the building.

"What?" Thad didn't sound any less tense. "*Why?*"

"Because I'm a joy to be around."

"Did she tell you she's grounded? She's not supposed to be anywhere except school, the pool, and her room. And she's *definitely* not supposed to run off somewhere without telling me where she went."

"She's practicing being a rebellious teenager." I raised my eyebrows toward Amber. "Why are you grounded?"

"It's not my fault," she said at the same time as Thad said, "She got in a fight at *school*."

Amber rolled her eyes again. I wondered if it was medically possible for them to get stuck in that position. I seemed to remember being Amber's age and having my mother threaten me that such things could happen.

"She punched a boy," Thad added.

"Oh, good," I said before thinking better of it. Thad sounded distressed about the situation.

"*Good?* He has a black eye. The principal called me and said she would be suspended, if not *expelled* if it happened again. The only reason she's not in more hot water is because she gets good grades and *usually* never gets in trouble."

"Do you want me to talk to her about it?"

"*No.* You'll encourage fighting."

"Well, I'd want to know *why* she punched the boy. Maybe she had a good reason."

Amber nodded firmly.

"Whatever the reason, that doesn't mean she can punch people. Val, I don't think you should do the sword stuff anymore. Not if she's going to use what she learns to hurt *normal* people."

"I'm teaching her to stab people, not punch them. She probably learned the punching from *Teenage Mutant Ninja Turtle* reruns."

"You're not funny, Val. She's grounded. Please tell her to come home."

Amber slumped lower against the wall. Maybe she *had* inherited some better-than-average elven hearing.

"She's taking me dress shopping. Don't you think that's more torturous than sitting in her room with her Xbox and her computer?"

"I do, but that's not the point."

"Thanks for the agreement there. I'll give her a ride home, okay?"

"Good." He hung up.

"Someone's in a grumpy mood," I muttered.

"*Teenage Mutant Ninja Turtles,* Val? Really?" There was the scathing/pitying look again. She'd mastered it.

"They were popular when I was a kid."

"The eighties were epically weird."

"You've seen the hair, I trust."

"I heard kids used to brush their bangs against the wall and hairspray them so they would be big and poofy and flat in the front."

"That's possibly true. I didn't have bangs, so I couldn't be that trendy. Why'd you punch the kid?"

"None of your business." Amber hustled toward the front door of the bridal shop.

"Does it have anything to do with why you want to quit swim team?"

"That's none of your business either." She opened the door and jerked her head for me to follow.

"I said I'd drive you home."

"You didn't say *when*." She strode inside, trusting I would follow.

Maybe I should have been less cheeky with Thad. Raising a teenager had to be *at least* as trying as battling invisible monsters in a haunted artifacts room.

CHAPTER 5

AS I STOOD IN A strapless bra and slip with my arms raised, the bridal-shop seamstress taking my measurements, Zav's familiar aura pinged my senses.

Greetings, my mate. Are you ready to go to the dwarven home world?

Uhm, not at this particular moment, but soon. I have to put on my clothes, give Amber a ride home, and pick up my supplies from the house. I also didn't know if I should leave before hearing back from Willard about the spy camera, the finger bone, and if her team had located the thief lurking in a nearby van.

You are naked? Leave it to Zav to focus on only one part of that sentence.

Not entirely. I'm wearing... I looked down at the strapless bra, having been told that my current underwear wouldn't work under a wedding dress and that all the measurements had to be taken with the right undergarments on. This experience was already more tedious than I'd imagined. *Things,* I finished.

When I am in my human form, I enjoy seeing you in things. And also out of things.

I'm glad to hear it. I need a few hours before I'm ready to go.

I must inform you that I scouted Dun Kroth after informing my clan about the wedding. I hoped that I could find an appropriate dwarven master for you to question about your sword and that your trip would be simple and painless.

That's thoughtful of you.

Yes. Unfortunately, it was the same as the last time I visited their world. No dwarves were about, and the entrances to their underground cities were sealed. It may be challenging to find someone, even with me as your guide.

Any chance they'll be more likely to come out if you're not *my* guide?

What do you mean?

Didn't you say before that they're hiding from dragons because of the strife between your clan and the Silverclaws? Maybe if I show up without a dragon, they'll stroll out to greet me.

The seamstress laid a couple of rectangles of fabric over my bare shoulders and *hmmed* as she studied them against my skin. She was in her sixties, her black-dyed hair swept back into a bun with two chopsticks and a pencil sticking out of it. It was possible there were other accoutrements in there—earlier she'd appeared to produce a measuring tape out of thin air. I trusted she'd done this a few thousand times, so I didn't question anything, but I did look to Amber, wondering if she had an opinion on the fabric swatches.

Once Amber had picked out the underwear and pointed to a few dresses she liked as inspiration—and had been certain I wouldn't balk at being asked to remove my clothes—she'd taken a seat and was fiddling with her phone. Now, she had her text messages open and wasn't paying attention to my procedure.

Before, I believed that was the reason for the dwarves' disappearance, Zav continued, *but it has been several months now since our clan defeated the Silverclaws, and there has not been a war or anything that should be worrying the dwarves overmuch, so I am no longer certain that is the reason for their continued hiding. Also, I must go with you. There are dangers on all the worlds, even the relatively civilized ones, and you need a guide.*

I sensed Zav landing on the roof, and Amber looked up. She ought to be able to detect his aura too.

The seamstress removed one fabric swatch and replaced it with a slightly different shade of white. "Oh, that's nice. Yes." She wrote a few notes on a clipboard.

"How much longer will this take? My fiancé is coming."

"He wants to be involved in your dress fitting? That is unorthodox but sweet. Of course, he cannot see you in the final dress until the big day, as that would be unlucky. I won't show him my sketches."

I sensed Zav striding through the front door. We were in a private area in the back, but he walked straight through the curtain and into view, the familiar power of his aura flowing over me and, as always, making me tingle with awareness of his presence.

"Oh, my," the seamstress said, taking in his chiseled jaw, elegant black elven robe, and... the yellow Crocs that Thad had lent him, assuring Zav they were lucky. It was unclear whether the *Oh, my* had been for his handsomeness or the strange shoe choice.

Why, oh why, did Zav have to find Crocs comfortable? I wondered if Amber would help me get some footwear custom-made for him and if he would actually wear it.

Amber stood up and stuck her phone in her pocket, then didn't seem to know what to do with her hands. She'd stopped calling Zav *scary* and *weird* since he'd saved her from that fae guy, but the only time she seemed comfortable around him was when she was too busy picking out jewelry to notice his aura.

Not that Zav noticed her aura either. Not at the moment. He was busy ogling me.

"This is what you will wear to the wedding? It is excellent. I can see much of your flesh."

The seamstress drew back, her mouth forming a scandalized O. "That's her *underwear*."

"Technically, it's *your* underwear," I told her.

"Actually, you bought it, Val." Amber smiled at me. "To go with your future dress. You can pay on your way out. I picked out some shoes for you too. You need to wear them for the dress fitting so we make sure you won't trip over your hem."

"The dress is going to be long enough that I need to worry about that?" I didn't return the smile. I was too busy wondering how I would kick someone in such a long dress. With the guests that Zav was inviting, a brawl or two was inevitable.

"You're not getting married in Vegas," Amber said. "You're not supposed to show off your legs."

Maybe I should have taken my mother's advice and eloped to Las Vegas after all.

"The legs are nice." Zav stepped forward and slid a hand down the outside of my thigh.

That roused a tingle that promptly had me thinking bedroom thoughts, but I swatted his hand away. "No fondling in front of family members, please."

"Ew, Val." Amber wrinkled her nose. "Nobody says fondling anymore."

"Groping?"

The nose wrinkle grew more pronounced.

Zav clasped his hands behind his back and turned to regard her.

Amber straightened her nose—and her face—and stuck her hands in her pockets.

"Offspring of my mate," he said, "you are schooled in the ways of human fashions?"

The seamstress's mouth made that O again. Or maybe she was mouthing *human*.

"You can call me Amber. Uh, what do I call you?"

"I am Lord Zavryd'nokquetal."

"Val calls you Zav," Amber pointed out.

"Yes. I allow this familiarity because she is my mate. And she has a tongue impediment."

Amber looked at me. "Is that like a speech impediment?"

"No. It means my brain and my tongue agree that his dragon name is stuffy and hard to pronounce." I tapped the seamstress on the shoulder. "Will you give us a minute?"

"Yes, I believe so. I'll… go select a garter." She hustled through the curtain.

"Sindari and Freysha call him Lord Zavryd," I suggested to Amber while wondering if that garter was for me or for her. If I wore anything on my leg, it would be Fezzik's holster.

"What's up with the lord?" Amber asked. "Do you own a lot of land or something? Are you like an English nobleman? Or a knight?" Her eyes brightened, as if being a knight would be quite romantic.

"My mother is the queen of the Dragon Ruling Council and commands all of dragondom throughout the Cosmic Realms."

"Doesn't that make you a prince?"

"No."

"It's a dragon thing," I told Amber. "Just call him Zav. Or Zavryd. He'll allow it because you're my daughter and you managed to select an engagement ring for me that makes me a better cook."

SECRETS OF THE SWORD II

"Yes." Zav beamed pleasure at me. "You have smoked ribs in anticipation of my return?"

"I keep the smoker going around the clock, filling the entire block with scents of slowly cooking pork."

"Excellent."

"I'm fairly certain the vegan neighbors want to leave angry signs on my door or perhaps toilet paper the house, but the dragon topiaries you regrew with impressive speed force them to stay on the sidewalk."

"Excellent," he repeated. "The new topiaries have sturdier root systems than the last ones. They will be extremely difficult for assassins to destroy." His eyes narrowed. "And we will not invite your meat-hostile neighbors to the wedding."

As a carnivore, Zav had been extremely perplexed when I'd explained the vegan movement to him. He hadn't been at all amused when I suggested he try tofu sausages because one never knew… one might like them. Not surprising from someone who incinerated the breading whenever we got chicken strips from drive-through restaurants.

"Given that you're planning to serve carcasses, that's a good idea." I planned to have a variety of salads for my elven kin, but I doubted a table of greens would be enough to remove the taint of heaping piles of meat nearby.

"I must discuss the wedding with you."

"Let me put on my clothes. I think the seamstress got all the measurements she needs."

"For the first fitting," Amber said as I hopped off the platform and headed for my clothes.

I eyed her over my shoulder. "*First* fitting? What does that mean?"

"She said there would be four to seven."

"Four to seven *fittings*? For *one dress*?"

"It's your wedding dress, Val. You want it to be perfect."

I looked at Zav, wondering if he would care if I grabbed a dress off the rack. What did it matter if it was a little short and my ankles showed? My ankles were sexy, damn it.

His eyes were glazed, and he didn't appear to be paying attention.

"You're thinking of those ribs right now, aren't you?" I asked.

He smiled at me, his fantasizing-about-meat eyes not that much different from his bedroom eyes. "Perhaps if you make a few extra kilos, I could take them back to my world so that the queen, my sister, and my cousins could taste them. Such a sampling could entice them to come to the wedding."

"Are they not planning to come currently?" I tried to sound disappointed rather than relieved and turned my back to change into my much more comfortable underwear. The strapless bra had a band that dug into my torso like wyvern claws.

"They are not. The queen has removed her objection to me choosing you as a mate, but she sees no point in human ceremonies. We are already mated in the dragon way. I told her there would be races, a great hunt, and aerial acrobatics competitions, but even these magnificent events were not enough to entice her."

"Uh, right. We may need to talk about the festivities you're planning. They're not traditional in human weddings."

"This will be a *cross-cultural* wedding," Zav said, the emphasis he put on the term making me think he'd heard it somewhere else and appropriated it. "I will permit human festivities, and you will permit dragon festivities. Is this not fair?"

"I don't know. Are dragon festivities legal?"

"They are legal to dragons. You will inform your wedding planner about this fair approach to the occasion."

"Willard? She'll be thrilled." I had to admit that I didn't disagree with Zav. I would prefer it if his odious family did *not* come, but it would be fair to include festivities that both our peoples enjoyed.

"One need not be thrilled to serve a dragon; one merely needs to be respectful and obedient."

"Oh, yeah. That's Willard. Obedient."

"I will inform her that you agree to the changes. We must find an appropriate place for the hunt. I will arrange for more suitable prey to be brought to your world. The great herbivores of your past have gone extinct. That is most unfortunate."

"You're going to import animals?" I imagined something like woolly mammoths and mastodons thundering through the streets of Seattle, stampeding past Nin's food truck. Was that my chest tightening with an incipient asthma attack or pure panic?

"Large and fast animals capable of defending themselves and putting up a fight to a dragon while also being most succulent and satisfying to the stomach."

That sounded *worse* than mastodons.

"Where would be an appropriate place to drop off the prey?" Zav asked.

"Canada," Amber said.

I nodded agreement. "Make it the Yukon."

Far fewer people to be trampled there than in Seattle.

"The wedding will be located there?"

"No, but it's heavily forested. It'll be a great place for mastodons or whatever you're bringing. And you can fly down to the wedding after the hunt. That's the appropriate order of events, isn't it?" I looked at Amber. "Hunt, wedding, wedding reception, right?"

"Don't forget the races," she said.

"Oh, I won't."

"The races will be after the hunt," Zav said. "After all that exertion, the dragons will be famished and ready for the feast. When is the feast?"

"I guess that would be at the reception."

"That is after the wedding?" Zav asked. "That may not do. There should be a feast before and after. Or concurrently throughout."

I imagined dragons lined up noshing at the buffet table and watching with vague interest as Zav and I walked down the aisle.

"Why don't you see if you can talk your family into coming before we get too far into planning for them?" I tried not to sound hopeful that he would fail at that.

"They *will* come. I am a master at politics among my people."

"Don't you just challenge anyone who pisses you off to a duel?" I asked.

"Dueling is a foundational part of dragon politics."

"Of course." My phone buzzed as I finished dressing. "Hey, Willard. Is there a law against importing animals to Canada? I know they're not big on agricultural products at the border crossing, but what are their feelings on giant succulent prey animals?"

"Livestock has to be inspected, cleared of pests and diseases, and possibly quarantined," she said without missing a beat. "I take it your dragon has returned to Earth."

"He has. We're discussing the wedding. He has some updates for you."

"I can't wait. I have an update for you on the thief."

That nervous flutter of unease returned to my stomach, and this time, it had nothing to do with mastodons. I was obligated to hunt her down, since I'd told Willard I would, but what if I found her and learned she was the legitimate descendant of Chopper's true owner? Chances were it was all a ruse, but... what if it wasn't?

I wasn't a thief. If I found the true owner, I would feel obligated to return the sword.

"Oh?" I asked warily.

"We traced that camera's signal to a van a half mile from our building, but it was already leaving the area when we got a team together to try to surround it. She probably stuck around only long enough to see if you defeated the whatever-they-weres or were sucked into that box. We managed to get a partial plate number, ran a search, and found a van matching the description with the full plate number. It belongs to a car-rental agency in Seattle. The keys and the van disappeared two nights ago and were reported stolen to the police."

"A thief didn't legitimately rent the van? Shocking."

"Indeed. We think she's in the country illegally. We've run facial recognition software on the photos my agent managed to get, but if she's in a database in the US anywhere, we haven't found her yet."

"So we don't know her name or anything about her except that she steals stuff and has a portal generator. And a box of evil that can possibly suck a person into another dimension."

"Only you saw the box, so I can't verify the last."

"*I* can verify it."

Willard grunted. "Since the police are also looking for the van, we've got some help. Oh, we figured out what she stole."

"Some heinous artifact with instructions on how to ensnare innocent half-elves?"

"A book."

"That might get me if it's a scintillating fast-paced fantasy novel with a suitable amount of romance and snarky banter."

"It was written in dwarven by one of their famous explorers from centuries past. Freysha translated it a couple of months ago. It has chapters on the haunted world of Nagnortha."

"Uh." That unappealing place was coming up way too often.

"It was deposited in the artifacts room before I was stationed here," Willard said. "Our agents originally found it in an abandoned mine up near Granite Falls. A dwarven colony lived there once and left some of their belongings behind when they cleared out."

"What kind of thief steals a book?" Amber asked, standing close enough to eavesdrop. Apparently, my day's drama was more interesting than her text messages.

Willard must have heard because she said, "An erudite one. Be careful, Thorvald. It could be someone smarter than you."

"I've stolen books, too, you know," I said, though that was perhaps not the best thing to admit with my daughter standing by. It had been during my wayward youth when Mom hadn't had enough money to give me an allowance, and I'd been too young to get a job.

"Your mom's Jackie Collins collection when you were a kid doesn't count," Willard said.

Amber snickered.

I shook my head. "You said there were other chapters on other things? Anything in it about weapons smithing? I thought the thief might be researching my sword."

"She'll be disappointed if that's why she grabbed it. Freysha didn't find anything in that book or any of the others she translated that referenced dragon blades. I know because I specifically asked her to look for that. It's one of the reasons I wanted her to translate the dwarven books we've got."

"I didn't know you cared about the history of my sword."

"I thought *someone* should know how it works. Hold on." Willard stopped speaking while someone in the background reported to her. It sounded like Captain Brisco. "They found the van parked downtown near Occidental Square," Willard told me. "The police have checked it out, but it's empty with no sign of the thief."

"Occidental Square?" Unease settled into my gut for a new reason. "That's where Nin's food truck is."

"There's no reason a thief from another country should be aware of her."

"No? She's aware of *me*. Since she failed with the box, she might think kidnapping one of my friends is a way to force me to give my sword to her."

"Well, go check. I was going to ask you and Zavryd to try to find her anyway. I'm positive the police won't have any luck capturing anyone sneaky enough to have gotten into our office and past the magical alarms."

"I'll get down there as soon as I can." I cared more about making sure Nin was all right than finding the thief, but I had a feeling I'd have to confront this woman sooner or later.

I turned toward the exit and almost smacked into Amber. Ugh, I had to drive her home first, and Thad's house was in the opposite direction.

"Zav? Will you do me a favor and fly down to Nin's food truck and make sure she's okay? There's someone new trying to get my sword, and we know she parked her stolen van in that area."

"I have only just returned to this world, and you wish me to leave you? Darkness has fallen outside. I assumed we would go to your abode, consume food, and enjoy carnal pleasures."

"Ew," Amber said.

"We will," I promised. "Just make sure nobody bothers Nin until I can get there, please. Traffic willing, I'll be there in an hour."

My phone buzzed with a text from Thad.

Are you almost here?

Almost. We stopped for teriyaki takeout, and they messed up our order.

"Make it an hour and a half, Zav. I have to get dinner along the way." And hope they got the order wrong so I wouldn't be a liar.

I don't think you understand how grounding works, Val, Thad replied.

You can explain it to me when we get there.

"You are acquiring food?" Zav asked.

"Yes. Watch over Nin, and I'll bring you skewers of meat."

"That is acceptable."

As I led Amber to the Jeep, I told myself that Zav would protect Nin and that she wouldn't be endangered—again—simply because she knew me. I hoped I was right.

CHAPTER 6

"I'M MISSING MY POT STICKERS," Amber said, rummaging through our bag of takeout as I drove her north toward Edmonds.

"Good. That means I didn't lie to your father."

It was too dark to see the eye roll, but I knew it was there.

"I'd rather have my pot stickers than you have a clear conscience."

"Pot stickers are ephemeral. A conscience is forever."

She snorted. "Nice vocabulary word."

"It was on one of Nin's word-of-the-day apps." I eyed her. "Why'd you punch the kid in school? Do you need me to show up and grow roots around his ankles?"

"I *knew* you did that."

"Old dog learning new tricks."

"Uh huh. Please don't show up at my school. It was bad enough that Dad had to come. At least he doesn't dress like Rambo's girlfriend."

"You'd have bigger problems than my lack of fashion sense if he did."

"That's the truth." She noshed on an eggroll and didn't answer my question.

Since I hadn't really been her mother for more than ten years, I didn't feel I had the right to advise her or order her to be a good girl, but I worried that she would get into more trouble. I also worried that this boy had been harassing her and would continue to do so. The idiots from the skate park popped into my mind, and I clenched my jaw, furious anew that twenty-something guys had been hitting on her.

"Did they get all of Zav's chicken and beef skewers?" It wasn't the question I wanted to ask, but if I kept the conversation going, maybe what I *wanted* to know would slip out of her.

"I didn't count them all."

"I thought you liked math."

"Counting isn't math. I can't believe you ordered *twenty* of them and spent over a hundred dollars. Who spends a hundred dollars at a teriyaki place?"

"Someone dating a dragon."

"Does he turn into a dragon to eat?"

"No."

"Then where does it all go? It's not possible for a human stomach to hold twenty chicken skewers."

"Magic is a powerful thing."

Amber hunched lower in her seat. "Wish I knew some. Then I could make roots come up out of the ground and pin dumbasses to their lockers. And rip their pants off."

"You're radiating hostility." I kept my tone casual, hoping she wouldn't see this as prying. "Any dumbass in particular?"

"The soccer team."

"The whole team?" I turned off Highway 99 and drove as slowly as I reasonably could, not wanting to reach the house before getting to the bottom of this.

"All except two. The guys I know from debate are okay. The rest are pigs. One of them has made me his special project. They've probably got bets going, like in all those stupid teen movies."

"You should watch science fiction. The plots are more stimulating."

"Like where Princess Leia is in a bikini and chained to Jabba the Hutt?"

I *knew* Thad had made her watch *Star Wars*. "That's more futuristic fantasy than sci-fi. Try *2001*, the *Matrix*, or *Gattaca*. Your dad would be beside himself with adoration if you said you wanted to watch them with him."

"Dad's not talking to me."

"Did you tell him why you punched the kid?"

"It's not like he can do anything. He won't let me go to a private school."

"They have soccer teams at private schools too."

"I'm just tired of the kids at mine."

"I felt that way about high school too." Maybe commiseration would get me further than prying. We turned from 212th onto Main Street. I was running out of driving time. "You may find this shocking, but I wasn't one of the popular kids."

"You just gave me a list of your favorite science-fiction movies. Why would I be shocked?"

"Because in your movies, the tall blonde girls are always popular." I was a little surprised Amber wasn't, or at least that she was having trouble this year. My excuse was that I'd grown up in the woods in Mom's converted school bus and had barely known how to have conversations with normal people when I'd gone from homeschooling straight into public high school.

"Not when you're six feet tall. And in the AP classes. And don't *want* to date anyone. Why does that make you every horny guy's special project? Everything was fine last year, but then I got boobs and became more interesting or something. And the girls I thought were my friends are annoyed because the guys are asking me out instead of them. Like it's my fault. I'm not even *charming*."

"Really." I didn't mean for Willard's deadpan to infuse my voice, but it might have happened.

"Was it like that for you? You must have been hot. I mean you still are. You know what a MILF is, right?"

"Yeah, we had that term even back in the nineties. How lovely that it's still trendy." I turned the Jeep onto Thad's street, slowing it to a crawl. "So, I've got a couple of ideas for you if you're interested."

"From personal experience?"

"From personal experience."

She fell silent, and I imagined wheels turning as she decided if my experience could possibly be relevant and if she truly wanted advice from me. I was encouraged that she'd opened up as much as she had.

"Go ahead," she said grudgingly. "But don't say anything stupid or after-school-special-ish."

"I'll use my vocabulary words if you want."

That earned another snort. I couldn't tell if it was derisive or appreciative of my humor. Probably the former.

"Well, I never found that turning your back and walking away was that useful. You usually just get jeered at and harassed more, despite all the advice out there to do just that. Having a quick wit can be a great weapon—I *know* you can whip that out—and if you can insult them cunningly enough to make them look like idiots in front of their friends every time, they'll probably stop approaching you, but you may make an enemy for life, and that won't help with popularity."

"I don't care about popularity." Amber didn't sound that convincing, and I guessed that her existing friends being annoyed with her stung more than the drama with the boys. "And I get flustered when they're bothering me. I always think of the witty insults five minutes *after* they've gone away."

"That's pretty typical." I pulled into the driveway. All the lights in the house were on, and Thad's silhouette was visible at the living-room window. "Another option is the decoy boyfriend."

"And that is what?"

"Make a deal with a boy who's been a friend for a while, who also isn't dating anyone, and who's just cool enough that the soccer team won't try to beat him up. Pretend you're dating, and then the other guys will get that you're not available and should leave you alone."

"You want me to *lie* about dating someone?"

"Just make sure he knows about it and doesn't care. Maybe you can offer to do his homework or something."

"Val, parents aren't supposed to give advice like that."

"What did you expect from the woman who ate your pot stickers before we got in the Jeep?"

"You did *not*." She squinted at me. "*Did* you?"

"I told you. Pot stickers are ephemeral."

"You only get bonus points for using a vocabulary word once."

"You're a tough audience."

Thad opened the front door and stepped out onto the porch, his hands on his hips.

Amber sighed, grabbed her practice gear and one of the takeout bags, and slid out of the Jeep.

"Make sure to leave Zav's skewers," I said.

"Don't worry. Nobody wants your dragon's meat."

"Well, not *nobody*," I murmured before considering Amber's above-average hearing.

"Gross, Val. Parents also don't make sex jokes in front of their kids."

"No? I bet you won't compare me to an after-school special again."

"That's a fact." She shut the door and walked through the elegantly landscaped front yard, muttering a response to Thad's query asking if she was okay, but not pausing. She disappeared inside.

I wished I knew if anything I'd said had helped.

Though I was tempted to peel out of there, both to avoid a lecture from Thad and because I hadn't heard from Zav yet and was worried about Nin, Thad headed toward the driveway. I'd missed my opportunity for a swift departure.

I stepped out of the Jeep, leaned against the door, and asked, "Eggroll?" as he approached.

"No. Look, Val—"

"I'm sorry." I lifted my hands. "I should have brought her back right away. I was trying to suss out what was wrong and why she was punching boys."

"Yeah? And how'd that go?" His voice dripped with sarcasm, which was unusual for him. He had to be frustrated with the whole situation.

"She told me a few things."

He rocked back, losing some of his bluster. "She *did*?" The surprise turned to a scowl. "She wouldn't tell me anything."

"You two probably didn't have a similar high-school experience. I seem to remember you admitting that nobody hit on you, not the other way around."

"Not *nobody*, just... not many. Wait." Thad shook his head. "They're hitting on her? Like *harassing* her?"

"You don't punch a boy who politely takes no for an answer and walks away."

Maybe I shouldn't have said that. Fury blazed in his eyes, and he looked ready to punch someone himself. But he walked that back, visibly loosening the fists he'd balled. "I'm going to talk to her principal tomorrow. And get the names of those kids. And talk to their *parents*."

"Ugh, don't do that. They'll definitely harass her then."

"What would you have me do then?"

"See if she can figure it out. I gave her some advice."

"Great. She'll switch from punching people to shooting them."

"That wasn't my advice. Just start tossing out *decoy boyfriend* when you pass her around the house."

"I don't know what that means, but I'm positive it's not the correct answer."

"Hey, my advice is brilliant. Aren't things going better with you and Nin since you got her the rice maker?"

He slumped against one of the landscaping boulders, some of the stiff anger draining out of him. "That was a good suggestion. And I don't know what exactly happened that night Amber... came to your house." He'd been about to say *ran away*, I gathered, but couldn't bring himself to say it. "But she's been less hostile toward Nin since then. They muttered *hi* to each other the last time Nin, uhm, came to breakfast."

Stayed the night and was *there* for breakfast, he meant.

"That's good." I didn't expand on what had gone on that night—I'd been terrified Amber would tell Thad about everything, including the naked-fae orgies we'd been marched past, but she must have decided to take that story to the grave.

"It's better anyway," he said. "It's still... awkward."

I thought about mentioning my blunder with the dragon-meat joke—speaking of awkward—but decided that would horrify him instead of reassuring him.

"She'll get used to Nin. I'm glad you two are enjoying spending time together."

My mate, Zav spoke into my mind, distracting me from Thad's response. *I am protecting your acquaintance from the odious vermin encroaching on her territory and await your excellent company and your arrival with dinner.*

I'm heading that way now. Is everything okay?

None of the vermin have dwarven blood. We will have to look elsewhere for the thief.

Good. I hoped that meant the thief hadn't been by to see Nin at all, but I worried that the choice of parking places hadn't been a coincidence.

My phone buzzed with a text from Nin.

Val, why is Lord Zavryd standing on top of my food truck and roaring to scare away my customers?

He's protecting you.

I do not need protection from people who wish to give me money in exchange for food.

Sorry. I'm on my way, and I'll explain everything. Someone new is after me.

Will you need more magical ammunition and grenades?
Probably so.
Thad was looking curiously at the phone.
"Nin says hi. I have to go." I waved and added, "Decoy boyfriend," as I climbed into the Jeep.

CHAPTER 7

*Z*AV *WAS* PERCHED ATOP NIN'S food truck when I arrived, sitting on his haunches in his dragon form as he gazed alertly at the square and the street, his tail draping down to the ground in the back. I imagined the framework creaking and groaning as Nin and her assistant grilled beef and scooped rice.

Three customers stood in line at the window, oblivious to and unable to see the dragon, even though Zav's talons were curled over the edge of the truck, three feet above their heads. Hopefully, Nin had conveyed to him that the *odious vermin* should be allowed to approach if they had money.

Thank you for protecting my friend so assiduously. I stopped on the sidewalk and held up the teriyaki takeout bag.

Willard had texted me the cross streets where the van had been left, and I intended to check it soon—I might sense something the police hadn't been able to—but not until I made sure nobody had bugged Nin.

Yes. I am a good mate. Zav sprang off the roof, wingbeats rattling the handful of leaves remaining in the nearby trees and startling the people in line. By the time he landed next to me, he had shifted into his human form. *I look forward to spending time with you. And consuming the contents of that bag.*

He peered down at it.

I smiled and hugged him. *I'm glad you enjoy spending time with me.*

As you enjoy spending time with me. He hugged me back, but one hand slipped into the bag and opened one of the boxes.

"Yeah, I do." I handed him the bag, so he could gorge himself to his heart's content. "There's a table over there. Have at it. I'll be right back."

The door on the end of the food truck opened before I knocked.

"I have prepared your order for you," Nin said, inviting me in. "Here is the invoice."

"You didn't charge me for the customers Zav scared away? That's thoughtful."

"He informed me that he believed I was in danger from them."

"Hopefully not, but have you by chance seen a half-dwarf woman today?" I described the thief based on the camera footage I'd seen.

"I have not, but…" Nin frowned, leaned into the kitchen portion of her truck, and asked her assistant something in Thai.

I thought about activating my translation charm, but it was a quick conversation.

"Someone who matches that description came by a few hours ago when I was gone shopping for supplies." Nin waved to the truck's large refrigerators. "She asked about the blonde half-elf woman with the stolen dwarven sword."

"Huh, I wonder who that could be."

"Your sword is not stolen, is it?"

"Not by *me*. I won it in battle with a bad guy, but I have no idea where he got it. I assume the dwarven smith who made it didn't originally intend for it to go to a zombie lord."

"Oh." Nin frowned, perhaps not finding this answer reassuring.

I didn't either. After ten years with Chopper, I didn't want to give it up. Especially since I'd run into several magical baddies of late who had defenses powerful enough to deflect even Fezzik's magical bullets.

Nin's assistant, an older, motherly lady named Tida, peeked through the doorway. "She also asked where to find Val," she said in accented English. "I do not think I told her, but…" Her brow wrinkled. "My memory of the conversation got a little fuzzy. Also I was busy serving people because we had a late-afternoon rush."

"Do you know where Val lives?" Nin asked.

The assistant brightened. "No. Even if she used some magic on me, I would not have been able to reveal your address." Her face fell again. "But I do know where your coffee shop is located."

I grimaced and pulled out my phone. "I'll warn Dimitri to watch out for her." I would have to check in on him later, too, to make sure nobody had questioned him and fuzzed *his* memory.

"Sorry, Val," Tida said.

"It's not your fault. If I didn't spend time with you guys, she wouldn't know about you." I stared glumly at the screen as I texted Dimitri, remembering the good old days when I hadn't allowed myself to get close to people.

No, those hadn't been *good* days. Those had been lonely days. I just wished I could have friends and also not endanger their lives. Was that too much to ask?

"I'm going to look around the area for her." I grabbed the ammo and grenades Nin had packed up for me, and hopped out. "Let me know if you see anything suspicious, please."

Nin looked toward a tree and park bench that Zav had claimed. "More suspicious than Lord Zavryd incinerating skewers of meat?"

"What?" I spun in time to see flames and a puff of smoke. "Those aren't breaded. What is he *doing*?"

"I do not know, but there is no need to leave him to protect me. I appreciate the sentiment, but I also want my business to continue."

After waving an acknowledgment, I trotted over to join Zav. The smoke around him was an odd mix of sweet and charred, but the skewer of chicken cubes he held was still intact. What had he burned?

"They're not to your taste?" I noticed a dozen empty bamboo skewers in the bag, so he must be eating them.

"There is an unpalatably sweet glaze on the meat."

"That's the teriyaki sauce. It's delicious."

"I do not like it." He used magic to float the deglazed chicken strips off the skewer and into his mouth like a squad of soldiers marching to their doom. "Why do humans insist on enrobing everything in sweetness?"

"It's a failing of the species. Want to go for a walk to…" I checked Willard's directions. "Second Street? The thief left her van there."

"I will walk with you." He hoovered the last of the chicken cubes and opted for incinerating the bag and skewers instead of throwing them away. At least my dragon wasn't a litterbug. "But it is dark. Soon we will mate."

He rose to his feet, giving me a sultry look that reminded me that food always made him horny. Even if it didn't have a similar effect on me, that look and having his aura crackling around me did. The memory of him sliding his hand along my bare thigh in the bridal shop came to mind, fingers leaving trails of heat that flashed along my nerves. If Amber and the seamstress hadn't been there...

Zav leaned in, and I made myself lift a hand to his chest to stop him from kissing me—and whatever else he had on his mind.

"We will," I said, taking my gaze from his lips, "but let's find our thief first, okay?"

The rumble that came from his throat might have been reluctant agreement or a growl of anticipation. It sent a shiver through me and made me wish this thief problem would disappear, and that Zav and I could go home and do what engaged people were supposed to do at night.

A buzz came from my phone, Dimitri's reply.

I patted Zav and started walking as I read it. As soon as we finished this task, Zav and I could go home.

I'm setting up an Etsy store to sell my dragon door knockers online, his text read.

I see you've been traumatized by my enemies.

I haven't seen her. There was a police officer who came by earlier, but it was a guy.

Are we in trouble?

Nin had pointed out that selling door ornaments that shot flames at intruders was possibly of questionable legality. Though I wasn't sure if the police handled yard-art regulations enforcement.

I don't know, Dimitri replied. *He came in, looked around for a while, and left without asking anything.*

How weird did the shop look when he came in?

You mean how many ogres, goblins, and trolls were hanging out slurping coffee?

Yeah.

Well, it's always busy, and that's our clientele.

So as weird as usual. We reached the intersection and turned down Second Street. The top of a white van was visible above the cars parked along the street.

Pretty much. He was pure human, as far as I could tell, so it's surprising that he found us. The glamor Inga and I put outside doesn't exactly camouflage the building, but it's supposed to make it so normal people don't notice it.

Let's hope the psychic next door hasn't reported you for being associated with gangs of vampires again.

She came in for coffee the other morning and waved to Gondo. I don't think she's a nemesis anymore.

Gondo *charmed her?*

I gather the goblin-fuel brew did. Everyone is a fan. You should try it.

People try to kill me on a daily basis. I don't need anything else that jolts my heart.

I stopped in front of the van. "Do you sense anything magical about it?"

I didn't, but Zav's senses were far superior to mine.

"I do not. Nobody is within, and the inside is hollow."

"It's a cargo van." I opened one of the unlocked doors and found it as empty as promised. "I wonder if she chose it because it was the easiest thing on the lot to steal, or if she needed it to carry around her loot. Or large artifacts such as portal generators and boxes that try to suck you into another dimension."

Zav gazed blandly at me. "You have not fully apprised me of your encounters with this individual."

I filled him in while I poked into the door pockets and glove compartment, hoping to chance across a brochure or a notepad with a to-do list of nefarious plans. Alas, I found only a map of Seattle, with nothing circled or highlighted.

"If she'd only come to question Nin—or Nin's assistant—then she wouldn't have unloaded the van, right? Maybe she's got a hotel room or bolt hole somewhere around here."

Zav tilted his head. "I sense… your enchanter acquaintance with the gnomish blood in the area, as well as two people with perhaps one-quarter elven blood. Two trolls are in a bar. An orc is fishing off one of the piers to the west. Those are the only beings with magical blood that I sense in the area."

"I think she has a cloaking charm or something similar."

"Inconvenient."

"Especially when the bad guys have them."

I gazed thoughtfully at the buildings up and down the block. "She's half-dwarf, so she'll be stronger than typical, but she still wouldn't want to tote her cargo miles, right?" I pulled up the map on my phone to see what was nearby. "Logically, she would have parked somewhat close to wherever she's staying, especially if she didn't know we would be able to track down her van. What's around here? Pub, bar and grill, a bunch of restaurants, billiards…"

"I am uncertain what types of establishments humans prefer for *bolt holes*. This means hiding place, yes?"

"Yes. The Cadillac Hotel is nearby." I lifted my head. "Why does that sound familiar?"

"A Cadillac is a type of human conveyance."

I smiled and patted his arm. "Don't worry, Zav. You'll get to excel when it's time to fight."

"Are you teasing me?"

"A little bit."

"We have discussed that it is inappropriate for humans to tease dragons."

"We've also discussed how atypical and special I am." I leaned into him and kissed him, forgetting that he was in his postprandial lust phase.

He wrapped his arms around me, pulling me against his chest, and made me completely forget what I'd found, what I'd been searching for, and why I'd been searching.

You are atypical. I like this. His hand slid into my jacket and under my shirt as his magic ran hot along my nerves.

You must also like it when I tease you then. I leaned into him, letting my own hands explore. We were in the middle of the sidewalk, with people exiting the nearby bar, but so far, nobody had hooted at us. An enemy might sneak up on us, but it was hard to be afraid of such possibilities when being embraced by a dragon. Surely, even the sword-coveting thief wouldn't dare approach my ferocious mate.

It is inappropriate. The queen would insist I punish you until you learn proper respect for dragons.

Can't we just have sex instead?

Yes. Now? His finger tugged at the waistband of my jeans.

Not in the middle of the street.

"Get a room!" someone called.

I'd expected that, and I made myself break the kiss, more than a little breathless, and pat Zav on the chest.

He looked toward the heckler, and his eyes flared with violet light.

"Don't incinerate anyone, please. Willard won't help with the wedding if you slay Earth citizens."

"They must learn to be respectful of dragons."

"Incineration will make that happen?"

"I might incinerate only his clothes. And his body hair. His face is covered in it, and it is not trimmed. Odious vermin."

I clasped Zav's hand and pointed him in the other direction. "Let's check the Cadillac Hotel. Maybe she's staying there."

"A hotel is a place where mates may spend the night and enjoy each other's company," Zav stated, forgetting the hairy heckler and gazing down at me as we walked.

My body was already flushed and highly aware of him. I didn't need a sultry gaze or thoughts of exploring the bounciness of a hotel bed with Zav, but then again… why couldn't we spend the night here? It wasn't as if I had to go home, and it might be fun to have a weekend fling downtown. Besides, the hotel was a lot closer than my house.

"Maybe after we check to see if the thief is there," I said.

"I will do this swiftly and efficiently while you acquire a room for us. A private room with no drunken voyeurs."

"I think most hotel rooms are free of that amenity." While we waited for the crosswalk light to turn, I looked up the Cadillac, trying to remember why it rang a bell. I'd never stayed there. "Oh, that's right." I sighed.

"Problem?" Zav asked as we crossed the street.

"Yeah. It's not an operating hotel anymore, and it's haunted."

CHAPTER 8

"HAUNTED?" ZAV ASKED.

"So the internet informs me." I summed up the description of the hotel to him. "Back in the late 1800s, it was popular with loggers, fishermen, and shipyard and railroad workers. It fell into disrepair in the 1900s and was trashed in the Nisqually Earthquake of 2001. It's since been restored and is the Klondike Gold Rush National Historical Park."

"A park may be in a building?"

"Apparently. Here's the haunted part: Apparitions reputedly wander the offices in the upper floors, strange sounds are heard now and then, and a ghostly presence is felt in the elevator. At night, the ghost of a woman and her child can be heard crying in the halls. Some say she's a prostitute who performed her own abortion and bled to death in her room." I grimaced. What a story.

"What does this have to do with thieves?" Zav asked.

"Probably nothing." After the morning's events, I was more squeamish than usual at the idea of hauntings, and my neck throbbed in memory of skeletal fingers wrapped around it. "She wouldn't have been able to get a room there." I stopped at the corner of the restored brick building. It still had a sign that read Cadillac Hotel, but Klondike Gold Rush signs were by the front doors, and the building was dark inside. "Let me see if there are any other hotels around here."

"Hotels with beds available for mated couples."

"Yes, yes, I'm horny too."

"Excellent." Zav reached for me but paused and looked toward the building's third-story windows.

I started to ask him if he'd seen something—such as apparitions haunting the offices up there—but my phone buzzed.

Dear robber, Zoltan texted, *why have you left this ghoulish parcel on my front door?*

You, of all people, are bothered by ghoulish things?

When they're left on my door, certainly.

I left a note to explain it. I'd like to know what person, magical being, or creature the bone came from. It attacked me earlier.

It attacked you, and you weren't able to identify it?

No. It was invisible.

It's not invisible now.

I know that. I managed to cut off some of the fingers grabbing me, even though they were invisible. I decided the story sounded implausible to anyone who hadn't been there. Hell, Willard *had* been there, and she found it implausible. I was fortunate she'd seen me floating horizontally and being pulled toward the corner by an invisible force.

You are my strangest client.

Aren't I your only client?

You forget my legions of fans that support my YouTube alchemy channel.

Those aren't clients; they're stalkers. I've seen the emails.

Such judgment. I will examine this bone, but there will be a fee.

I expect no less.

"I sense something." Zav was still gazing at the windows.

"Ghosts?"

"No. It is either a magical artifact that is being camouflaged, only partially effectively, or it is some magical residue."

"You think it's related to a certain half-dwarf thief?" It was possible my thief had decided to use the place as a bolt hole—a museum that closed at five might be a better place to lie low than an actual hotel. It was also possible that magic left by a passing mage or enchanter accounted for the place's supposed hauntedness, and that this residue had nothing to do with my problem.

"I do not know. We will investigate."

"I'm sure the door is locked, and breaking and entering is a crime in Seattle. Especially on a busy, well-lit intersection." I eyed the cars zipping past us, the late hour doing little to diminish the traffic. Maybe there was a back entrance we could use.

"The door is not locked." Zav stepped under the covered entryway and opened one of the glass doors.

"Did *you* do that or was it unlocked?" If the latter, our thief might have come this way after all.

"Dragons are versatile."

Guess that answered my question. I joined him in the doorway. It would only take a minute to investigate whatever residual magic he sensed. As of yet, I didn't sense anything.

I paused before entering fully, holding my hand up to stop Zav. In this neighborhood, any commercial—or historically significant—building would have an alarm system. Yup, a little red LED glowed from a wall-mounted detector. We could probably be in and out before the security company showed up, but I would rather not trigger anything at all.

"Alarm." I nodded toward it, then spotted a larger unit on a back wall, beyond displays of information and faux artifacts from the late 1800s. "I might be able to disarm them with my lock-picking charm." I'd never tried to get through an alarm system before, but the magic had proven versatile.

Both units disappeared in flashes of flame, leaving only smoke and ashes wafting down to the floor.

"Or you could utterly destroy them with your magic. Was there teriyaki sauce on them?"

"There is no reason to waste time on human impediments." Zav strode into the room, his elven slippers—thank goodness, he'd made the Crocs disappear—barely whispering across the hardwood floor.

"Someone's grouchy because this isn't a real hotel and there aren't beds," I muttered.

"I do not require beds." He gave me a smoldering look over his shoulder, but that might have been left over from lighting things on fire.

I drew Chopper, using its blue glow for illumination rather than drawing attention by turning on lights, and trailed Zav toward an elevator. Halfway through the bottom floor of displays, my nerves started itching, and I thought I detected wisps of fog similar to what had been in Willard's artifacts room.

Maybe it was my imagination. The haze wasn't as dense or nearly as obvious as what I'd experienced that morning.

"Do you sense something?" I asked.

Zav was waiting at the elevator, a sign saying it was for staff only. "Residue."

"What does that mean?" I couldn't put a finger on it myself. As before, it registered to some other sense than my built-in magic detector. More like what normal humans would call a sixth sense. A seventh sense? A hunch or intuition that something unnatural was here...

"Magic was here and left evidence of its presence." The elevator doors opened for Zav, and he stepped in. "Come. It is stronger upstairs."

Worried we would be attacked by more invisible enemies, I touched Sindari's charm and summoned him. Even though I believed Zav could take care of just about anything, it wouldn't hurt to have a second ally if we ended up battling enemies on multiple fronts.

Zav lifted his chin. "You summon the tiger because you do not believe I can sufficiently protect you?"

"I'm sure you can. I wanted his opinion on whether the rations stacked on that display shelf are originals or reproductions." I pointed to crates of canned beef and pancake flour.

By now, Sindari had formed at my side, and he gazed at the display. Zav didn't even bother looking. He was giving me an I-am-disappointed-by-your-lack-of-faith look.

Canned meat sounds loathsome, Sindari said. *Lord Zavryd would agree.*

"Depends how much sugar is in the sauce." I smiled at Zav, hoping he would forget to feel affronted.

"Come." He pointed at the elevator floor.

"Yeah, yeah."

Your dragon seems grouchy this evening. Sindari walked at my side to the elevator. *Is Lord Zavryd disappointed because there haven't been any glorious battles lately?*

He's disappointed because there hasn't been any glorious sex. I smiled again as we stepped inside and kissed Zav on the cheek.

I did not require that information, Sindari said.

Now you'll know not to comment on Zav's mood.

Indeed.

The elevator rose without anyone touching anything. Hopefully because Zav was using his magic, not because it was haunted. So far, I didn't hear or see any signs of ghosts, but the hairs rose on the back of my neck as we ascended to the third floor. The doors opened, and the mystical fog lay thick before us.

"Hell," I muttered. "You still think there's just residue here?"

It is the same fog as before, Sindari said, not yet stepping out. *Do you suspect the thief and the box are here?*

It's possible.

"The residue is more pronounced here. And as I said, it *is* possible that there is a magical artifact that is camouflaged to make it difficult to detect and pinpoint." Zav didn't hesitate to step out. Could a dragon be sucked into an interdimensional realm? "I will deal with it."

He strode off down a wide hall. Before I'd taken more than two steps after him, a cold breeze whispered at my cheek, and a faint crying reached my ears.

"Maybe we'll wait here while he deals with it," I murmured.

Sindari's tail swished. *I did not enjoy the morning battle against enemies I couldn't see.*

"Tell me about it."

Zav disappeared into an office at the end of the hall. A few seconds later, a scraping noise came from another office. It sounded like furniture being dragged across the floor.

"You guys hear that, right?" I called softly, not wanting to yell in case our thief was lurking nearby and also camouflaged. I eyed the walls for cameras, but there was no sign of a security system—pre-existing or recently installed—on this floor.

Zav didn't answer me.

Sindari lifted his head and sniffed. *Someone has been here within the hour.*

"Do ghosts have scents?" I joked.

I do not believe so, he answered seriously.

"Someone may have worked late."

I doubted it. What kind of museum required its employees to work this late? The hours listed on the door hadn't been expansive.

Sindari padded halfway down the hall, turning into the office that the scraping noise had come from. The faint crying continued as I followed him.

The office smelled musty, and dusty drop cloths covered the furnishings. I was surprised the door had been open.

Fog curled around Sindari's legs as he looked at something behind a covered desk. He picked it up with his teeth and backed toward me.

"A food wrapper? That's what you smelled?"

Someone has been sleeping back there.

I accepted the wrapper and checked where he'd been looking. A couple of the furniture cloths had been made into a bed on the floor, with one of the fake bags of flour from downstairs leaned against the wall like a pillow.

The person I smelled slept here, Sindari said. *It was a woman.*

"A half-dwarf woman?"

I cannot determine that from scent. She smells like someone from this world.

"A cookie connoisseur apparently." I held up the wrapper to Chopper's glow. "Or maybe biscuits. This isn't in English. Our thief must have imported her favorite snacks."

Had she traveled all the way here to try to get my sword? Maybe she'd sensed it earlier in the month when the fae taint had turned it into a beacon detectable for hundreds, if not thousands, of miles.

The scraping sound came again, from the other side of the desk.

I spun with Chopper raised, not sure whether to expect a mouse or a ghost. Sindari went to investigate first. I was too busy staring at a familiar purple glow that now filled the hallway outside. More hairs rose on the back of my neck.

"That wasn't there before." I raised my voice. "Zav?"

I do not smell or see what made that noise. Sindari eyed the ground beside the desk.

More worried about Zav, I returned to the hallway. The purple glow flowed out of the doorway to the office he'd gone in.

Moving shadows danced on the walls, and cold chills stroked my cheeks. I swatted Chopper at the air around me and ran toward the office, anticipating invisible grips would try to stop me.

A whoosh of magical power flared from inside of it. The purple glow disappeared abruptly.

I made it to the doorway without being grabbed and lunged inside, half-expecting to find Zav gone, sucked into another dimension and that box yawning open.

He stood in the corner, gripping his chin and gazing down at the exact box I'd seen earlier. The lid was open, but the glow had disappeared.

"Did it sense your mighty dragonly approach and short out?" I lowered my sword.

The fog was fading, along with the creepy chill drafts that had teased my cheeks. Only the woman's crying remained, faint and far off. Maybe the old hotel truly was haunted, and the noises had nothing to do with the box or my thief.

"No. After removing the camouflaging spell to locate it, I turned it off."

"You didn't have to close the lid?"

Sindari joined me inside, curling a lip and showing a fang to the box.

"By using my power to depress the dragon sigil." Zav gripped the box, tilting it so we could see the bottom. The profile of a dragon's head was etched into the surface, and it glowed a faint purple.

"*Dragon* sigil? Is this a dragon artifact?" I'd assumed it was either dwarven or came from that haunted world.

"Yes. I recognize it. A *Zhapahai*. It is for trapping interdimensional creatures to study."

"It almost trapped me this morning."

"It can trap anything, but it was designed to work on the wild worlds that have creatures that can shift in and out of our dimension. There was a time when dragons wanted to master the skill of these creatures to use as a weapon against our enemies."

"And that time is gone?"

"We have grown more adept and powerful with our magic over the generations, and few enemies exist who can challenge us openly. As far as I know, the studies ended, and the *Zhapahai* were all placed in museums."

"Klondike Gold Rush museums on Earth?"

"No. This should not be on this world. It was likely stolen."

"By our thief? How has she gotten all these magical devices?"

"How have you gotten all of *your* magical devices?" Zav looked pointedly at my charm necklace, then at Sindari.

Sindari sniffed. *I am a magical tiger, not a magical device.*

"Not by stealing them." I folded my arms over my chest, not pleased by the insinuation. I'd thought Zav was past calling me a criminal.

"My point is only that many artifacts have been stolen and found their way to this world." Zav lowered his hand. "I am suspicious, though, that this may have been *given* to your thief as a way to assist her in getting you."

"Not another Silverclaw that wants to see my demise, I hope."

"There are many Silverclaws, some who are scientists and who would have known about such devices."

"What would have happened if I'd been sucked into it?" Maybe I didn't want to know.

"It would take a scientist to read the settings," Zav said, "so I cannot say for certain. It may have delivered you to a cage in a dragon scientist's laboratory."

"Maybe I should let it take me so we can find out who's responsible."

"It may also have dumped you into a *xrackaw*-filled swamp on Yagobar. Or into the magma of an active volcano." He scowled at the box.

"On second thought, I'll stay here, and we can leave that thing turned off."

Magic tickled my senses, and the box started to fade. Disappearing just like the one that morning had?

Zav rested a hand on it, and his own magic surged. The process halted, and it solidified again.

He lifted it from the floor and, with another rush of power, opened a portal. There was barely room for it between a desk and a filing cabinet.

"I will take this to an ally who may be able to tell where it came from and what the settings are. I will return in the morning and take you to Dun Kroth to find the provenance and secrets to your sword. It is important for you to learn this information since so many seek to claim it for themselves. We will delay no longer in researching it."

The provenance. That meant we might find out who it truly belonged to, and I would have to say goodbye to it. I gazed sadly down at Chopper.

"I suggest you return to your abode where the defenses are sound. This thief may have more tricks under her talons."

"I'm certain of it."

Zav strode toward the portal but paused to look at me, his gaze softening. "I will return in the morning," he repeated, "and tomorrow night, we *will* enjoy *tysliir*."

"Won't we be on the dwarven home world?"

A hint of a smile touched his lips. "They allow sex there."

"Good to know," I said as he sprang through the portal.

Do you and Lord Zavryd speak of things other than mating? Sindari sat on his haunches, probably wondering why I'd summoned him.

"Occasionally. Want to stick with me for a while in case a thief jumps out with powerful artifacts and tries to slay me on the way home?"

Will Dimitri be at the house?

"Are you only staying with me if he'll be there to pet you when we get there?"

No, but it would be a perk. He has a crafter's hands.

"What kind of hands do I have?"
They are brusque and rarely adoring.
"I'll work on that."
Do.

CHAPTER 9

THE NEXT MORNING, I GATHERED all of my gear and headed to the coffee shop to see if the thief had been by and to wait for Zav there. I'd sent a text to Amber, letting her know I would be out of contact for a while but that she was welcome to send updates about her school life and that I would read them when I got back. That had earned me a yuck face.

"It's *fine*," a whiny boy voice was saying as I walked into the shop, drawing out the single-syllable word to at least two. Reb slouched by the coffee kiosk with an ice pack to his eye while his surrogate mother, at least until she found him a full-blooded troll mother willing to take him in, frowned down at him.

"Did you pound them mercilessly into the ground?" Inga asked. "You know trolls will keep striking if they sense weakness in you."

"I know that. I *am* a troll. You're just a big human with troll hair." Reb wrinkled his face at her, then seemed to regret it as he winced and adjusted the ice pack.

Our barista, Tam, was making drinks and pretending not to pay attention to the exchange. Dimitri was in the back, with semi-professional lights shining down on a row of dragon door knockers in different colors as he took photos of them. He probably didn't have to *pretend* not to pay attention.

I swung by the kiosk for a couple of sparkling waters to take with me to dwarf land—hey, a girl had to have a few luxuries—and asked, "Everything okay?"

Even though I hadn't been responsible for Reb's father's death, it had been tied in with the dark elves I'd been investigating, and I felt some guilt over not being around to keep them from killing him. I was glad Inga had volunteered to take care of the boy, even if troll mothering techniques would have given Child Protective Services fits—had they acknowledged that trolls existed.

Reb slouched further. "Fine."

"Fine." Inga managed to sound almost as sullen and surly, but that was a typical tone for her.

"Need help with anything? Beating up trolls is a specialty of mine."

"So I've heard." She gave me a dark look.

At least she didn't call me Ruin Bringer. We'd come to a semblance of peace, though I doubted Inga would ever adore me.

"I could show him a few moves. I'm teaching my daughter to fight." I wondered what Amber would think about having a troll sparring partner.

"I will instruct the boy," Inga said. "And teach him enchantments that could be useful."

"I don't want to learn magic," Reb said to the floor at her feet. "I told you. I'm going to be a warrior. Like Sinjar the Bold!"

"That is a troll folk hero," Inga explained to me.

"Did he have a cape?" I paid for the bottled drinks and swung my backpack to the floor so I could make room for them. It was jammed full with my extra ammo and grenades as well as less-explosive supplies, such as food, water, a multi-tool, rope, a blanket, a first-aid kit, and chocolate. The necessities.

"A what?" Reb asked.

"A cape. Like superheroes on Earth."

"Capes sound sissy." Reb pointed at my open pack. "Are those grenades?"

"Yes. I'm going somewhere dangerous. I'd wear a cape if I had one. They're not sissy. Haven't you heard of Superman?"

"Sinjar the Bold could kick Superman's ass!"

Inga cuffed him. "Language."

He spat a stream of words in trollish at her that likely involved more dubious language. Inga lifted her hand in warning.

"You're not my real mother," he blurted, then ran off—or tried. He tripped over my pack on the way, cursed again, and charged for the back exit.

Inga sighed. "Troll males are difficult."

"Are the females easy?" I arched my eyebrows.

Given that she was six-and-a-half-feet tall and a perpetual grump, I couldn't imagine that her human mother—I supposed I didn't know if she'd *had* a human mother—had found her easy.

"They are more reasonable." With a stiff back, Inga strode off after Reb. "It is time for your schooling."

A distant shout came from the end of the hall, something about warriors not needing schooling.

Most of the time, I regretted that I hadn't been around when Amber had been growing up. But sometimes, I was secretly relieved that all I'd had to deal with had been murderers and rapists.

"She better be careful if your police officer comes back around," I told Dimitri as he joined me with his iPad open, photos in the process of being edited. "It's not legal to hit kids anymore, at least not in this country."

"Must be a new rule," Dimitri said. "My dad clobbered me regularly. To man me up."

"No, it was illegal ten years ago too. As Thad informed me when we were still married and raising toddler-Amber. If she was misbehaving, we were supposed to talk to her about actions and consequences and then have her sit on the naughty step as punishment."

"It must have worked well. She's so polite and well-mannered today."

"I didn't know your voice could get that sarcastic."

"Please. Sarcasm is the official language of New York. What do you think of these pictures? Nin is going to help me get an online store up and running, so we can keep selling dragon door knockers even after all of our regular clientele have them."

I sensed Zav's aura, not near the shop but back at the house. He must have expected to find me there instead of checking on the shop. Well, he would figure out where I was.

"Make sure to include a photo of the pink one," I said as Dimitri finished showing me the digital camera roll. "You want buyers to know all of the options available."

"That option isn't available."

"We've made three."

"Not willingly." Dimitri swiped through the pictures, which looked pretty good. At the least, they were better than the blurry, shadow-engulfed images I took with my phone's camera. "I'm sticking with black, blue, and green."

"Girls will want pink and purple."

"Girls don't buy dragon door knockers."

"We've sold a bunch to girls."

"*Troll* and *orc* girls. They're not who's going to be shopping on Etsy."

"Have you asked them?"

"Val, they live in caves. UPS doesn't deliver to caves."

"Are you sure? They delivered to my mother's school bus at the campground we stayed at one year."

"I'm sure the campground had an address," Dimitri said, his jaw set in a study of mulish obstinacy.

I trusted Nin would talk to him and fix him of his delusions about who did and didn't shop online for dragon door knockers.

The door opened, and a uniformed police officer walked in.

"Uh oh." Dimitri lowered his iPad. "That's the same guy as yesterday."

The officer, buzz-cut and in his thirties, gazed around the shop, looked at me for a moment, then spotted the door knockers lined up for the photo shoot and squinted at them. Interestingly, he didn't have an iota of magical blood, not that I could sense. But he was wearing a bracelet that didn't look regulation but *did* emit a faint magical signature. It might be designed to help him locate things—or buildings—camouflaged from mundane humans by magic.

He frowned and strode toward the door knockers.

I nudged Dimitri. "Maybe he's a customer."

"I doubt it," Dimitri said glumly.

"If he is, ask if he has any daughters and how they feel about online shopping and pink dragons."

"You're not funny." Dimitri gazed wistfully toward the front door, like a man ready to go on the lam.

I turned him toward the officer. "I'll go over there to talk to him with you."

As we headed over, Dimitri still throwing longing glances toward the front door, my phone buzzed.

Where are you? Willard texted.

At the shop. Where are you?

At your house. I went for a short run at Green Lake and decided to stop by.

To use my shower? How many laps is a short run for you? It was just shy of three miles around the lake on the paved path.

Four, and it's cool out, so I didn't sweat much.

You ran twelve miles and didn't sweat much? You're a machine.

Ha ha. I got that wedding footage I told you about. I was just going to drop it off, but... hang on, I'm getting sass.

Sass? Nobody's home.

Wait, my senses told me that Zav was still at the house. Why hadn't he flown over here? Maybe he had paused to trim the topiaries.

Your dragon lover is here giving me sass.

I'll be right there.

"...implicated in the murder of one Charlie Wu," the officer was saying, and my ears perked up. Murder?

Distracted by Willard, I hadn't paid much attention when he started talking to Dimitri, but now, I hurried over to join them. The officer—a detective, his badge said—faltered and seemed startled by my approach. Maybe he'd heard of me. Or maybe he liked blondes and thought I was hot. With a big nose and big ears that the buzz-cut only enhanced, he was on the homely side. Female attention might fluster him.

Just in case it helped, I put my hands on my hips, adjusting my jacket so more of my chest would be on display, and slid my ring finger into a pocket. "Hi, Detective. What's going on here?"

"Who are you?" He had a Midwestern accent and had to be a new transfer. Most of the Seattle PD knew me by sight. I'd even consulted for them on occasion.

"Val Thorvald. I'm one of the owners here."

"The door knockers were her idea," Dimitri said.

I elbowed him. "*I* simply said to survey the customers and see what they wanted. You came up with the winged T-Rexes all by yourself." I lowered my voice to whisper, "It's not nice to throw your business partners under the bus."

"You have armor and a badass sword," he whispered back. "You can survive being hit by a bus."

The detective held up a hand, appearing more annoyed than amused by our banter. What was new? He *did* steal a glance at my chest, so maybe he was attracted to me. I smiled warmly. Whatever helped keep Dimitri—and our shop—out of trouble.

"I'm Detective Sutherland, here investigating a murder."

He pulled out a tablet similar to Dimitri's, managed to fumble it, but recovered it before it fell to the floor. He swore, took a breath, and showed us a photo of the cement walkway up to someone's house, the wood of the porch charred, the bushes to either side blackened and skeletal, and the door itself charred and warped by fire. The only thing in the photo that wasn't damaged was a familiar green dragon knocker mounted below the peephole in the door.

"The body was found underneath that *thing*, that thing that spat a stream of fire at me when I walked up to investigate." He scowled at me *and* Dimitri, then pointed to the knockers lined up on the display case. "It's exactly like those, and the homeowner, after we questioned her, said she bought it here."

Dimitri didn't reply. He looked like a man accepting that a noose had been dropped around his neck and there was no way he could escape.

"The knockers don't spit out enough fire to have done all that." I pointed to the destroyed bushes and porch in the photo. "Just a little gout about a foot long to scare off intruders who don't know the password."

"Because Charlie Wu didn't know the password, he is now dead," Sutherland said.

"I'm sure something *else* killed Charlie Wu. Do you have photos of his body?" I wanted to see where he'd croaked and in what position.

"Not that we'll disclose to suspects."

"*Suspects.*" Dimitri's sarcastic New York voice had gone squeaky. "At the worst, we built a defective product. We didn't *murder* anyone."

I elbowed him again and switched to telepathy to say, *Don't say anything to incriminate yourself. He might be recording this. We'll get a lawyer if we need to.*

Dimitri only looked glummer at this promise of a lawyer.

"*Very* defective," Sutherland growled.

"Do you have proof of that?" I asked. "Clearly, the knocker didn't blast an inferno at *you* when you walked up. You're here, and your eyebrows are even intact."

"Just because it doesn't do it every time, doesn't mean it didn't do it once. And once was all it took." Sutherland tapped handcuffs on his belt, as if he was ready to arrest us at any second.

Well, he could *try*. I had a date with Zav to visit another world, and I wasn't going to miss it.

"If it *did* harm someone," I said, "it had to have been modified to do so. We don't sell anything capable of murder. Well, maybe the goblin-fuel coffee blend, but that's only a risk if you have a heart problem and drink more than one cup."

"You're not helping," Dimitri muttered to me.

"Who's the homeowner?" I asked.

If we knew that, we might have an idea about whether that person was the type to modify yard art for inimical purposes. Had one of the goblins purchased it, I wouldn't have doubted that a door knocker might have been modified, but I wouldn't classify any of the goblins as inimical. Nuisances, yes. Inimical, no. They also tended to live under park benches, not in suburban houses.

Sutherland scowled at me, as if sharing this information was highly classified and would get him in trouble. It wasn't as if I couldn't check the social-media sites, where death-by-dragon-door-knocker stories would trend to the top immediately. Would stories of our knockers help sales or hurt them? All press was good press, right? Assuming I kept Dimitri from being arrested, his online shop might blow up like dragon fire in an arsenal.

"Maggie Kohler," Sutherland finally said.

Not recognizing the name, I raised my eyebrows toward Dimitri. Did he keep a list of customers? Or just trade cash for knockers, no questions asked?

She's a part-fae baker with a shop here in Fremont, Dimitri replied silently. *She comes in early and gets a coffee every morning.*

He didn't have telepathic skills of his own, but mine had improved, and when I was paying close attention, I could hear his thoughts.

Almost *every morning,* he added. *She hasn't been here the last few days.*

The fae weren't known for their tinkering tendencies, but maybe her human side had driven her to modify the knocker. Because… because why? She wanted to murder someone in front of her own home? Maybe she'd only intended to scare the guy. Though the original knocker should have been sufficient for that.

"Have you asked her what happened?" I asked aloud, aware of the detective frowning suspiciously at us as we communicated telepathically. If he had that bracelet, he had some knowledge of the magical community and might know that some beings could speak silently to each other.

"Yes. That's how I knew to come *here*." Sutherland pointed at the floorboards. "She said her friend, Charlie Wu, was coming to visit, knocked using the ring attached to the belly, and then the dragon torched him. She didn't see that, since she was inside, but she—and her neighbors—heard the ghastly scream. They're all horrified."

"Nobody saw the death, you say? Then you can't arrest Dimitri or anyone else. For all you know, an assassin with a blowtorch was hiding in the bushes when this Wu arrived."

"Nobody in the neighborhood saw anyone running around with a blowtorch."

"Assassins tend not to flamboyantly stroll down the middle of the street with their murder tools."

You do, Dimitri thought.

My strolling isn't flamboyant. You might want to visit the baker's shop and talk to her, see if there's anything shifty about her story.

That will be hard to do from jail.

He's not going to arrest you.

Are you sure? He keeps fondling his handcuffs.

That's because he's single and lonely. I smiled to the officer. "We'll be happy to cooperate with your investigation, of course, but we will have to get our lawyer involved if there truly are accusations made against Dimitri."

Not commenting on the lawyer threat, Sutherland pointed at a black door knocker. "I want to take one of these for the forensics lab to study."

I imagined people who usually dusted for fingerprints and ran DNA tests on strands of hair presented with one of the T-Rexes. What would they think when they took it apart? Since I'd helped assemble some of them, I knew they ran on magic, not propane or anything else flammable.

"Sure." I picked up one of the black ones. "They're ninety-nine dollars, plus tax."

Sutherland had been lifting his hands to accept it, but he froze. "You're going to charge me?"

"For something worth a hundred dollars? Of course we're charging you. Being a cop doesn't give you the right to confiscate our inventory, not unless you're considering it for safekeeping, evidence, or contraband. Besides, don't tell me your people didn't already take the one on Ms. Kohler's door." I beamed another smile as I shifted to thrust my chest toward him.

Sutherland stood with his hands out for a long moment, hopefully too enamored by my beauty to debate whether the knocker fell into any of the categories that would give him the right to confiscate it. "I'll be back," he finally said.

"You might want to take that trip to the bakery soon," I told Dimitri as the detective walked out. "Sutherland may come back with someone who's less enchanted by my boobs."

"You think they're what kept me from being arrested?" Dimitri quirked a skeptical eyebrow.

"Possibly what kept him from remembering that forfeiture is also a legitimate reason for the police to take stuff and that it might apply to a door knocker wanted for disassembly purposes."

"Even though I'm not an admirer myself, I'll admit that the female anatomy has interesting powers."

A text came in. *Your dragon is being difficult.*

"I'll see you later, Dimitri. I have to go use my anatomy on a dragon."

"Will you bail me out of jail if I'm arrested by the time you get back from your trip?"

"Yes, but don't get arrested. Call a lawyer."

"Do you know one?" He waved toward the window, the detective visible getting in his car, which he'd parked in a loading zone across the street. "You implied you have someone."

"I was bluffing. I've asked for legal representation before, but lawyers find me difficult to work with."

"Huh."

"I'll pretend not to notice your lack of surprise." I clapped him on the back and headed home to see what Zav was doing to vex Willard—and if he was ready for our trip.

CHAPTER 10

I FOUND ZAV IN THE LIVING room with Willard, sitting and watching the TV while she stood beside him with the remote and... was that a pointer? She flicked her hand, and a red laser beam highlighted a table with elegant place settings, plates with dainty portions of an exotic salad, and a voluminous flower arrangement in the middle, all over a lacy white tablecloth that draped to the floor.

"You'll note the small portions brought out by caterers from the kitchen," Willard said. "There's no buffet laden with animal carcasses."

"That portion is minuscule. And it is of leaves."

"My niece is vegetarian. There were no meat products at her wedding."

Zav rose to his feet as if he'd been slapped on the cheek and challenged to a duel. "No meat! Why would you show me such a ridiculous festivity? Dragons would not be satisfied with anything like this."

"I'm just trying to impart that a wedding should be elegant." Willard had noticed me come in, and she shot me an exasperated look. "You can have meat, but it should be prepared in a kitchen by a chef, not roasted over a spit. This is a wedding, not a reenactment of Neanderthal times."

I rubbed my face. Maybe employing Willard to help hadn't been the best idea.

"I've interviewed a priest," she said, as Zav turned toward me, his fist on his hip, "and found someone who's willing to do the ceremony outdoors and says he has officiated over *quirky* weddings before. I'm not sure he meant ogres, per se, but I'm hoping they'll get distracted by something else and won't show up. Do you have a wedding photographer booked yet?"

"No. And I was thinking of a secular wedding, so maybe we don't need a priest."

Now *Willard* put a fist on her hip. "Even if you're not that religious, don't you think you should play it safe? Have your ceremony blessed by a priest in case it helps in the eyes of God." She looked at Zav. "This union could use God's help."

"Dragons are not theists," Zav informed her. "My mate, I have checked on the artifact and brought back news. I did not expect to be waylaid by your employer when I arrived."

"I'm here to help," Willard said. "Val wants a respectable wedding."

"Is that a harpist?" I pointed to the TV.

"Yes, she was quite lovely. I've found someone local who is also willing to play outdoors, as long as there's a gazebo or other covered structure so her harp strings don't get wet if it rains."

What happened to my request for a DJ? And a buffet?

"I've spoken to the florist and selected four possible flower arrangements for you to select from—no, make that three. Bouquets overflowing with ranunculus are too cliché. Besides, you're too strong a woman for such ruffly flowers."

What the hell was a ranunculus?

"Who are you and what have you done with my boss?"

Willard squinted at me. Why did I have a feeling she was planning the wedding *she* wanted instead of mine? I needed to try harder to get her hooked up with Dr. Walker. Maybe if she were busy with a new relationship, she would want to spend less time on my wedding plans. I hadn't envisioned anything this elaborate when I'd asked her to help.

"Someone who's attending and doesn't want your parents—or your mother at least—to feel like she's walked in on a freak show."

"Val's father is coming," Zav stated. "I told him about the wedding."

"Oh?" Willard asked. "That should be… interesting."

"Yeah. I haven't told my mom yet." I walked in and clasped Zav's hand. "What did you learn about the artifact?"

"According to our scientists' records, that particular *Zhapahai* had been missing for a long time. Several generations ago, it was lent to a dwarven scientist, but he disappeared during a research trip, and the artifact was

SECRETS OF THE SWORD II

never returned. It was believed to be on Dun Kroth somewhere, but the dragon scientists had other *Zhapahai,* so nobody went searching for it."

"So... it was hanging out on a shelf in some dwarven laboratory until our thief found it?" I asked. "Is she stealing on the dwarven home world as well as on Earth?"

"It sounds like we can only speculate for now," Willard said. "Until you capture her and have a chat with her."

"Won't that be fun?" I muttered, hoping she didn't have access to any more magical boxes. "I'm ready to go when you are, Zav. Unless you want to discuss flowers further, Willard."

"Not at this time." Willard looked at Zav. "Do you have any way to determine if the thief activated her portal and went back to Dun Kroth? Or if she's still here on Earth?"

"I do not," Zav said.

"If she's after my sword, she'll probably go wherever I go," I said.

"You think she can track it through dragon portals?" Willard asked.

"I don't know, but once I learn all the secrets of my sword on Dun Kroth, maybe it'll lead me to her." I didn't mention that getting answers about Chopper's complete capabilities was of more interest to me than catching the thief. If she was hunting me, she would find me sooner or later.

"You're asking a lot of a piece of metal," Willard said.

"A dragon blade is a superior weapon of great craftsmanship," Zav said. "I do not see the point in plucking flowers from the ground for a festivity, but if this is a necessary human custom, perhaps the flower arrangements at the wedding should be bundled to look like Val's sword. Would this not be more aesthetically pleasing than blobs on a table?"

"No," Willard said, even as I thought a sword-shaped bouquet would be cool. I wondered if it was possible.

"I don't know if you can do that with flowers," I said, "but I bet we could get a sword-shaped cake. There'll be a dessert, right, Willard?"

She lifted the remote and fast-forwarded to dessert being brought out on small plates. "My niece had individual tiramisu cups served to all of her guests."

Judging by Zav's expression, he was even less impressed by the delicacies than I was.

"Dragons will not eat sweets," he said.

"More for the rest of us," Willard said.

Zav gripped his chin and contemplated me. "We could shape one of your meat cubes in the likeness of a sword."

"That is technically true," I said. "As long as they fit in the smoker."

"Meat *cubes*?" Willard touched a hand to her chest. So that was what the word *aghast* looked like on a person.

"Meat loaf," I explained. "Without bread crumbs. He keeps forgetting what they're called."

"Why don't you just leave the planning to me? Here, I'll leave the video for you. Maybe you two can watch it together and see what weddings are supposed to look like. Good luck on your trip." Willard grabbed her exercise jacket and headed for the door. "Don't piss off a dwarf king and get humans blacklisted from visiting their world."

She paused to send a worried frown in my direction, and I could tell that she'd gone from joking to worrying that such an outcome was possible.

"I'll be circumspect and polite," I promised.

"You know how to do that?"

"Sure. My mom taught me when I was sitting on the naughty step."

Willard's you-are-extremely-strange expression was different from Amber's but equally interpretable.

"A dwarf king should be honored to serve the mate of a dragon," Zav said. "I will ensure it."

"Don't let *him* get us blacklisted either." Willard pointed at Zav, then walked out.

"It is unlikely that humans will be invited to Dun Kroth under any circumstances," Zav informed me.

"We're already blacklisted, huh?" I checked my phone to make sure nobody important had messaged me and was putting it back in my pocket when it buzzed, not a text but a call. "Hey, Mom," I answered, worry dropping into my gut like a rock.

I remembered how the elven assassin had made a point to let me know with his coin placement that he knew where my mother lived. What if this half-dwarven thief had also learned where she lived and threatened her in some way?

"Val," Mom said, sounding a touch shaken. "You didn't tell me the elves would be at your wedding. You didn't tell me *he* was coming."

"King Eireth? How'd you find out? Did he come to see you?" I grimaced, imagining how hard it would be for her to see Eireth looking exactly the same as he had when they'd been lovers, while she'd aged more than forty years.

"One of his scouts came to question me. He just left."

I hadn't expected that. Now I felt bad that I hadn't warned her, but how could I have known Eireth would send a scout? And why now? The wedding was months away.

"What did he want?" I asked.

"To ask me questions. I... got the feeling he was doing a preliminary security check. To make sure it would be safe for Eireth to come to Earth."

"And he checked *you*? Mom, half the ogres and trolls from the coffee shop are threatening to come, not to mention Zav's family, if he can get them to. What does he think a barefoot woman in her seventies is going to do?"

"I *just* turned seventy, Val," she said tartly.

"Doesn't that make you in your seventies?"

"No. *In your seventies* refers to someone of seventy-five or six. *Much* older than me."

"My apologies, Mother. You are clearly still middle-aged." I nobly resisted adding the line *for a tree*. "Did you pass the interview? Did he say if he would be interviewing the ogres at the coffee shop that Zav invited?"

"Why would your dragon invite ogres?"

"He's inviting everyone. He seems quite pleased to let the world know that we're getting married in the human way."

Zav lifted his chin. "Yes. Your employer also informed me that it is typical for guests to bring wedding presents."

I stared at him. "Is *that* why you're inviting everyone? What kinds of presents could you possibly want? You're an all-powerful dragon who can use his magic to poof things into existence."

"The ogres may bring interesting prey to hunt. The goblins may build a bubbling hot-water box for our domicile—you have not acquired one for us on your own yet. One of the trolls is a cobbler and has noticed my interest in human footwear. He may know how to satisfy a dragon's preferences more than a human shoe peddler."

I made a mental note to go hot-tub shopping before Zav could ask any goblins to *make* one for us. I'd already seen what their handiwork created. I refused to sit in water heated by open flames.

"Val," Mom said quietly, the tartness replaced by something less certain. "Do you truly think Eireth will come? I... know he is married now and there won't be anything between us, but… I don't know. I would like to see him, but I'm also apprehensive about seeing him. Does that make sense?"

"Yes. I think he'll come. Once, he offered to wed Zav and me in the elven way. It's too bad he can't do it in the human way. I'd rather have him than Willard's priest who officiates over quirky weddings. I have no idea what that means, but he can't possibly have experience with dragons, ogres, and trolls."

Eireth wouldn't bat an eye at ogre or troll guests; I was positive.

"You wish your father to wed us?" Zav asked.

"I don't think that would work. It might be legitimate in the eyes of other elves, but here on Earth, you have to have be ordained."

"How does one become ordained?"

"Uhm, good question. Probably by being a citizen of Earth first." I ran an internet search while Mom murmured worried sentences about how disappointed Eireth would be to see how old she'd gotten, and what if his wife was snooty and rude to her? Maybe she shouldn't come at all.

The mutterings were more to herself than to me, but I tried to be encouraging. "He's a king, Mom. He'll be diplomatic and friendly and give you a big hug. I'm sure of it." I decided not to mention that the wife *was* snooty and rude, or had been when she'd considered me a suspect in the poisoning of Eireth. With luck, she wouldn't come.

"I hope so," she said. "I *do* want to see him. I think."

"He'll want to see you."

"Oh, I don't know about that."

"Trust me. He likes you a lot more than me. I'm mouthy and weird. Just ask Amber."

"She's already informed me of that."

"Imagine that. Bye, Mom. Let me know if anyone else shows up to pester you in your cabin in the woods."

After she hung up, I read the search results. "In Washington, any ordained or licensed clergyman or justice of the peace may officiate a wedding."

"A clergyman is a religious leader?" Zav asked.

"Yeah."

"King Eireth is a religious leader among the elven people."

"There's not going to be a checkbox for the elven religion. I suppose we could just fill out a marriage application online ahead of time and then it wouldn't matter who officiated. I haven't quite figured out how we're going to explain your... nationality." I studied his face. "Can you make yourself a fake ID?"

He tilted his head.

"Never mind." I put my phone away and patted him on the chest. "Let's go find some dwarves. The sooner we find Chopper's secrets, the sooner I can come back and figure out how to make you a sword-shaped meat loaf."

His face brightened. "Excellent."

CHAPTER 11

A SMOKY BRIMSTONE SCENT TAUNTED MY nostrils, and I started sneezing as soon as we passed through the portal into Dun Kroth. Not a good sign. I'd packed my inhaler and a first-aid kit—this time, I'd also remembered a winter coat, since legions of fantasy novels had educated me on the fact that dwarves lived in the mountains—but if I had an asthma attack, I was a long way from a hospital. Zav would take care of me to the best of his abilities, but dragons seemed better at healing punctures and gashes than ongoing medical issues.

You didn't accidentally bring us to a volcano world, did you? I asked silently as Zav flapped his wings, the portal fading behind us.

He banked, giving me an alarming view of craggy peaks, tree-filled canyons, and a tiny river far, far below. I gripped his scales as tightly as I could from the broad expanse of his back. He'd warned me that we would arrive in the air, but I hadn't imagined it being quite so high in the air. Or that one of the nearby peaks would be emitting plumes of smoke.

I did not, but the mountain ranges that run across great swaths of Dun Kroth contain many active volcanos. The intermittent foulness of the air is one of the reasons that the dwarves burrowed tunnels, using magic to filter out the gases and protect their lungs as they built their cities underground. We are fortunate to come during an epoch when the air is much improved.

If you say so. I bet elves don't visit a lot.

This is true. Dragons are sturdy and do not mind a little ash and brimstone in the air. We find it invigorating.

And yet my air fresheners for the Jeep turn you green.
They are repugnant.

Zav flew down the back side of a mountain and into a canyon. The trees were a normal shade of green, unlike the oddly colored ones on the elven world, but they were short and squat. I didn't see anything like the towering pines or firs of Washington.

We soared low over a stream trickling between the trees and past a clearing dotted with stone houses that looked like something Fred Flintstone would have built. Tangles of briars and brush hugged their walls and overran the paths in a way that would have made me suspect the place was abandoned even if my senses hadn't told me that nobody magical was around.

Zav flapped his wings to take us out of the canyon and flew across a scree-covered slope at the base of a mountain. A beautiful road built with stone blocks wound toward an archway in the side of the cliff.

"Tolkien must have spent a couple of summers here," I murmured.

Definitely not the winters. Even with a white-yellow sun shining through the hazy smoke from the volcanos, there was little warmth. Frost glinted in the shadows.

Stone doors sealed the archway, and tufts of broad-leafed grass stuck up between the pavers here and there. As with the village, it seemed like the dwarves had abandoned this place months, if not years, ago.

I can sense the dwarves deep within this mountain. Zav landed on the road, facing the double doors. *I have informed them that the great Lord Zavryd'nokquetal is here and requires they send an enchanter to speak with us.*

"Requires it, huh?" I patted his scales and slid off his back, landing harder than I expected. "That's sure to work."

Unfortunately, my own senses didn't extend far enough for me to detect anyone inside the mountain. I'd seen a few small animals skittering through the leaf litter under the trees, but so far, this entire world seemed abandoned to me. Abandoned and strange. Aside from the pervading brimstone odor, the air was thick and heavy.

No, I realized, jumping a couple of times and coming down hard. Not the air—the gravity.

On the elven home world, it had been close enough to Earth's gravity that I hadn't noticed it. This was a different story, and I made a mental note that my arms might grow fatigued quickly in a sword fight. Would I be able to swing Chopper as fast as usual? I dredged through my memories of heavy gravity explained in science-fiction novels, but the authors had rarely brought up sword fights.

Do you have an alternative plan? Zav asked.

I walked up and knocked on the door.

I tried that already.

"Yes, but you're a fearsome dragon. They would be foolish to answer the door for you. I'm a charming half-elf."

You are more likely to vex them than charm them.

"Only if they prove themselves our enemies. Or say something that requires ridicule."

They have not responded to me at all.

I rested my hand on the cool stone and gripped my lock-picking charm with my other hand, willing the magic to open the doors. I didn't expect it to work—Zav's magic was far more powerful than any of my charms, and he'd surely tried this—but it would tickle me if it did.

I already tried that, Zav informed me dryly. *Ancient dwarven masters enchanted the doors long ago, perhaps the very ones who worked with smiths to make the dragon blades.*

"I'd like to talk to them then." The doors didn't budge—I didn't see hinges and wasn't even convinced that they were legitimate doors instead of slabs of granite placed to permanently bar the way.

Zav let out a long breath, the dragon equivalent of a sigh. *That would be ideal. I do not know why they have ensconced themselves in their mountains and will not answer the summons of even a Stormforge dragon. My kin and I are known to be reasonable.*

For dragons, I thought but didn't share. "The fae queen said Mount Crenel is where my sword might have been forged and that there are caves and temples inside that might hold information. Can you take me to that mountain?"

I have heard of Mount Crenel, and that there are tombs among the temples and also that there is a repository of knowledge, so that is a logical place to check, but I am not certain which mountain it is. The name is from dwarven lore, not dragon lore.

I took that to mean that one dwarven mountain looked like another to a dragon.

I have flown over the various mountain ranges of this world a few times, and I can make some guesses, Zav added.

As I returned to his side to climb on his back again, he spun around, almost whacking me with his tail. His back stiffened as he peered toward another mountaintop, his nostrils quivering.

"Problem?" I stayed crouched low in case the tail whipped around again. Whatever he saw or sensed, he was on full alert.

I sense powerful creatures flying this way.

"*Flying?* Like dragons?" I drew Chopper.

They are not dragons. They are not... Climb on my back.

"No offense, Zav, but I'd be more comfortable fighting from the ground."

There are many of them. We will need to find a defensible place to face them. Climb on now.

He levitated me in the air before I could say anything else. It was just as well. I didn't want to argue further, not when he was worried about whatever it was. I couldn't remember ever seeing him worried about *anything*. Dragons were the supreme predators in the Cosmic Realms.

Weren't they?

Zav sprang into the air and, instead of flying in the opposite direction of the approaching threat, flew *toward* it. He didn't soar straight toward the mountaintop but stayed low and headed for that canyon we'd passed. As he tilted his snout downward to fly into it, I sensed the creatures for the first time.

A creepy graveyard chill came over me, reminding me of the touch of the invisible fingers in the artifacts room. But this couldn't be related to that, could it? We weren't even on the same *planet* anymore. Or had the thief followed us here and was sending this attack?

If so, she had access to even more powerful magic than I'd suspected. These beings had extremely strong auras.

As we dipped into the canyon, eight winged creatures came into view, flying out from behind the distant mountain. They traveled in a V formation, like ducks, but that was their only resemblance to something natural. Huge and made from yellow bones, they reminded me of skeletons of pterodactyls in museums, but even from a distance, I could tell they were much larger than pterodactyls had been.

We descended before I got a better look, and I wondered if my eyes were playing tricks on me. They weren't *really* skeletons, were they? Maybe they were relatives of wyverns or something of that ilk with a pale-yellow coloring. After all, the air was hazy. Maybe I *hadn't* seen through their rib cages.

What are those things, Zav?

Whatever living creatures they once were, they are that no longer. Now, they are only someone's undead minions. He flew over the trees in the canyon and back to the abandoned settlement of stone dwellings.

Undead minions? I had a vampire for a roommate and had battled a few zombies in my life, so the concept wasn't unfamiliar, but I didn't run into many such beings on Earth and had been told they were even rarer on other worlds. Dwarves, elves, trolls, and many other races stamped them out when they sprouted up through someone's deal with the underworld. The undead were dangerous and had a tendency toward proliferation. Those who wanted to remain under the radar didn't make pests of themselves by raising armies.

Yes. They were altered with the powerful death magic of the underworld. Do not let them touch you or break your scales. Your skin.

That might be easier said than done. Any idea why they're after us?

The creatures flew into view again, a couple miles up the canyon from us. Their yellow skeletal frames and pale leathery wings stood out against the hazy blue-gray sky as they soared in our direction.

And would it make sense for you to make a portal and for us to leave instead of fighting them? I added.

The no-breaking-the-skin rule might be hard to obey, and I worried about what would happen, especially since Zav hadn't gone into detail. My mind filled in dreadful possibilities.

I am considering that in order to send you back, but their presence here is alarming. I should investigate.

Hey, if you're staying, I'm staying. But tell me why you *need to be the one to investigate.*

Neither today nor the last time I came to this world, looking for information on your blade, was I able to make contact with Braytokinor, the dragon who rules Dun Kroth. It is not uncommon for dragons to leave for a time, but had he known about these creatures, he should have done something. If necessary, he should have come to the Ruling Council and gotten help to deal with them.

Zav landed on one of the stone buildings and levitated me off his back.

"We're fighting here?" I landed on the flat slab of a roof, grunting again at the heavy gravity, and drew my weapons.

You will hide among the buildings and may vex them from afar if you wish, though it is unlikely they will respond to your words. I will destroy them. Zav sprang into the air before I could utter a protest. *They cannot shift into smaller shapes, so it should be difficult for them to reach you if you stay inside the buildings.*

"Zav! You can't take on eight by yourself." And how the hell was *destroying* them investigating anything?

I will take on no more than two at once, Zav assured me, flying not toward the creatures arrowing toward us but for a dark cave or depression in the wall of the canyon. He landed in it and turned to face them, his back and flanks protected by the rock.

From what I'd always seen, Zav's fighting style was akin to aerial martial arts with magic thrown in. Would he be able to defend himself effectively from the ground? From inside a cave?

Seven of the creatures veered toward him. One flapped its leathery wings and streaked toward me. Its power preceded it, battering my senses with the same intensity of Zav's aura. That scared me. Were we facing enemies equivalent to a dragon? To *eight* dragons?

"This may not go well," I muttered.

CHAPTER 12

THE WINGED CREATURE DOVE CLOSER, its empty eye sockets glowing as they fixated on me. Its jaw opened, sword-like fangs looking every bit as deadly as the teeth of a living animal—a living predator.

I rubbed Sindari's charm to call for his help as I pointed Fezzik between those eye sockets and fired.

The creature didn't erect a magical barrier to bounce my bullets away, and they struck its skull, right where I'd aimed. They ricocheted off the bone as surely as they would have a magical shield, and the creature didn't flinch or alter its path. Could undead skeletons feel pain? Probably not.

Sindari formed at my side and groaned into my mind. *A little more time for preparation would be appreciated, Val.*

Sorry, I was on Zav's back until a few seconds ago. I holstered Fezzik as the creature came in, talons outstretched, and crouched with Chopper in both hands, ready to *vex* the creature. *Don't let it cut you.*

The undead have the power of the grave.

Which I assumed was bad. I had no experience with *death* magic, and I didn't want it.

I timed the creature's approach and jumped to one side of the roof, dodging the grasping talons. Sindari sprang to the opposite side to avoid them. I leaped back in, hoping to slash at the creature's back end before it passed out of range, but a blast of power hit me like a tornado.

Before I could get my own modest magical defenses up, the attack knocked me from the roof, turning me in somersaults. The power had the chill of death, and it numbed my skin as I tumbled through the air. I glimpsed Sindari, who hadn't been struck by the power, springing for the creature's flank.

I twisted and managed to land on my feet in the undergrowth, but the heavier gravity made it more jarring than I was used to. Pain stabbed my ankles and made me pause instead of climbing back to the roof. Maybe I could fight the creature from the ground.

Sword raised, I turned to track it, hoping for another shot. This time, I would use Freysha's teachings to create a shield around myself.

Sindari had caught the beast's side and now hung from its skeletal flank, gnashing at one of its huge ribs. It flew past the abandoned village and over the trees, and I lost sight of them.

"Come back over here and face me!" I yelled, frustrated to find myself on the ground and unable to help.

Off to the side of the village, the other seven creatures descended on Zav in a flurry of magic and wingbeats. Their dark auras surrounded his, and I could barely sense him through the malevolent cloud. Because of the trees, I couldn't see much of the battle either, only catching glimpses through the leaves.

Several blasts of pure power slammed into the side of the canyon where Zav crouched, throwing his own magic at his attackers in waves. Two flew backward, somersaulting as I had, skeletal tails flying over skulls. That didn't keep the others from attacking.

Zav's magical barrier protected him, but shards of rock the size of boulders split off the canyon wall. The creatures were trying to bury him in that cave.

I took a few steps in that direction, but a surge of power came from the one that had attacked me. A second later, Sindari flew back into view, tumbling through the air. He got his feet under him, but like me, he came down hard, his breath expelling in a grunt that turned into an angry snarl.

The creature flew back into view, coming for us as I ran to Sindari to help him if he needed it. It dove toward us, and I raised Chopper, determined to get in fast enough to strike at it this time.

But the yellow eyes focused on the sword, and the creature didn't come within range. It flew over us like a bomber, hurling down magical blasts of energy.

I hurried to form my defenses, imagining mental fern fronds matting together in a dome-shaped barrier over Sindari and me—and hoping it would work. I'd never tried to extend my shield and protect someone else before, and I had no idea how effective my magic would be on this world.

Power railed at us like a hailstorm wind, tearing up the undergrowth all around us and slamming into my barrier. One of the stone structures crumbled as if a wrecking ball had crashed into the roof, and the noise almost startled me into dropping my defenses. Chunks of stone struck the barrier—would have struck *us*—and bounced off. The creature sailed out of view over more dwellings.

Dwarven buildings are usually indestructible, Sindari noted of the crumbled stone near us.

"I'm glad I didn't take Zav's advice to hide in one."

I lowered my barrier and drew Fezzik again. If the creature wouldn't come close enough to strike with my blade—maybe it was even avoiding Chopper—I had to figure out a way to make the bullets work. Assuming the creature came back and wasn't going to join its buddies.

With buildings and trees in the way, I couldn't see Zav's fight, but the raw power being expended by both sides clawed at my senses, so intense that it made me want to crawl under a rock and put my arms over my head. Not that doing so would help.

A dragon's roar thundered through the canyon, echoing from the walls. Zav was not pleased.

It is returning. Sindari shook his fur and crouched to face our foe again.

I started to raise my barrier, but I could only focus on using my power for one thing at a time. In the past, I'd managed to use my magic to burrow holes in the defenses of enemies so that Chopper could slip in and strike. Could I do the same for Fezzik? Or could I weaken the creature's body? It didn't seem to have a magical barrier; it was the bones themselves that were impervious.

Our attacker returned, arrowing toward us from above, talons outstretched. I willed my mental fern fronds to combine and twist into spears, then visualized jamming them into the creature's skull. Faint cracks appeared, and I fired Fezzik's magical bullets, hoping they would do more damage this time.

Nothing came of the cracks, and the bullets bounced off. I cursed in frustration. The creature's wings blotted out the sun as it dove straight at me.

I sprinted to the side, leaping behind one of the standing structures for cover. The creature landed instead of flying up into the air again. Seeing an opportunity, Sindari rushed in, leaping for its back while it looked at me.

But the creature sensed him and shifted focus quickly. It spun around, jaws snapping and a taloned limb raking toward him.

Now, its back was toward me, so I rushed in with Chopper. It crouched to spring. I focused all of my magic on the root spell, willing entangling tendrils to grow from the ground and grab it while I swung my blade.

As on the fae world, my magic worked more easily here, and long roots thrust from the ground, grasping its legs before it could spring away. It startled the creature, and it lurched sideways.

I smashed Chopper's blade into its rib cage. It was far harder than bare bone should have been, but Chopper flared blue, and its magic let it slice through.

On the creature's other side, Sindari dodged its jaws and clawed his way onto its back. He ran up the vertebrae toward the skull as I sliced Chopper through another rib bone.

A wing lifted and tried to pound me into the ground. I dove under the creature's rib cage an instant before it struck me, and I came up in a crouch. Shifting my grip, I drove Chopper up into its breastbone. A satisfying crunch filled my ears, even though the creature didn't react. It felt nothing. Would we have to hack it into a thousand pieces to destroy it?

Another crunch came from above. Sindari sinking his fangs into the creature's skull, I hoped.

As I tugged Chopper out to strike again, the creature lowered itself.

Startled, I dove to the side, yanking my feet out of the way before it could crush me. A wing smashed down from above, and this time, I didn't have time to dodge it. It swatted me to the side, and I rolled into one of the buildings, thudding hard against the wall. I avoided cracking my head but lost my concentration, and the magical roots disappeared.

With a blast of power, the creature hurled Sindari off its back and into the trees. Then it turned and stalked toward me.

I leaped to my feet and faced it with Chopper raised. The creature left behind bones and a piece of its skull that we'd cut off, but its eyes still glowed, and its sharp fangs were still intact. What did I need to do to kill this thing?

I formed a barrier around myself again but didn't trust that it would be enough to stop those fangs, so I crouched to jump out of its path. A burst of magic came from it, hefted me into the air, and pinned me to the wall, my feet dangling several feet above the ground. I managed to keep my magical defenses up, but it didn't matter. The creature had trapped me with the barrier still around me.

Less than five feet away, it lifted its head, jaws spreading wide. Though pinned to the wall, I could lift my arms. I brought up Chopper and willed all of my energy into my barrier.

The fangs descended like jackhammers. They struck my magical shield and slowed but not enough. The tips drove through and toward my face, the piercing of my barrier jolting my brain like a snapped rubber band.

I sliced upward and sideways with Chopper, cutting through the tips of both fangs. One of them drove down and caught my shoulder, punching me to the ground. The now-blunt fang didn't pierce my skin, but bruising pain pummeled my body.

A roar came from behind the creature, and Sindari flew out of the trees and landed on its back. Its head turned to face the new threat. I dropped my barrier so I could try to remake the roots, though my head was throbbing almost as much as my shoulder.

Frustrating seconds passed before I could coax them out of the ground. Finally, roots snaked up and grasped our enemy's legs again.

Distracted, its power disappeared, releasing me from the wall. I fought the instinct to rush away from the creature before it could strike me again and instead leaped in with Chopper. I swung at its skull from beneath, frustration and pain adding strength to my blow. The blade severed the bottom of its jaw, and the bone tumbled free. The blow did not stop its attack.

Sindari avoided its wings and talons and ran up the creature's back again, this time targeting the vertebrae of its neck instead of its skull. Would severing its head destroy it? I rushed in from underneath and leaped up to reach those same vertebrae from below. With another blast of magic, our foe hurled Sindari away again. But the wave didn't catch me this time. The tip of Chopper's blade reached the vertebrae and sliced through them, my sword flaring a bright blue, as if to add its own power to the blow.

Bone crunched, and the skull plopped off. I leaped to the side, barely avoiding being struck by it.

Not trusting that was the end, I whirled to face the creature again. But with the skull detached, the body stopped moving. The bones shuddered, swayed, then collapsed into a pile.

Finally. Sindari stalked out of the trees, moving tenderly. *I have not been thrown around so many times since I was a cub wrestling with my uncle.*

"It's hard to imagine such a regal and noble predator as a cub." I'd met a cub from his kind before, and she had been a big goofball that ate my seatbelts. "I bet you were cute and goofy."

I was regal, even as a cub.

"Even while you were being thrown through the air?" I released my magic, and roots slid back into the ground. The remains of the creature did not move, and its aura disappeared.

Yes.

I was about to run over to check on Zav—the cracking and roars of his battle promised it was still going on—but Sindari glanced at his side, drawing my eye to red blood.

"It cut you," I blurted, rushing over and dropping to my knees beside him.

I rested a hand on his flank, Zav's warning ringing in my mind. The creature's talons had raked three deep gouges in Sindari's side, splitting fur and flesh and revealing muscle. My senses told me there was something magical about the wounds, and there was a faint purple glow over them that reminded me uncomfortably of the box.

Yes, and it feels like icicles burrowing into my torso. Sindari twisted and started licking at the wounds.

"I'm sorry." I needed to go help Zav but didn't want to leave if the gouges could get worse quickly—what if they turned out to be fatal? "Will you be able to heal? Zav said..."

I am certain he warned you not to let an undead creature cut you, yes, Sindari finished for me. *I will need a healer's touch, and I am uncertain if those among my kind know how to handle this type of wound taint. Without an experienced healer, such wounds turn necrotic and can take over your body and either kill you or turn you into one of them.*

"We won't let that happen." I hoped Zav was a good enough healer to keep that from happening. Fortunately, the noises and magic-flinging from his battle were fading—I sensed several of his foes flying away. "Dimitri wouldn't pet an undead tiger. Too creepy."

Then I most assuredly do not want to let that come to pass.

"Stay here. I'll get Zav."

I ran through the trees, having to vault over trunks that had been torn from their roots by the power flying around during the fight. Others had been slammed to the ground by massive boulders tumbling from the canyon wall.

Zav was on his feet amid a mess of bones and skulls scattered among rock rubble. Gray stone dust coated his black body and wings—the cave had collapsed behind him—and his enemies were vanquished. Relieved that he appeared more irritated than injured, I ran up and flung my arms around one of his forelegs.

Four got away, he informed me with disgust, though he lowered a wing and gently rested it around my back.

"Scared by your ferocity, I'm sure."

Scared by me blasting away their defenses with my power and destroying them, he growled into my mind. *They do not feel fear, as living creatures do, but they are not without thought. When they realized their victory was uncertain, they fled. They will report our presence to whoever created them.*

"Your presence is hard not to notice. I imagine that their creator already knows you're here."

Perhaps.

"Sindari is hurt. Can you help him?"

Sindari hadn't remained behind, instead trailing me through the trees, and he sat on his haunches, his flank dark with blood.

He allowed them to pierce his flesh. Zav gazed toward Sindari.

"Not on purpose. He was helping me. Since the creature was knocking over buildings, we had to fight it instead of hiding inside."

Hm. Zav gazed at Sindari with consideration. *I believe it will take a more skilled healer than I to repair his wound, but let me inspect it.*

I stepped out of the way, and Sindari came closer. My heel clunked against one of the skulls, causing it to roll down a rubble pile and land next to a skeletal leg, the foot and talons still attached.

"Your eyes aren't glowing now, punk." I glared at it.

A few more bones dusted the rubble underneath me, smaller pieces that might have been shattered from a foot. Reminded of the finger bones from the artifacts room, I picked one up. All the bones I'd encountered in my life looked similar, so it wasn't as if this had some proven link to the invisible wraith-beings that had attacked me, but the faint purple glow around Sindari's gashes reminded me so much of that box that it was hard not to wonder if they were tied in somehow.

But what would undead creatures flying around on another world have to do with a box made by dragons? Could they all have been created with the same type of magic?

"Are those skeletal wyverns—or whatever they were—native to this world?" I asked, though Zav was gazing intently at Sindari, beaming healing magic at him.

Then I remembered Zav had said the creatures were an oddity and that the dragon ruling this world should have done something about them. That implied they weren't natural occurrences. Maybe they'd come from that haunted world.

They are not, Zav replied without taking his focus from Sindari.

"So someone could have brought them here? After capturing them there? Or *making* them there?" I wondered what Zoltan's response would be if I taped another bone with a note to his door. I'd left before learning if he'd discovered anything useful about the other one.

That is correct. Someone undead.

"Only undead people—er, beings—can make undead... minions?" I'd known that it took a vampire to make another vampire, but I knew less about zombies, and I'd never even encountered an ambulatory—or aerial—skeleton before.

Powerful beings. The presence of such a being here may account for the dwarves going into hiding.

"A whole *planet's* worth of dwarves?"

Perhaps. It is not a hardship for them to remain underground—they have ways to farm, hunt, and fish down there—so it may be something akin to waiting out a storm for them. It is also possible that the being is particularly wide-ranging and heinous and has been preying on their people.

"Comforting." I took some comfort in the fact that Zav, Sindari, and I had defeated the skeletal army, but if those had simply been minions, they'd been powerful ones. How strong did that mean the creator was?

Sindari shifted from sitting to lying on his belly, his head between his paws. That didn't bode well.

"How's the healing going?"

I have repaired the physical wounds, but the undead taint remains. It must be driven out by a more versatile healer than I, someone with experience with such injuries, or it will turn necrotic and damage his body from the inside.

"Can Zondia help? Or another dragon?" I could hardly believe I'd have to give up my sword quest less than an hour into arriving on this world, but Sindari was far more important.

I do not believe Zondia'qareshi has experience with the undead. She is young. The most experienced healer I know is a curmudgeon of a female dragon from the Silverclaw Clan. She is ancient and has peculiar habits.

"What constitutes peculiar habits for dragons?"

She preys upon dwarves, elves, humans, and the other sentient races, even though the meat is unpalatable.

"Uh." This did not sound like the dragon I wanted healing Sindari—or anyone else. "Why would someone like that become a healer?"

She is a healer of dragons. She wishes to remind the other races that dragons are all-powerful and to be obeyed. She eats their kind to make a statement.

"Wouldn't she just eat Sindari?"

That made Sindari look over at me, green eyes bland. *Nobody eats Del'nothian tigers. As I've informed you previously, we are apex predators.*

"Uh huh. Worms and insects eat even predators when they die. Circle of life, buddy."

The Del'nothian tigers have long been allies to the dragons, Zav said. *She would not eat one. I believe she would even heal one, though she would hate to help a Stormforge dragon, especially one who has battled so many of her kin.*

"Yeah, this sounds like a bad idea. Are you *sure* Zondia can't heal him?" Never would I have thought that I'd long for her to help me.

Maybe Zoltan has a potion that would do. Sindari must not have been eager to be treated by a grumpy old dragon.

You may not have time for experimentation, Zav said. *Once you return to your world, if the wound advances far enough and the magic of the realm charm believes you are an undead creature rather than a tiger, it may keep you from traveling again from your realm. You would be stuck there.*

Where I would die—or be killed by my people.

That is possible.

I tried to swallow a lump of emotion swelling in my throat. It didn't work. "He'll go with you, Zav. I know you can find a way to help him."

Very well, Zav said. *I must also ask my people about Braytokinor and if anyone knows what's going on here. If he has been slain, or this world is truly threatened, my kind should act. They should be willing to come deal with the situation here.* Zav's head turned, his long neck shifting as he looked over at me. *I must return you to your home. I cannot leave you here. It is too dangerous.*

"Wait, I'm coming with you. I *have* to go with Sindari." I waved to the feline-shaped charm on my thong.

Would the magic allow Sindari to travel through a portal without me? Or would he poof back to his world? We could usually only be separated by a mile, so it was hard to believe that being on different worlds would work. And if he got stuck back there…

It will be safer for you at your home. Lend me the charm, and I will take Sindari to the dragon home world.

"Why can't you take both of us?"

Did you not hear his warning about the human- and elf-eating dragon, Val? Sindari asked.

"I'll poke her in the ass with Chopper if she tries to eat me."

Sindari and Zav exchanged looks, as if they both thought it was a bad idea for me to go along.

You and your blade are now known among dragon kind, Zav said. *As you know from your incident with the assassin that a Silverclaw dragon hired, you are most hated. I believe the Silverclaw healer would go out of her way to slay you. Of course, as your mate and protector, I could not allow this, and we would do battle, but if I slew or incapacitated her…* Zav extended a wingtip toward Sindari.

"She might be disinclined to heal my buddy?"

She will be disinclined to heal him if she learns that he is linked to, and an ally to, you. It will be better if I claim that his charm belongs to me.

"Wait, if she's a Silverclaw dragon, doesn't she hate you as well?" Though I had questions and concerns, I removed my leather thong, the charms clinking against each other, and unthreaded the feline one.

She loathes me, yes.

"And that's not a problem?"

I will have to promise a return favor in exchange for her help. Zav's lips rippled back, revealing his fangs.

"That doesn't mean having sex with her, does it?" I thought of the assassin's *favors* for the fae queen. To save Sindari's life, I would look the other way—extremely *far* the other way—while he got jiggy with a dragon, but I wouldn't like it.

No. Dragons are not like fae. I will have to bring her meat or, more likely, she will expect political favors in future court sessions. There was the lip ripple again. Who would have guessed a dragon could do that?

I held the charm up for Zav—he used his magic to lift it from my hand and store it in some invisible pocket—then rested a hand on Sindari's back. *Will you be all right?* I didn't want to delay things, not when he had to get this healing treatment before the magic dictated that he return to his realm, but I was worried and felt guilty. *I'm sorry I brought you out to fight when this was a possibility.*

Injuries are always a possibility in battle, and I live to hunt prey and destroy enemies. Sindari tilted his head in consideration. *I would always rather fight than not. Unless it is in a bog, pond, lake, or under torrential rainfall.*

Yes, I've noted your aversion to water except on warm sunny days. Good.

With a swell of magic, a portal formed.

Zav pointed his wing at it. *You will return to your world.*

"I could stay here while you take care of him," I offered, hating the idea of sitting back home and twiddling my thumbs. "Isn't it possible the dwarves would come out and talk to me if no dragons were in the area?"

I envisioned camping out in front of those stone doors in my tent, but then I remembered Zav's words, that it probably wasn't the *dragons* keeping the dwarves in their mountain.

It is too dangerous for you to stay here alone. Zav pointed at the portal again. *You will stay in the protection of your abode, and I will bring Sindari back to you on Earth when he is healed.*

He was probably right—even if he was getting uppity and making it a command—but I was curious about one thing. *Do you think the big bad sensed your arrival here—your dragonly aura—and that was why the, uh, minions were sent? If I activated my camouflaging charm, would I be able to travel around here unnoticed?*

I supposed there was little point. If I was camouflaged, the dwarves wouldn't know I was here, either, and nobody would come out and chat. Also, Mount Crenel could be a thousand miles away, and I didn't see any public transportation systems.

Possibly, Zav said as I returned my thong, bereft of my favorite charm, to my neck, *but it is still too dangerous and there is little you could do here on foot. I will bring you back after this world has been dealt with and made safe again. If dragons defeat whoever is responsible for the undead minions, then perhaps the dwarves will come out, and it will be easier for you to find someone to answer your sword questions or guide you to that mountain.*

"I understand. Thanks for helping Sindari." I hugged Zav's leg and my furry ally before stepping through the portal.

My last thought before the swirling tunnel of magic enveloped me was that this had not only been a waste of time but that I'd gotten one of my best friends hurt. That crusty old dragon had *better* be willing to heal him.

CHAPTER 13

RAIN AND DARKNESS HAD DESCENDED on Seattle by the time I returned. A text message from Amber informed me that she'd scheduled my next dress fitting, making me wish I'd argued harder to stay on Dun Kroth. Who wouldn't want to battle creepy skeletal enemies instead of being poked and prodded and tape-measured by a seamstress while half-naked?

Dimitri wasn't home, but I sensed Zoltan in the basement, and surprisingly Freysha was down there too. I hadn't seen her since visiting our father in their homeland. Maybe she'd returned to finish her engineering class.

If she stayed awhile, maybe I could talk her into teaching me a little more magic. The roots and mental defenses were nice, but what I would really like to learn was how to hurl fireballs. Wizards did that in books, and it seemed terribly useful. Freysha, with her forest magic, might not be able to create flames, but maybe she could introduce me to a helpful pyromaniac elf who owed her a favor. I would be happy to pay for tutelage, but so far, I hadn't found the elves any more interested in currency than dragons. Maybe, like the fae queen, they could be enticed by chocolate-covered caramels.

After making sure the new toe bone had survived the trip through the portal with me, I headed around to the back of the house and down the basement steps. Usually, Sindari's charm bounced against my chest under my collarbones when I did that, and I noticed the lack. An uncomfortable feeling washed over me as I worried that Zav's plan wouldn't work and I would never see Sindari again.

I knocked on the door and was answered by two muffled shouts, the words "don't come in!" being decipherable in the mix.

"Fine, but I'm leaving another gift-wrapped piece of bone stuck to your door."

A rustling and a startled gasp came from the yard next door. Maybe I shouldn't have called that quite so loudly. There were so many trees and bushes, in addition to a six-foot wooden fence, between the properties that I tended to forget that we were in an urban neighborhood and that sound carried.

Oh, well. If the rumors of the house being haunted hadn't warned the neighbors to expect oddness from this corner lot, then the dragon-shaped topiaries out front, now complete with glowing eyes, were a big clue.

One moment, please, Freysha spoke politely into my mind. *Zoltan is streaming a live recording.*

Do you know what that is? I hadn't noticed Freysha on my laptop, experiencing the fascinating vagaries of the internet, in the months she'd visited. She was much more inclined to study from ancient tomes in her room, peruse goblin-approved engineering texts for her class, or grow Jurassic foliage in the conservatory. Her class *was* online, however, so maybe she had learned about the joys of YouTube.

I am learning as I assist him, she replied.

This isn't something for his raving groupies, is it?

What is a groupie?

The teenage girls who send him fan mail and want to know how to turn their high-school nemeses into frogs.

Freysha digested that for a moment before replying. *I believe it is for them, yes. But this is a frog-free presentation. He is instructing his followers on formulas and tinctures that can be made using manzanita bark.*

I got him that bark, you know. Tell him I expect a cut of his advertising revenue from the video.

I had no idea if there *was* advertising revenue, but since, as far as I knew, I was Zoltan's only recurring client, he had to make money *somewhere* to buy ingredients.

You may enter now. Freysha didn't comment on the rest.

When I opened the door and walked into the dark basement, I almost crashed into another door two feet in front of it. "Dimitri found time to build the light-lock, I see."

Red light from Zoltan's special lamps flowed through a crack under the interior door, so it wasn't entirely airtight—*light-tight*. I closed the exterior door behind me before opening the next one.

In addition to the usual lab accoutrements, the magical anvil, Zoltan's coffin, and his various cases of books and scrolls, a recording setup had been erected on a table. In front of a laptop camera, a cauldron smoldered over a Bunsen burner, votives burned in a pair of holders made from monkey skulls, and an array of colorful liquids in vials filled almost every remaining inch of space.

"You're burning candles in monkey skulls, and you were squeamish about the bone I left taped to your door?" I asked.

"I ordered the skull candle holders from a catalog. They didn't appear in a mysterious package on the door." Zoltan, clad in a white suit, his dark hair impeccably combed back from his widow's peak, adjusted his red bow tie. He usually wore suits, but the black cape trimmed with ermine fur wasn't his typical basement wear.

"I left a note. How mysterious could it have been?" I headed toward Freysha, intending to give her a hug and welcome her back to Earth, but I paused and pointed at the cube of special red lights she was holding. "Have you been pressed into service as his lighting assistant? Can you even *record* videos by red light?"

"Certainly you can," Zoltan said. "It's perfect. The candles and the red lights create the ideal ambiance for an alchemist occasionally giving lectures on how to dabble in the dark arts."

"You were teaching them to make wart remover." Freysha balanced the light contraption on a shelf and came forward to hug me.

"I said there was *occasional* dark-art dabbling, not frequent. Practical alchemical solutions applicable to all are much more popular. They also don't result in my videos being de-monetized and de-listed. Instructions on how to use alchemical formulas to slay or incapacitate people can have that result."

"Weird." I'd *known* there was advertising revenue. "Got something for you."

I fished the bone out of my pocket and offered it to him. "Will you see if this is related to the other one? Not *related*, exactly, since it came from a flying skeleton instead of an invisible wraith, but from the same world. Shared DNA or whatever."

Zoltan used his forefinger and thumb to pluck up the bone and carried it over to the station that held his microscope and a variety of magnifying glasses. I didn't think he had a DNA sequencer over there, or that they were something that could fit in a basement, but maybe he had an alchemical alternative.

"It sounds like you've been in interesting places lately." Freysha tilted her head, a pointed ear poking up through her blonde hair.

"Yeah, the artifacts room under Willard's office."

Her elegant eyebrows rose.

"Also the dwarven home world. Zav and I were trying to research my sword but didn't make it far before eight undead, winged creatures waylaid us." I summed up the brief adventure for her and told her about Sindari.

"Ah, that is unfortunate. And also explains rumors that we've been hearing about Dun Kroth. Just two days ago, our father sent a scouting party to investigate and find out why we've lost contact with the dwarven king."

"I hope they don't run into the flying things. We only defeated four before the others fled. How is our father? Recovered from his dragon-inflicted illness?"

"Yes." Freysha smiled. "He has been telling people that you are getting married in the human way—which is deemed to be somewhat similar to the elven way and therefore acceptable—to a dragon."

"He tells people about me?" I touched my chest. "I'd assumed that my assassin career made me an embarrassment. Along with the fact that I'm a half-human mongrel."

Her smile shifted to a frown. "You should not use derogatory language to describe yourself. You are a strong warrior and have promise to one day be a decent magic user."

"Still, he didn't tell your mother about me, did he? I'm sure your people don't approve of dalliances with human maidens." I trusted my mother had qualified as a maiden back then. Or something close.

Whistling came from the work station. Zoltan had pulled down several thick tomes and opened them—biology tomes, judging by the illustrations visible—and had laid the new bone on a swath of fabric—or maybe that was an antimicrobial towel.

"He eventually told her," Freysha said.

"After I showed up on her doorstep? I guess it was more of a platform than a doorstep."

"Before then. He told *me* about you first though." Freysha smiled again. "I was surprised to learn I had a sister! He hadn't ever spoken to me about people, uhm, lovers he had before my mother."

"I don't think that's a conversation most parents have with their kids. 'Hey, kiddo, guess how many people I shagged before I met your mom?'"

"Shagged?"

"Never mind."

"I am taking a sample from the new bone fragment," Zoltan announced, switching his magnifying glass for what looked more like a hammer than a precision laboratory tool.

"Go for it. The owner doesn't need it anymore."

"Macabre."

"He's odd for a vampire, right?" I asked Freysha.

"He is my first vampire acquaintance. We don't allow vampires on my home world."

"Ghastly," Zoltan said.

"The elven embargo on vampires or the bone?" I asked.

"The former. The bone is simply a bone."

"It doesn't ooze insidious magic?"

"It does not." Zoltan grabbed a chisel and tapped off a shard. "I had to pulverize the other one you gave me. I hope you didn't want it back."

"Not really. Is that necessary to examine it fully?"

"No, but I have an interesting recipe that calls for wraith bones. I always assumed it was a joke, since apparitions can hardly have bones, but given the story you put down in your note… I'm curious if the formula will turn out."

Turn out? I imagined him baking muffins that failed to rise.

Zoltan put his sample on a slide to examine under his microscope.

"Hey, Freysha, are you aware that some elf was sent to question my mother?"

"I was not. Do you know who?"

"Mom didn't share his name, if he gave it to her. He told her he was investigating her as a precaution before Eireth comes for the wedding." I watched Freysha's face, concerned that she hadn't known about this. Was it possible the elf had lied to my mother and had nothing to do with Eireth?

I shivered, thinking of the elven assassin, but he'd given Zav his word—and accepted all that magical jewelry—that he wouldn't bug me again.

"That is possible," Freysha said thoughtfully, studying the cracked cement floor. "When Father leaves his suite, he has more bodyguards now than typical. Even though he's recovered from his illness, our people are concerned that someone will try again to harm him."

"Zav came back and explained to you what happened, right?" I hadn't been to the elven world since my showdown with the assassin, but Zav had gone and told my father about the wedding.

"Lord Zavryd did explain everything, including that the dragons Xilnethgarish and Quaresthee allowed themselves to be manipulated and used against their wills."

"Hm." That didn't paint Xilneth in the most flattering light, but I supposed it was better than having the elves believe he'd masterminded the plot. I had never met Quaresthee and had no feelings toward him, but I liked to think of Xilneth as an affable oaf and didn't want to see him in trouble or ostracized over that fiasco.

"Elves are wary," Freysha said. "It will be some time before they relax their guard again. There are also some who... don't trust you, because of your Earthen heritage. There's been some speculation that this wedding might be a plot, designed to lure my father off Veleshna Var where he might be more easily assassinated."

"*I'm* not the one who invited him."

"Do not be too bitter. It is a small faction of elves who believe this. Others heard that you bested the infamous assassin Varlesh Sarrlevi in battle and are impressed. Still others, mostly of the female variety, are impressed that you got a dragon to claim you as his mate and find the idea of a wedding most romantic."

I twisted my lips into what I hoped was a suitably disturbed expression. "Don't take this the wrong way, but I liked it better when your people didn't know I existed."

"But you are glad that your sister knows you exist, correct?" She touched her chest.

"Yeah, you're okay." I thumped her on the shoulder. "Hey, will you teach me how to make fireballs?"

Her mouth parted, but words didn't come out. Maybe that hadn't been the smoothest transition.

My phone buzzed. It was after eleven, but Thad was calling. That gave me something new to be concerned about.

"I'll step outside to take this," I said. "Freysha, make yourself comfortable if you're staying. Your room is still the same."

"I saw that you have been watering the plants. This is excellent."

"I do the indoor ones, and Dimitri does the outdoor ones. We have a system of shared chores around the house." I headed for the door, answering before the phone dropped to voice mail.

"What does Lord Zavryd do?"

"Topiaries." I passed through the doors. "Hey, Thad. What's up?"

"There's a *boy* in my house," he said in a tight voice.

"Like a burglar?" I glanced at the time again, making sure I'd read it right.

"A new *friend*. Amber said you knew about it."

"Oh, the decoy boyfriend? He shouldn't be anything to worry about." I grinned, tickled that Amber had taken my advice.

"I've told her he has to leave three times now, but she keeps saying they have homework they have to finish. It's Friday night, Val."

"Is it?" I'd lost track of days of the week. "Can't you be firm and put your foot down?"

"I never had to before. Amber is a good student, and she's so busy with swim team that she never had a… a… *social life* before."

Social life, I gathered, referred to boys.

"You can do it," I said. "You were in the army. I have confidence that you can get firm with a couple of teenagers."

"Do you?"

"Sure. Don't you have any baseball bats or other large sports sticks that you can wave around menacingly?" I knew he didn't keep weapons, but hadn't he played softball one summer?

"I have a reproduction cannon, but it's only eight inches long, and I'd be loath to take it off my Warhammer game board."

"Leave it. Your painted miniatures aren't going to scare teenage boys." I rubbed my eyes. It had been a long day. "Do you want me to come up there and poke him with my sword?"

"No." Thad sighed. Wistfully? "Sword-poking is a criminal offense."

"And menacing someone with a reproduction cannon isn't?"

"Not a small one, no. Never mind. I just wanted to rant."

"That's allowed." I bit my lip, feeling guilty once again that I wasn't around more. Should I offer to let him send Amber to my house for teenager vacations now and then? So he could have alone time with Nin and a break from sarcasm? The only problem was that he'd been at my house during one of the numerous attacks, and he didn't even think it was safe enough for Amber to visit for sword lessons.

"Thanks."

"How're things going with Nin?"

His voice turned shy and smugly happy. "Good."

"I'm glad. Look, just let me know if you need me to come up and menace the decoy boyfriend."

"Are you *sure* it's a decoy?"

"If it's not, things escalated from I'm-not-into-boys to dating-boys quickly."

"I think that's how it happens with teenagers. Okay, I'm going to get my cannon. Night, Val."

He hung up before I could decide if that had been a joke. I hoped so.

At your leisure, dear robber, a text came in from Zoltan.

You have something? I texted back before feeling silly because I could walk back inside.

"I have a great many things," Zoltan replied aloud as I entered the basement.

Freysha, who'd stayed inside, nodded at me.

"I'll trust that you will pay my consulting fee and that I need not withhold information," Zoltan said.

"Thanks so much." I looked at Freysha. "I guess giving him a stellar and rare ingredient wasn't enough of a payment."

"I haven't yet determined if that supposed *wraith* bone will work in my recipe. But I have determined that the two owners of those bones did not originate on Earth."

"Okay." I would have been more surprised if they had. "Anything else?"

"Do not rush me, dear robber." Zoltan straightened his bow tie. "I have also determined that they came from the same world, sharing the DNA that is common, according to my texts—" he waved to books that weren't written in English, or any other Earth-based language, "—in beings from the reputedly haunted world of Nagnortha."

"Is it odd that I encountered them on different worlds?"

"I cannot answer that question, other than to suggest that perhaps someone borrowed them from their home world. You may leave now. I must upload my video. I'll invoice you in the morning."

"Can't wait," I muttered, heading for the door again.

Freysha followed me outside.

"You know who I'd really like to talk to?" I asked.

"Lord Zavryd?"

"He's helping heal Sindari. I'd really like to talk to that thief. *She's* the one who put the box in the artifacts room, and I can't help but wonder if she's the one who sent those flying creatures after us."

"Perhaps if you wander around the city," Freysha said, "she will approach you again."

"By *approach* me, you mean set a cunning trap to ensnare me?"

"Yes. If you allow yourself to be trapped, I am certain you will get the opportunity to speak with her."

While she had me chained and was walking away with Chopper, right. "I would rather trap *her* and control the conversation."

"How are you going to do that?"

"I'll let you know when I figure it out."

CHAPTER 14

B EFORE DAWN, I WOKE TO a faint gonging in the house. One of Dimitri's alarms going off. Or was that one of Zav's? I couldn't remember, but nobody visited at this hour for any good reason.

After rolling out of bed, I stuffed my feet into my boots and grabbed Chopper. My window had a view of both streets leading to our corner as well as the sidewalks. A figure in a dark trench coat stood on the strip of grass on the other side of the sidewalk, looking toward one of the dragon topiaries. Its eyes glowed at him. It was too dark to make out his face or tell if smoke was curling up from the topiary's snout, a sign that it had sent one of its warning gouts of fire at the intruder.

Whoever it was didn't have magical blood, not that I could sense, but that didn't mean he wasn't trouble. Unfortunately, Zav hadn't returned during the night. That wasn't that atypical—it usually took him a while to travel to and from his home world and find the various dragons there—but I worried about Sindari. By now, the magic that let him travel outside of his realm would have run out for the day, forcing him to return. Had Zav found a dragon willing to heal him before that happened? Since Zav had my charm, I had no way to check on Sindari.

As I jogged down the stairs, I almost crashed into Dimitri coming out of his room on the first floor. He carried a wrench.

"Prepared to defend us from home invaders?" I waved at it.

"If necessary. I don't think you should mock me when you're wearing combat boots with a... is that a *Lord of the Rings* nightgown?"

"It's *The Hobbit*, thank you, and it has Smaug on it. I thought it would amuse Zav."

"Does it?"

"It amuses him to take it off me."

Dimitri curled a lip. "That's an even more disturbing image than the boots."

"Maybe it'll scare off our snoop."

"There is someone out there then?" Dimitri asked as we headed to the living room window and peeled the curtains open a few inches.

"Yup. That sketchy burglar is scoping out the premises."

Too bad it wasn't the thief I *wanted* to catch. Mr. Trenchcoat had advanced to the sidewalk and moved farther from the topiaries. He was studying the front door and didn't seem to have noticed our noses pressed to the living room window yet.

A car was parked a couple of houses away, the headlights on and someone sitting in the driver's seat. Were those the roof lights of a police car?

Dimitri groaned. "It's that detective that came to the shop."

"He's stalking you where you live?"

"Stalking or maybe he gathered the evidence that he needs to arrest me."

"Maybe he just came to see if we have one of the door knockers on the house."

We did. Dimitri had recently installed a green one on the front door, even though I'd suggested that the topiaries were sufficient. Zav had also installed numerous alarms around the property lines, including an invisible dome-shaped barrier that automatically flared to life if magical winged creatures flew into the area or an unfamiliar full-blooded magical being attempted to walk onto the property. The assassin had destroyed a few of the defenses when he'd attacked, but Zav had since restored everything.

The detective straightened his back and took a bracing breath.

"He's coming up," Dimitri said.

I reached over and rested my hand on an orange ball-shaped salt lamp that Zav had altered to work as the controller for the defenses. As soon as the detective took a step onto the walkway, he ran into the invisible barrier and stumbled backward.

"No, he's not," I said cheerfully, as the detective patted the air in confusion.

Dimitri shook his head, looking glum instead of cheerful. "I'm going to get in more trouble for resisting arrest."

"How are you resisting arrest? He hasn't made it to the door to read you your rights. And he won't."

"I can't stay in the house forever."

"No, but you can call Tam and ask her if she can handle the shop today. Get Inga to come in and back her up if there's trouble. Did you talk to that baker yet? The only way to make this problem go away is to figure out what actually happened—and prove it to the police."

"I went to her house, but she didn't let me in."

"Was she home?"

"Yeah. When I knocked, the curtains moved, and I saw her peeking out, but then she closed them and refused to answer."

"That's suspicious then. She doesn't want to talk to you."

"She may be afraid I'll threaten her because she threw me to the wolves by telling the police all about my door knocker."

"Maybe, but she may also be lying about what happened with the door knocker and her *friend*."

Dimitri regarded me. "Do you actually think my door knocker is innocent? I mean, that nothing went wrong? I don't see how it could have—Inga has been enchanting them, and she's way better than I am—but it's possible something *could* have gone wrong…"

"None of the stuff you make is deadly. Your most dangerous contraption hurls thorns into burglars' butts. I have faith that your door knockers are innocuous, except perhaps to poofy eyebrow hair."

He snorted. "Thanks. It means something that you don't think my stuff is junk that doesn't work right."

I thumped him on the back and thought about going back to bed. Since the barrier extended all around the house, the detective wouldn't get in. The driver of the police car had turned off the lights, gotten out, and joined him. They were patting their way along the front of the property, trying to find a hole in the barrier. One strayed too close to the corner topiary, and its eyes flared yellow, and fire streamed out of its snout.

The guy cursed and leaped back. Flames danced along the hem of his jacket, and he patted at it, then flung himself onto the grass on the other side of the sidewalk and rolled about.

"Zav's stuff, on the other hand, I trust less not to turn deadly." I shook my head.

"I shouldn't be amused by that, right?" Dimitri pointed at the guy as he finished rolling, climbed to his feet, and patted at the charred fabric again.

"No, that would be immature."

"I thought so. I just wanted to make sure."

The detective made sure his partner was all right, then held up a hand and jogged down the sidewalk.

"He's going to try the back," Dimitri guessed.

"He won't get in. You're safe as long as you stay here."

"What if they stake out the house, and I'm stuck here forever?"

"Maybe you can ask Nin to talk to the baker. Has she ever met Nin? If not, she might answer the door for her."

"That's a good idea. Do you think she'll mind doing my dirty work?"

"Questioning suspicious people who are trying to get you thrown in jail isn't dirty work. It's smart work. Besides, she won't want the majority owner of our business to be arrested. Who would run the shop and make the dragon door knockers if you were in jail?"

"Inga could."

"She's not an owner, and she's busy raising a rowdy troll boy."

"True."

My phone buzzed. "Call her before she goes to the food truck for the day," I suggested, then wandered back to the kitchen and peered out the back window as I answered the phone. "What's going on, Mom?"

I almost asked what prompted her to call this early, but she was usually up by five, even this time of year when it was dark until seven. The detective had forced his way through the neighbor's privacy bamboo, climbed our fence, perched atop it, and was trying to jump down. But the barrier bounced him back over the fence and into the bamboo. The tall stalks rattled and shed leaves as he tumbled down out of sight.

Even though I'd told Dimitri being amused was immature, I might have smirked.

"Is there anyone stalking you who might have an interest in me again?" Mom asked.

My smirk vanished. "It's possible. Why? Did someone come to your house?"

I envisioned Dimitri's police showing up there to question her, but she wasn't tied in any way to the door knockers or the shop, except vaguely by being related to me. What if my *thief* had been there? It was probably too late to set a trap.

"I'm not sure, but Rocket started barking at around four this morning. He was positive *something* was out back. I never saw anyone, but I did hear a clattering at one point, and he went on for a good fifteen minutes. I didn't let him out. I was worried it might be someone with a gun. I was also worried the elves were spying on me and that they would have unfavorable things to say to Eireth if I sicced Rocket on them."

"*Sicced* Rocket? Mom, your dog runs up and leans on strangers' legs. That's not siccing."

"He would do more than that if someone was threatening me."

"Knock them over and stand on their chests while wagging everything?"

"I called you for advice," Mom said tartly, "not to mock my dog."

"Sorry. I'm just pointing out his affable good nature."

"I haven't gone out to look for tracks. It's not light enough yet. I just wanted to see if I should take more than my Glock when I go."

"What *more* do you have? No, wait. I don't want to know. Stay inside, and I'll come over to help you look around. Maybe Dimitri has a few of his defenses that I can bring over to install around your yard."

"I've *seen* his yard art, Val. It's hideous. I allowed it when he was paying rent because I didn't want to hurt his feelings."

"It's not just decorative. It's useful. Right now, I'm watching a barrier knock an intruder off our fence and into the neighbor's aggressively growing bamboo. Oh, wait. Now he's moved to the other neighbor's yard, and, yes, he was just dumped into the rose garden. I hope the thorns tear his pants off."

"I didn't realize his yard art was that effective."

I didn't mention that Zav's magic was responsible for the barrier I'd described. Dimitri had some useful stuff, after all. "It's improving. There's a troll enchanter schooling him in the ways."

"Hm."

That wasn't a ringing endorsement, but I would see if Dimitri had anything I could take out to her place. It bothered me that this could be the second time in as many months that people had gone out to see her because of her association with me—the *third* if one counted the elf interrogating her about the wedding.

"I'll grab something to eat and head out there now," I said. "Don't wander off until I get there, please."

Her second *hm* was even less committal, and I had a feeling she and Rocket would be sniffing around out back as soon as it was fully light.

"Is everything all right?" Freysha walked in as I hung up and peered toward a different section of the fence, where the detective was trying again.

"Nothing that Zav's magic can't handle, but someone may be pestering my mom again."

"My people?" Freysha touched a hand to her chest.

"I hope not. Last time, it sounded like they came to the door during the day instead of skulking around in the backyard at night like a raccoon ravaging garbage cans."

Freysha frowned. "That doesn't sound like my people."

"I'm going out to visit her." I paused on my way up to my room to dress. "Do you want to come? You two haven't met, have you? She likes elves. She'd like to meet you." At the least, Mom would be interested in asking Freysha questions about Eireth, whom I knew she'd never entirely gotten over.

"I can come with you. If elves *did* visit her in the night, I may be able to determine who and why."

"I'm more concerned that it was my half-dwarf thief who visited her in the night, but thanks." Maybe Freysha could help me make a trap to ensnare that thief. I would ask her in the car.

Freysha nodded. "Dwarves would be more likely than elves to knock over trash cans."

"Not everybody can be agile and graceful."

Unfortunately, I had a feeling the sneaky thief was more like an elf than a dwarf. She'd eluded everyone so far, and I had no idea how I would trap her.

CHAPTER 15

"THERE ARE *SO* MANY WAYS to make a trap." Gondo gestured expansively from the back seat of the Jeep. He was wedged between a couple of enchanted metal gargoyles and manticores that Dimitri had parted with, defenses that were redundant at our place now that Zav had done his upgrades. "How long is this drive? I will make a list for you. And read you the list. It will be thorough, with footnotes and appendices. I learned about footnotes and appendices in my human university class."

"A list is good. No need to read it aloud. I can scan it later." I took the Woodinville exit off 405 and drove toward Duvall, wishing Mom had picked somewhere less remote when she'd opted to move up here to be closer to Amber. Duvall was three hundred miles closer than Bend, Oregon, but with traffic, it didn't seem like it.

"Oh, I should read the list to you." Gondo rummaged in the beat-up briefcase filled with tools that he'd shown up to the house with, arriving less than a minute before Freysha and I had been headed out. Since he'd had homework and notes for Freysha from the class they were taking together, it hadn't seemed appropriate to take off and leave him standing on the sidewalk. Besides, he could help install the yard art. "That way," he added, "I can extrapolate when necessary. Do you have any coffee?"

"No." I looked at Freysha in the passenger seat, wondering if she enjoyed the company of overly chatty goblins or was simply too polite to shoo them away.

She only smiled. She *had* been studying to go to their world and learn from their engineers. Maybe her readings had prepared her for goblin chattiness.

"I went first to the Coffee Dragon," Gondo said, reaffirming my suspicions that nobody ever used the word *sable* in the name, "where I'd hoped to acquire some of the special blend, but the fearsome trollish woman was there and said I couldn't come in because the goblin occupancy capacity had already been crossed."

"She's turning away customers?" I might have to talk to Dimitri about that. Even though the goblins slept under bridges and in parks, they somehow always had money to pay for numerous cups of coffee.

"Yes. And there were only *eighteen* goblins inside. I counted. They didn't even have *all* of the tables. A surly orc was swigging espresso shots at the little table by the window."

Hm. Maybe I *wouldn't* talk to Dimitri. Nineteen goblins did seem like it would exceed some maximum-occupancy law somewhere. There were probably dice ricocheting off all the walls by now.

"Why so many goblins so early in the day?" I asked. "I thought you were night people."

"Last night was the Ratchet Festival, so we were up all night," he said. "We will nap in the afternoon."

I almost asked what the Ratchet Festival entailed but was afraid he would tell me.

Gondo pulled two smashed aluminum cans out of the plastic garbage bag I kept in the back of the Jeep and tucked them into his briefcase. I wondered what second life the lemon La Croix cans would have.

He asked Freysha something in the goblin language.

"No." She made a hand gesture that looked like using a screwdriver.

"Hm." Gondo tapped a ruler to his chin.

What had he been measuring in the back of my Jeep? I didn't ask about that either.

"Can you two engineers help me figure out how to trap a half-dwarf thief?" I asked instead.

"Is your dragon mate not capable of such a simple task?" Gondo asked.

"He's busy. And he doesn't know I want to trap her."

"Her? A *female* dwarf thief?" Gondo's green ears perked. "Dwarf women are buxom and sturdy and know about tools. They're most pleasing."

"Uh huh. This one is from Asia and is half-human. She might not know about tools."

Instead, she knew about undead minions, which was much less appealing.

"Disappointing," Gondo said. "I will sketch some trap ideas. Freysha will help."

"There's some rope in the back." I pointed a thumb over my shoulder. "If you haven't already used it for something."

"Rope? Our traps will be sublime and sophisticated. We have no need for simple rope."

"But aluminum cans are okay?"

"Aluminum cans are a fabulous invention unique to this world." His voice had grown dreamy. "*Fabulous.*"

I drove through Duvall, continuing past larger mostly wooded properties, and finally turned onto the gravel dead-end street where my mother had rented a cabin. Tall pines and firs filled the yards and provided privacy. The homes were all on acreage, so I understood why my mother had chosen the area, even if I wished it were more conveniently located to the city.

"Do you think she'll like me?" Freysha whispered as we passed a wooden bear-holding-a-trout mailbox, followed by a mailbox with foxes painted on the side. Maybe Dimitri's yard art would fit in here.

"Sure," I said. "Why not?"

"I'm the offspring of… the other woman."

"I think my mom is the other woman."

"Not from her point of view."

"You're making my head hurt."

I turned onto Mom's gravel driveway and parked the Jeep, noticing that she'd added a new outbuilding since the last time I'd visited. Between the pottery shed and the wood shed, a wooden cylinder with a door in the end now rested on its side. It looked like a giant whiskey barrel had fallen over.

"What is that thing and why is it a circle?" I wondered.

"The bottom is flat," Gondo said. "That means it's an arc, not a circle. The arc is the strongest structural shape."

Freysha nodded. "In an arc, stress is distributed equally instead of being concentrated at any one point."

"Thanks for the engineering tips. Maybe Mom got a new storage shed. An unstressed storage shed." I stepped out of the Jeep.

The door on the strange wooden building opened, and my mother walked out. Naked.

I almost fell over.

She lifted a hand to wave, then realized I hadn't come alone. She stepped back into the building, wrapped a towel around herself, and came out again.

Rocket barked from inside the cabin, and I spotted golden fur and a nose pressed against a window by the front door.

"Your warning is a little late," Mom called to him.

"I'm positive I told you to stay inside until I got here to help." I waved for Mom to go into the cabin and put on clothes. "Not wander the premises naked. You're an easy target."

"I am not. The sauna is sturdy. Besides, I checked the tracks, and it looks like a bear came to visit." She waved toward the dense trees behind the cabin. "Not an assassin or anyone else nettlesome."

Gondo jumped out of the Jeep with his tool briefcase. I had no idea where he'd gotten that thing, but it was stained on one side, dented on the corners, and looked like it had been fished out of a mud puddle.

"This is very exciting," Gondo said. "I did not know there would be nudity."

"If you find my mom exciting, you're weird."

"Really, Val. I've aged well, and I keep myself in shape."

"She is a silver coyote," Gondo said, fortunately more with reverence than lust, though he definitely checked her out.

"Silver *fox* is the term," I said, "and she's way too old for you."

"*Really*, Val." Mom sniffed and started for the house, her bare feet hardened enough not to mind the gravel. She couldn't truly be irked that I was trying to keep a goblin from ogling her, could she? Maybe I shouldn't have said she was too *old* for Gondo but was instead too regal, or sophisticated, or *sane*.

Mom paused when Freysha stepped uncertainly out of the Jeep. She glanced at me. "Did you bring another elf to interview me?"

"No. This is my half-sister, Freysha. I brought her to help me trap a thief."

Freysha did the typical elven greeting of a bow-curtsey. "Good morning, Lady Thorvald." Then she switched to elvish and said something else.

My mother nodded. "I only remember a little, but yes. You're Eireth's daughter?"

"Yes. It is nice to meet you. I have been teaching Val to use her magic."

"Oh?" Mom looked at me again, eyebrows rising.

I hadn't spoken much to her about my lessons, knowing she had always loved elven culture and abilities and wished *she* had the ability to learn magic.

"Is she a good student?" Mom asked.

"She tries hard."

Mom snorted.

"Thanks, Freysha," I said dryly, though I doubted Freysha had meant that as an insult.

"Sometimes, my gentle forest magic is not to her tastes," Freysha explained, seeming confused by my sarcasm. "She wishes to hurl fireballs and scorch enemies to ash."

"Shocking," Mom said.

"Only the really *bad* enemies," I said. "For nuisances, I'd only torch their clothing or their eyebrows. Just enough to teach them not to mess with me."

"You wouldn't torch tools, right?" Gondo asked. "Tools should be respected by all."

"Wrenches don't usually piss me off. Though pliers can be pesky."

"Why is it that you think I'm the strange one in the family?" Mom asked me.

"You're standing naked and sweaty in the driveway, and you have to ask me that?"

"I was using my new Finnish sauna. It's the key to health and longevity. Perhaps you should try it."

"Is nudity required?"

"Yes."

Gondo raised his wrench. "I'll try it."

"No," I said, relieved when I sensed Zav approaching, not only because his presence should put an end to the awkward conversation but because he could give me an update on Sindari. A *good* update, I hoped.

"Come inside, everyone." Mom extended an arm to the door. "I have coffee and tea."

"Coffee?" Gondo's ears rotated and perked like a German Shepherd's. "What kind?"

Mom seemed puzzled by the question but had a better answer than I would have. "It's the After Dark blend from River Trail Roasters."

"After Dark sounds perfect for goblins," I said.

"I haven't tried them before." The ears perked further with keen interest. "I love trying new roasters. Organic? Fair trade?"

"I believe so. You can look at the bag."

I imagined Gondo stuffing his nose in it and inhaling deeply.

"Will Lord Zavryd be joining us?" Freysha looked toward the western sky, the direction he was flying in from.

"Probably. After he lectures me for leaving the house. Mom, will you go put some clothes on, please? *Before* making the coffee?"

"I suppose, but it's not like making bacon. Burns are uncommon."

"You *burning* yourself isn't my primary concern," I said as Zav soared in over the trees, his wings spread, his black scales gleaming under the morning sun.

"Oh, my." Mom gaped up at him.

I tried to shoo her inside again—toward the direction of her closet—but she seemed enthralled by his magnificence. Zav *was* magnificent—I assumed he wasn't bothering to hide himself from mundane humans this morning—and I supposed it didn't matter if he met my mother naked. He had few qualms about nudity, as evinced from his perpetual lack of underwear under the robe.

Zav shifted into human form as he landed next to my Jeep, violet eyes focusing on me. "My mate, you did not wait for me in the safety of your abode."

"Sorry. My mom was visited by a bear. I thought it might be a thief. You've met my mother, right?" I extended a hand toward Mom, who wasn't doing as good a job as she should have been using her towel to cover herself. With a flash of insight, I knew what it was like for Amber to go out in public places with me. To her, *I* was the embarrassing one. Well, at least I clothed myself.

"Yes," Zav stated. "First in Greemaw's valley. She had fantasies about shooting me."

"We all did," I said. "You were kind of a dick then."

"I was pursuing a mission and believed you were a criminal and an obstacle." Zav smoothed a hand down his silver-trimmed black elven robe, looking much the same as he had back then, save for his footwear. Once again, he was in the hole-filled yellow Crocs.

I had a terrible suspicion that he found them more comfortable than the elven slippers or any of the other footwear he'd tried on. Horrific.

"Now, you know how delightful I am. And my mom…" I wasn't sure what to say about her. Her nudity had me flustered. "Just got a new sauna."

"What is a sauna?" Zav asked.

"That thing." I waved toward it. "It's hot inside, and you sweat. It's not sexy, and there aren't bubbles, not like the hot tub. I doubt you'd like it."

"It is *hot*?" Why did he sound intrigued? "This part of your planet is damp and chilly. *Often*."

"Uh huh. You can check it out later. Any news about Sindari?"

Zav gripped his chin thoughtfully and gazed at the sauna.

"I will go and look around to see if elves beyond those your mother knows about have been here," Freysha said. "With my magic, I may also be able to detect if a half-dwarf was here."

"Thank you, Freysha." I poked Zav in the ribs. "Sindari?"

"Yes." He clasped my hands. "He has been healed. By the dragon I spoke to you about."

"The Silverclaw matriarch who hates Stormforge dragons and would eat me if we met?"

"Yes. I came to give you this." Zav produced Sindari's charm from some magic pocket. "Then I must return to my world. To *five* worlds. In exchange for this small favor, she has demanded the still-warm liver of a *branoth*, the succulent bone marrow of a *fran-fran*, the eyeballs of an *ornax*, the rare Cerunian ink fish, and the testicles of a *yorak*."

"What lady doesn't like *yorak* testicles?"

Zav tilted his head. "Is this something you desire at the wedding feast? Perhaps I could capture *yorak* and bring them to Earth for the hunt."

"No, no." I lifted a hand, reminded that I had to be careful with my sarcasm around the not-from-around-here Zav. "Not necessary."

"You are certain?"

"*Very* certain."

I took Sindari's charm, eager and also nervous to summon him. Even though I believed Zav spoke the truth, I worried that Sindari might have been irreparably damaged or that the undead taint had changed him somehow.

It might not have been long enough for him to recover on his home world before being called forth again, but I rubbed the charm to summon him, hoping he could come for a few minutes.

"I am still attempting to get my brothers and mother and sister to agree to come to the wedding," Zav said. "They were unwilling to discuss it once I informed them of the problem on Dun Kroth. A meeting is being called. In addition to hunting for Vanishna-kova's required foods, I must return in time to attend it."

"I'm sorry you have to fly all over the world—*worlds*—to do favors for the grumpy dragon, but I do appreciate you helping Sindari. And me." I hugged him as Sindari's familiar silver mist formed.

"You will show me your appreciation later." Zav hugged me back and pressed his cheek against my hair, lips brushing my ear.

Oh, that was appealing. It made me regret that we were at my mother's cabin instead of back home.

"I will." I kissed him on the neck.

Sindari sighed telepathically—and out loud. *You brought me into your world to see you nuzzling your mate?*

No, to check on you. I released Zav and turned to hug Sindari. The nasty gouges in his side were gone, as was the evil purple glow that had hovered over them. *Are you well?*

Well enough to go into battle again. He gazed around the driveway, cabin, and... Why was my mother still outside and still naked? Now she was just taunting me; I was sure of it. She'd stopped to point at a couple of sparrows flitting around one of her feeders. Gondo stood beside her, though he shifted from foot to foot, and I was positive he didn't care about birds and only wanted coffee.

Your mother is unclothed, Sindari observed. *Humans lack fur and are unappealing naked.*

I agree, but don't tell her. She gets huffy.

"Let us go inside to your coffee maker, Lady Thorvald." Gondo reached up and clasped her hand—fortunately the other hand was keeping the towel up, save for an alarming droop—and led her up to the covered porch and the front door.

Is that goblin wooing your mother? Sindari asked.

Just trying to get some of her coffee. I hope.

Val? Freysha spoke into my mind from somewhere in the woods behind the house. *I've found something.*

More than bear prints?

Yes.

I'll be right there. I lifted a finger toward Zav, intending to let him know, but he'd wandered over, opened the door of the sauna, and was peering in. Well, he had a big day or days of hunting ahead of him. If he wanted to relax in a sauna for twenty minutes, who was I to stop him?

"Can you stay long enough to fight if there's trouble?" I asked Sindari as I headed around the cabin to join Freysha.

Always. Will there be more of those vile skeletal creatures?

"I hope not."

CHAPTER 16

THERE WEREN'T ANY OTHER HOUSES behind my mom's cabin, just trees. A muddy trail led off toward Moss Lake and a huge forested recreational area. Fortunately, my senses told me that Freysha hadn't wandered far. I headed off the trail toward her, passing what even my meager tracking skills told me were bear prints among the soggy brown fir needles.

It must have been something else that interested her. Had the bear been a coincidence? Or someone's cover?

"Up here," Freysha called softly from ten feet up in the crotch of an alder tree. She nodded toward my mom's cabin, the back door and deck visible through the branches.

"Someone was up there?" I gritted my teeth at the idea of the thief or any creeper peering through my mom's windows from the woods. I'd brain the sucker if I found him—or her.

"Yes." Freysha closed her eyes, one hand resting on the damp bark of the tree. "An elf."

I eyed the ground, but the faint indentions in the leaves and mud might have belonged to Freysha. Or my mom, for that matter, since we were so close to the trail and the house. I picked out a few Rocket footprints.

I agree. Sindari was prowling through the undergrowth, leaving a few big prints of his own. *It is faint, but the scent of an elf lingers on the foliage.*

I sniffed the air, but all my substandard mongrel nose smelled was someone's wood stove burning fuel nearby. "That assassin was here a few weeks ago. Sarrlevi. Could he have crouched up there?"

It was bad enough he'd visited my mother's place and left his signature coin where she could find it. The idea of him peeping at her made me wish I knew where he lived so I could go wrap magical roots around him again. Around his throat this time.

"This was a more recent visitor," Freysha said. "The tree is sharing its memories with me."

"How does that work?"

"The magic of the forest."

"Are you going to teach me how to access that?"

She smiled without opening her eyes. "I thought you were more interested in hurling fireballs. Trees don't approve of fire."

"Not *more* interested. Just *also* interested."

I would not be able to detect the scent of someone who passed through weeks ago. Sindari was currently sniffing a wild blackberry bush, the fruit long since devoured by critters. *Whoever was here is not familiar to me. Since we crossed paths with the assassin, I know his scent.*

Freysha jumped down from the tree, landing lightly beside me. "I believe the elf who visited your mother to ask her questions may have observed her from here before approaching her cabin. Perhaps to ensure she is not dangerous or to see how she acts when she is not in the presence of others."

I scowled, not appreciating quasi-friendly spies any more than assassins. "All because they want to make sure she's not a threat if Eireth comes to my wedding?"

Freysha hesitated. "It may be more that they are concerned she will be... inappropriate in his presence, especially if his wife comes along."

"She's not invited." I folded my arms over my chest.

"I was there when Lord Zavryd extended his invitation. He invited... almost everyone within his telepathic range, which is vast. Our entire city, essentially."

I dropped my arms. "He invited thousands of elves we don't know to our wedding? How many *presents* does one dragon need?"

We were going to have a chat before he went off on his exotic-animals hunt. A thorough chat.

"The impression I had was that he was pleased and proud and wanted everyone who was interested to come and witness the festival."

"Oh." I was glad he was pleased about the whole affair, but it had been bad enough when he'd invited the ogres.

"If it soothes your mind, I am certain that few of the elves who aren't related to you will come. It is possible that my mother will to ensure that *your* mother will not attempt anything… untoward to our father."

"Make a pass at him, you mean? My mom is seventy. I'm positive she can control her libido."

Freysha nodded. "I also do not believe that she—or my father—would do anything inappropriate. It's possible that *my* mother is the one who sent someone to observe and interview your mother. If that is true, it is…"

"Petty? She got the guy, and she'll live centuries longer than my mother. Why is she even worried about it?"

"She should not be. If Lord Zavryd will deign to open a portal for me, I will go home and discuss this situation with my parents."

"Let me know if I can send an electric cattle prod along."

Freysha probably didn't know what that was, but she smiled. Then she looked around thoughtfully. "This may be a better place to set a trap for your thief than your well-defended home in town. It is likely she has already visited it and noticed the various protections around it."

I imagined an identical tree in my neighborhood with a half-dwarf crouched on a branch, peering through the windows at *me*.

"She would be foolish to attempt to breach Lord Zavryd's defenses," Freysha added.

"I don't know about that. The assassin tore them down."

"He has substantial magical training. If this thief was born here on Earth, she is likely similar in talent to you, perhaps even less able if she has not found a teacher." Freysha splayed her hand on her chest.

"She's just got a lot of powerful artifacts."

Someone had created those undead minions.

"Not unlike you. You may be facing off against your—what is the human word?—doppelgänger."

"Except she's short, dark-skinned, and dark-haired instead of lanky and blonde. *And* a thief. I'm not a thief." No matter what people kept saying about my sword…

"Of course not," Freysha agreed politely. "But if she wants your sword—that is her goal, yes?—and if you're willing to stay here and visit with your mother for a time, perhaps she would be lured in to attack you in this place with few magical defenses."

"Are you forgetting the gargoyles in the Jeep?"

"Perhaps you could take your time setting them up."

"Yeah, I see what you're saying. And there's no reason I couldn't stay for a bit. Mom should appreciate having a little company."

"Excellent. Before leaving, I will set a few traps and ponder a way to lure her to those specific places." She eyed the tree, her expression thoughtful again.

"How do half-dwarves feel about chocolates?"

A few days back, per my agreement with the fae queen, I'd left some boxes of caramels and fudge in the fairy ring in the front yard. With no way to communicate to the fae that they were there, I hadn't expected anything to happen to them, but someone had activated the magical doorway in the middle of the night, only for a few seconds, and the boxes had been gone by the time I looked out the window.

"I do not know," Freysha said, "but that would be suspicious, would it not? I believe the sword itself may be sufficient bait. And she may wish to spy upon you before attempting to get it, so I will seek out the places such as this that offer good vantage points."

"Do you need me to get the ropes out of the Jeep? Or anything else? Gondo thinks highly of aluminum cans."

"I will make my own ropes." Freysha wiggled her fingers and didn't comment on the cans.

"Vines aren't native to the area."

"They will blend in."

"All right. Thanks. Anything I can do to help?" I felt guilty about standing around while someone else did work for me.

"It would perhaps be better if you are not near me and do not draw attention to what I'm doing." Freysha lowered her voice. "She could be out here even as we speak. I will be stealthy."

Exuberant woofing came from the trail, and Sindari sighed into my mind.

Rocket bounded into view, tail wagging hard enough to knock leaves off the bushes, and ran to greet us. I patted him, Freysha patted him, and Sindari made a point of sniffing things and keeping his back to the dog, his tail high in the air in a show of aloofness.

That didn't keep Rocket from leaving us to bound all around Sindari, then drop his forelegs to the ground in a bow, tail swishing as he woofed. Sindari turned his back on him again. Rocket scooted back, still in the bow position, and woofed again.

"So much for stealth," I said.

Sindari gave me an aggrieved expression. *What is wrong with this slobbering canine?*

"You know he wants you to play with him."

And you know *that regal, majestic tigers of the Tangled Tundra Nation do not* play.

"Are you sure? Rocket looks fun."

The golden retriever bounded to a leaf pile and dove into it. Even though the leaves were soggy, he managed to fling them all over the place as he flopped down and rolled on his back, all four paws in the air.

That is not fun, Sindari informed me. *That is ridiculous. It is possible he is afflicted with mental impairment.*

"Not everybody strives to be regal, you know."

They should. No prey would take that seriously.

I waved for Sindari, and hopefully Rocket, to follow me back to the house, so Freysha could set her traps. Before we made it to the entrance of the backyard, my phone buzzed with a text from Nin. I saw that I'd also missed a call from her. I hadn't heard it; the reception out here was sketchy.

I am investigating the baker, Nin's message read. *I believe I am barking up the right tree.*

A squirrel chattered at us from a branch, and Rocket ran over, put his forefeet on the trunk, and barked at it.

An appropriate thing to do today, I texted back, not trusting the reception to let me make a call. *What did you find? Did you question her?*

I only managed to speak to her for a moment before she closed the door and said she was not interested. She has four deadbolts on her door that she thunked into place. This neighborhood is not known to be dangerous.

She wasn't interested? Are you posing as a door-to-door saleswoman?

I am giving away buy-one-get-one-free offers for my food truck to the occupants of select houses on this street.

The street where the baker lives?

Yes. She refused to answer questions, especially when I brought up the coffee shop, but her neighbors like to gossip. It seems that her deceased acquaintance, Charlie Wu, was a former boyfriend. The neighbors believe from repeated noisy arguments, and sounds of things breaking, that he abused her. She broke up with him, but he did not take it well and kept coming back. He slept in his car in front of her house a few times. She started dating someone else, and the two men ended up fighting on the sidewalk in front of the baker's house.

Didn't she ever call the police?

The neighbors did not know. This is all gossip and rumors, mind you. But if the police would be cooperative, perhaps we could find out. Our baker had a reason to wish her ex-boyfriend to disappear.

Or be slain by fire?

Quite. I will attempt to find the name of the new boyfriend. Perhaps he will be interested in two-for-one coupons.

Any sane person would be.

Precisely.

A scream came from my mom's yard, and I almost dropped my phone.

Visions of the thief grabbing her and holding a knife to her throat popped into my mind. I yanked out Chopper and sprinted to check on her.

CHAPTER 17

I BURST INTO THE YARD IN time to see my mother staggering back from the sauna, the door flopping shut as she lifted her hands in horror. There was no sign of the thief or any other enemy. And I sensed Zav nearby, so if there had been trouble, he would have put a halt to it.

Wait a second... I didn't just sense Zav nearby; I sensed him *in* the sauna.

Oh, hell. Was he experimenting with nudity too? And here my mother had finally put on clothes...

"What's the problem, Mom?" I trotted up to her side.

"I..." She lowered her hands and cleared her throat. "I didn't mean to scream. I was just surprised. I'd left my coffee mug in there, you see, and when I went to get it..."

I opened the sauna door, and hot dry air washed over me, as well as a view of Zav, naked except for his Crocs, as he lay sprawled on his back on the bench.

"My mate," he said, beckoning to me. "This heat is fabulous. Join me. We must discuss whether you will come with me for my hunt and for the meeting with the Dragon Ruling Council. As soon as my kind deal with the undead interloper on Dun Kroth, we will be able to return and finally learn the secrets of your sword. Must you remain here? Is your mother in danger?"

"Only of having her retinas scorched out by dragon nudity." I spotted Mom's empty coffee mug and grabbed it. It had a lopsided rim and looked like something she'd made herself on the pottery wheel—her new hobby.

"Dragon nudity? Dragons are always nude."

"I meant *this*." I waved at him. Admittedly, his nudity was attractive—scorchingly hot, one might say—and I didn't mind it at all, but I could see where finding a naked man in one's sauna would be alarming. "What happened to your robe?"

"The air is a comfortable temperature in here. I do not need it." Zav sat up, draped an arm over the back of the bench, and patted the open spot beside him. "Join me. You may also remove your clothing." His eyes glinted as he envisioned this, reminding me that it had been a while since we'd had a steamy night together. Though I supposed a sauna was steam-free.

"May I? You're generous."

"Yes."

I started to step inside, but Mom cleared her throat behind me. I turned and offered her the mug. "I'll take care of the problem."

"No doubt. Please be aware that I just cleaned the sauna. Also, there's a no-bodily-fluids rule."

"Isn't the whole point to sweat?"

"*Sweat* isn't what I'm worried about." Mom peered in over my shoulder. "He's not even using a towel. Put towels down if you're going to sweat or do anything else in there. There's a stack in that box under the bench."

Her gaze lingered on Zav, even though she was pointing at a wood crate.

"Are you checking him out?" I asked.

"Of course not." She snatched the mug and stepped back.

"He's pretty sexy."

"That's why I'm worried you won't put enough towels down. Now if you'll excuse me, I must return before that odd green person drinks all of my coffee."

"I'm sure it's too late. I've seen how many cups he orders at the coffee shop." Maybe I should warn her that she should make Gondo aware of bushes in the backyard that she wasn't attached to.

"When I left, he was munching on the beans from the bag."

Gondo is now helping Freysha lay traps, Sindari informed me from where he'd taken a seat in a sunny spot in the yard. Well back from the sauna door and any chance of glimpsing Zav, I noted.

Did he take a bag of coffee beans with him?

That is possible.

Will you get it from him? Take Rocket. He'll think it's a delightful game. Pilfering back a goblin's pilfered coffee beans.

Sindari leveled a flat stare at me. *Will we engage in battle soon?*

Gondo might bop you on the nose with his wrench.
Sindari's eyes closed to slits.
If the thief shows up, you can sit on her.
Very well.
Sindari sauntered off. Whether he intended to rescue my mother's beans, I didn't know.
"Join me, Val," Zav rumbled from the sauna. "I can't stay long."
Mom lifted her eyes toward the heavens and headed back to the house with her mug.
I slipped into the sauna with Zav, using a nearby rock to prop the door open. I had no intention of stripping down and didn't want to swelter.
But I'd no sooner sat down beside him than a puff of magic stirred the air. The rock rolled away, and the door shut.
"It is drafty with the door open." Zav lowered his arm from the back of the bench to my shoulders.
Even though I had no plans to have sex in my mom's sauna, I leaned against his side, still appreciative that he'd taken on all this extra work to help me out.
Zav stroked the back of my head. "Do you wish to come hunt with me? We have not yet flown together to chase and slay fast and guileful prey. It would be enjoyable." His eyes closed partway, and he gazed at me through his lashes. "Mates hunt together."
It was getting hot in the sauna, and it had nothing to do with drafts. I turned my head so I wouldn't look into Zav's eyes and get distracted, but that left me looking at other appealing parts of him. Maybe I would focus on that crate of towels.
"Normally, I would be open to hunting with you, providing we could season and cook the prey once we caught it, but Freysha is setting up traps, and I'm going to try to capture the thief." I glanced warily at him, expecting him to tell me to stay in the booby-trapped house for my own good.
"The thief who attempted to trap you in another world and take your sword."
"Yeah, I'm a little irked with her."
"You are a superior warrior and will capture and defeat her," Zav murmured, shifting my braid aside so he could kiss the back of my neck. A trickle of magic zinged down my spine and lit every nerve in my body.
"I appreciate your confidence." I appreciated a lot about him. My hand strayed to his bare thigh to stroke him before I thought better of it.

"I also want to know what the link is between her and the creatures she sent after me in the artifacts room and the creatures that attacked us on the dwarven world. Zoltan says they're from the same place."

"Nagnortha is a place that is not governed and where few visit. The undead roam free there. I had thought the winged creatures were made from scratch with magic, but it is possible they were captured on Nagnortha and taken to Dun Kroth. This would not be the first time in the history of the Cosmic Realms that someone has gathered minions from there to use to further their power."

"You think the half-dwarf thief is responsible?" My mind boggled at the idea of someone like me figuring out how to gather undead minions. I couldn't even get the upper hand dealing with the vampire in my basement.

"Unlikely. She may be a minion herself."

I blinked. "You think she's undead?"

I'd seen pictures of her. She'd appeared to be living and breathing.

"Not necessarily, but she could be allied with whoever is behind establishing a presence on Dun Kroth."

"I told you that she claims she's a descendant of the dwarf who made Chopper, right? Since she's a thief, I assume she's lying, but there's a part of me that worries she isn't."

"You believe she may be the rightful heir to your blade?"

"No. I mean... probably not. What are the odds, right?"

Zav paused in his ministrations and considered me. I didn't think he was judging me, but knowing about his honorable nature made me feel guilty.

"If I find out she *is* the proper heir to the sword... what do you think I should do?" I *knew* what I would feel obligated to do, but I also knew how much harder my job would be without Chopper. If not for its ability to cut through magical armor—not to mention *dragon* scales—I would be dead by now. Dead a dozen times over. Fezzik was useful, but this past year in particular, I'd run into a lot of magical beings who could deflect the bullets.

A lot of magical beings who were criminals and who were dead or imprisoned now, thanks to the work I'd done with Chopper. What would this thief do with the sword? Break into the National Museum of Natural History and steal the Hope Diamond?

"When the time comes, you will know the right thing to do," Zav said, "and you will do it."

It wasn't an order. It was a statement of his belief in me. Hell, after that, I'd *have* to give the sword to her. But only if she *proved* it was rightfully hers. I wouldn't fall for some scam.

"I guess if I have to, I can borrow one of the magical swords in Willard's artifacts room. After all, I put a lot of them there." I forced a smile, though I knew none of the weapons in her basement could pierce dragon scales. There probably wasn't another sword on Earth that could.

"Yes. You are a strong warrior with or without that sword. Regardless, you will find a way to defeat your enemies." The corners of Zav's eyes crinkled. "And vex them while doing so."

His faith in me stirred up my emotions, and I leaned forward and kissed him before remembering that I shouldn't. He made a pleased noise of contentment as I slid my fingers through his hair. We wouldn't have sex in here, but a little cuddling couldn't hurt. Cuddling with kissing and stroking.

"Are you not hot in all that clothing?" Zav slid a hand under my jacket, fingers trailing across my stomach, teasing me through the fabric of my shirt. "You will feel better once you remove it."

I *was* breaking a sweat, but... "That could lead to us doing inappropriate things in my mother's sauna."

"Inappropriate?" Zav sounded offended, and I almost laughed. "It is never inappropriate to have sex with one's mate."

He peeled my jacket off my shoulders, and my body disobeyed my wishes to be proper, shifting to let him remove it.

"It is when you're in other people's houses. Or outbuildings." I attempted to sound stern. We *weren't* going to do this. Not here.

"You wish to go outside?" He shared an image of us pressed against the back of the sauna, grass under our bare feet as we writhed naked together, and warm excitement flooded me at the thought. I wasn't sure if it was my idea or he was sharing *his* excitement, but either way, it made me forget some of my inhibitions.

Surely, this place could be hosed down, right? I could clean it for Mom afterward...

"It would be cold out there." I shifted toward him, sliding a hand down his chest and letting myself gaze into his smoldering eyes.

That was a mistake. They flared violet, and his power flowed over me, heating my body in a way that had nothing to do with the sauna.

"Inside is better." Zav kissed me and pulled me into his lap, and I lost all interest in protesting his affection.

You're a bad influence, I thought, my lips too busy now for talking.

I am a dragon.

Is that supposed to be an explanation?

I am your mate, and we have not joined in the nest for ages. I will have you now. He pushed my shirt over my head, fingers exploring my sensitive flesh even as I let my hands roam over his.

Yeah, he would. After he'd helped Sindari, I wanted to reward him, and his touch and his magic felt so good, as it always did.

Until he paused, pulling his lips from mine and frowning toward the wooden ceiling.

"Zav," I groaned. His hands were cupping my bare breasts—I didn't even remember my bra coming off—and had been sending the most delicious waves of pleasure through me. "You can't stop now."

Someone had to be coming—someone important. Then I sensed the aura of a familiar dragon. His sister Zondia was flying this way. I groaned again, for another reason, and thunked my head down on his shoulder.

"She has come to retrieve me to appear before the Ruling Council. An emergency meeting has been called. I did not expect my people to come together to address this problem so swiftly."

"Can't she wait twenty minutes?"

Leave it to Zav to convince me that I wanted to have hot randy sex in a sauna only to stop once things got heated. I slid a hand down his abs to stroke him in case he could send her away for a while. I wanted the dwarves to get their home world fixed as much as the next person, but what difference would a few minutes make?

His gaze lowered to mine again, and he growled deep in his chest. "Yes. She will wait. I have informed her that we will mate first." He pulled me against his chest, kissing me hard. *Far too many nights have passed since we mated.*

It had only been a week, but maybe that was a long time to a horny dragon. Admittedly, I'd missed him, too, and waves of pleasure surged over me as we returned to kissing. I just had to get the rest of my clothes off…

But Zondia didn't do the polite thing and fly away. She kept coming, her presence ringing my senses like a gong. What was she doing? Coming to have coffee with Mom and Gondo?

Her approach didn't seem to bother Zav. Didn't dragons think it odd to have sex with their siblings nearby?

I tried to enjoy his ministrations, but Zondia glided over the trees and settled right atop us, talons scratching overhead as she settled onto the roof of the sauna.

I drew back from Zav. "You've got to be kidding me."

"What?"

"Your *sister*." I jabbed a finger upward. "Can't you send her somewhere?"

"She will not enter while we are mating."

"Yeah, but she'll be right up there, sensing and *hearing* everything. What if I scream?"

Hell, Mom and Gondo and Freysha—and Rocket and Sindari—would hear that too. This wasn't going to work.

"I like it when you scream." He smiled and slid his hand up my side. "A superior mate ensures that his female has intense pleasure before taking his."

"Yes, yes, and I do appreciate your thoughtfulness, but not with an audience." I squirmed off his lap and grabbed my shirt and jacket, turning a circle before finding my bra dangling over the heater.

"My sister is indifferent to our sexual activities."

"Oh, I'm positive."

"Val!" Mom called from outside. "There's a *dragon* on my sauna."

By that, I trusted Zondia hadn't shifted into her human form yet.

"We'll spend a whole weekend together once everything is resolved," I promised Zav, patting his knee as I tugged on my clothes.

Zav's eyes glinted with displeasure at this delay, and I worried he would use his magic to seal the door, but all he said was, "Then I will ensure it is resolved *extremely* quickly."

"Good. I look forward to it."

"Yes. You will."

His smoldering gaze had returned, almost making me rush back over to kiss him again, but then Mom added, "It's a huge *purple* dragon!" and the spell was broken.

I stepped outside, the cold air battering me unpleasantly after the warmth of the sauna. Mom and Gondo stood on the covered porch, gaping at the roof of the sauna.

"I believe she's a lilac dragon," I said.

Zondia's head came into view, lowering on her long neck. She looked at me, but only briefly before turning that serpentine neck to peer into the sauna.

Your mate is less foolish than you, Zondia spoke telepathically to Zav but included me. It was an unexpected compliment, though it was doubtless meant as more of an insult to Zav. *She knows the importance of maintaining order in the Realms and not allowing races that we rule to be harmed, nor delaying for the disgusting carnal pleasures of this species.*

I expected Zav to tell her to sod off, but he sighed and walked out, draping an arm over my shoulders. *Yes, she is a good mate.*

I patted his naked abdomen. "Is your robe ever going to reappear?"

"Yes. It is most chilly and damp out here." He released me and poofed the robe into existence, neat and tidy and unwrinkled as always. Even more impressive, it arrived *on* his body.

"Dragon magic is truly amazing," I said.

His eyes glinted. "*I* am amazing."

Zondia made a hawking noise deep in her throat, like a giant owl about to regurgitate a wad of mouse bones.

"That'll kill the moment," I muttered.

Fortunately, she didn't spew anything out. Maybe that had been the equivalent of a teenager saying *gag me.*

Freysha strolled out of the forest and must have spoken telepathically to Zav, for he nodded and opened a portal.

"I've built several traps in places I think a spy would perch," Freysha informed me, then shared images of certain trees in my mind. "I believe they are quite crafty, and the magic is well hidden—I have learned a few things about mechanics and physics from goblins and my engineering class—but they are not sophisticated enough to be selective about whom they ensnare, so do not walk near those particular trees."

"I'll stay out of the woods. And tell Mom to keep Rocket inside." An image of a golden retriever hoisted into a tree by one ankle came to mind. Mom wouldn't forgive me if that happened.

"Good. You may also want to remove your sword from your person, so its aura is more noticeable. It tends to camouflage itself when it's on your back."

"*Most* of the time," I said.

Freysha hadn't been involved in the fae adventure, but she'd seen my sword when it was tainted, so she nodded, knowing what I meant.

"Thank you, Lord Zavryd." She bow-curtseyed to him. "Val, I will speak with my parents and make sure no further elves pester your mother or come question any more of your family."

I hadn't even imagined them going to see Amber. Ugh.

"Thank you."

Freysha sprang through the portal. Mom and Gondo, coffee mugs in hand, watched this without comment. Apparently, seeing someone go through a portal wasn't as alarming as opening the door on a nude dragon.

"We will also go," Zav told me as the portal to Veleshna Var faded, and Zondia created another one, presumably to the hot, sauna-like dragon world. "I believe you can best this thief, should you get your wish and the opportunity to face her, but if she is like you, you must be careful and not underestimate her."

Even though I'd been thinking of the woman as similar to me, because we were half-human, being compared to a thief still made me twitch. I knew Zav didn't refer to our professions, but I couldn't help but think of Chopper and how he expected me to do the right thing if the rightful owner was found.

"I won't," was all I said.

"Good. I look forward to finishing planning our wedding festival and mating with you when I return." Zav kissed me, keeping it much more chaste than our earlier kisses. Maybe he didn't want to inspire more gagging noises from his sister.

Zondia flew through the portal, and after patting my butt, Zav turned into his dragon form and leaped through after her. I looked toward the porch to see if Mom reacted to dragons shapeshifting in front of her, but she'd gone inside. Gondo had opened the back door to the Jeep and was pulling out Dimitri's yard-art guardians to set up.

I headed over to help him. It would give me something to do while waiting for my thief to show up.

Before we got started, Mom reappeared, this time with a stack of towels and a big bottle of some cleanser. She gave me an unreadable look and headed into the sauna.

CHAPTER 18

MOM AND I SAT OUT on her covered porch, her in a rocking chair and me in an Adirondack chair made from recycled skis. We wore jackets and wool caps since twilight had come, and a mist had started falling. Fezzik rested in my thigh holster, an extra magazine in my belt in case I got in a gun-slinging match with the thief. I also wore the armored vest Nin had crafted for me.

Chopper was in its harness in the front seat of the Jeep. From here, I could keep an eye on the sword, but it wasn't so close that I could easily grab it. With luck, our thief would think she had a shot at getting to it first. In other words, it was bait.

Mom's chair creaked softly as she rocked in it, her feet up on the split log railing. She'd deigned to put on slippers, the air chilly even for someone with lots of callouses from walking barefoot. The fuzzy footwear was somewhat at odds with the Glock I'd seen her stick in her jacket pocket. I'd told her I would handle any trouble that came, and had deliberately placed my sword outside, so the thief shouldn't go into her cabin, but I couldn't blame her for being prepared.

Rocket sat alertly at the side of her chair, ears perked as we listened to nocturnal critters scuttling around in the brush under the porch while he gazed toward the property across the street. A porch light was visible beyond the trees at the front of the property. I had dismissed Sindari earlier in the day so I could summon him tonight if I needed him. And because he'd been scent-marking trees that Rocket seemed to believe were his.

"You don't have to stay out here with me," I said, looking up from my phone.

I'd been texting people and pretending not to be bored sitting out there, but it wasn't working that well. Everyone else seemed to be busy tonight. I was hoping for an update on the *decoy boyfriend*, but Amber hadn't responded to my hints for information. Only my therapist Mary had responded, replying to my query about whether it was normal to be worried about the guests that your fiancé was inviting to your wedding. She suggested I increase the days I attempted my meditation practice and sent some mantras on positive thinking that I could repeat when needed.

"No?" Mom asked. "I assumed we were bonding."

Earlier, Mom had been reading, but it had grown too dark. We hadn't turned on the porch light, though I supposed it was pointless to sit in the dark. I hadn't activated my cloaking charm, so the thief would sense me. *Should* I activate it? No, she wouldn't believe that I would leave the area without Chopper. What I was hoping was that she would see me here and think she was good enough to steal the sword out from under my nose. She had better not be.

"I'm just trying to catch a thief," I said.

Mom gave me a long look, though I don't know what she could have been searching for in the dark. Did she think I'd lied about my reason for staying? Did she think I was here because I thought she was too old and helpless to take care of herself?

"It was just a bear," she said.

Hah, I'd been right.

"I know." I decided not to mention the elf that had peeped at her from the trees before coming to question her. Hopefully, Freysha would talk to her mother, and nothing like that would happen again. "I really am here trying to catch the thief. A lot of weird things have been going on, and she's behind at least half of them."

"What makes you think she'll show up here?"

"I'm here."

"How... self-centered."

I snorted. "She'll be able to sense me if she's close, and she may be able to sense the sword from farther away. It's got a powerful aura for a magical item. It's also possible she has some way of tracking me with magic. She had no trouble finding me at Willard's office and setting up a trap in the basement." Though in retrospect, she might have gone to Willard's office to steal that book, and it had been a coincidence that I was there. Maybe she'd only set up the trap when she'd realized she had the opportunity. She could have simply had that purple box of doom in her van for emergencies, like normal people carried first-aid kits and flares.

I curled a lip in skepticism.

"The elf from your father's court found *me*," Mom said, "and I don't have a magical sword. I guess I can't be too skeptical. I just… I've never known what it is to have magic or *sense* things. I didn't believe you when you first said you could sense *hinky* things—that's what you used to call it as a kid."

"I *know*." This time, I gave *her* The Look. "Remember when we went camping at Lost Lake in Oregon? And I said a kid we saw buying candy in the store was hinky? You grabbed me by my ear and dragged me back to our tent and lectured me on racism and not judging other people by skin color."

"Well, that is an important lesson."

"I said he was hinky because he was part troll, not because he had brown skin. I didn't know how to articulate that at the time since I'd yet to meet a full-blooded troll. The kid was lucky he wasn't green."

"Isn't it just the goblins that are green?" Mom waved toward the kitchen window, the room where Gondo had guzzled half her coffee and munched on her beans earlier.

After installing Dimitri's dubious yard guardians, he'd gotten a ride back to town in a beat-up old truck with pool-cleaning tools mounted on the side. The driver had also been green and likely sitting on three phone books to see over the wheel.

"The trolls are kind of a bluish-greenish-gray," I said. "You'll probably see some at the wedding if you come. Ogres too. And goblins. Not sure about orcs. They're not as frequent at the coffee shop. Zav is working on dragons."

"Of course I'll come, but, Val, do you *know* all of those… people? I thought the magical community disliked you."

"You mean you thought they hate me with the fiery intensity of a thousand suns? Some still do, but that's calmed down a bit since I became a co-owner of their favorite establishment for acquiring coffee. All those years I thought ogres and trolls were grumps, and it turns out they were just caffeine-deficient."

"A terrible thing to be deficient in. I need to buy more beans. I don't know how your goblin friend was able to metabolize all that without exploding. Or without his *heart* exploding."

"Goblin anatomy is different from ours."

"Hm."

It started raining harder, and I was on the verge of grabbing Chopper and suggesting we call it a night, but Mom spoke again.

"I'm a little apprehensive about the wedding. About... *him* coming."

"Sorry. Zav invited Eireth. I guess I would have, but honestly, I don't know him well. We've only met twice and briefly both times."

"No, it was right to ask him. I'm glad he cares enough to take an interest in you. I always thought he would, if he found out about you, but there was no way to tell him."

"What are you apprehensive about? He's pretty mellow, from what I've seen. For a king." Rain spattered on the railing and bounced to my cheek. No way would a thief be skulking around out there in this weather.

But Rocket, who'd let his head settle to the wood boards of the porch, lifted it again. Faint snuffles sounded as he tested the air. It was hard to believe a bear would be out in the rain.

"The part where he hasn't aged and I'm... old," Mom said. "I'm afraid he'll look at me with sad pity in his eyes. I was the sexy, exotic human when we met. And now I'm... less exotic."

"I don't know about that. Gondo was kind of into you."

She didn't laugh. Maybe I shouldn't have made the joke when she was being serious, but I didn't know what I could say that would be comforting. She was worried about the same stuff I'd been worrying about with Zav. Maybe telling her about that would be the right thing to do, to let her know that I got it. Or would one day.

"I've had those concerns with Zav. What happens when I get old, and he's still a virile dragon in the prime of his life?"

"He is virile."

"I knew you were looking."

Mom snorted softly. "I'm not sure whether to feel scandalized or tickled that the image of him... *lounging* there will most likely be imprinted in my mind for the rest of my life."

"Was it his impressive nudity or the yellow Crocs that were responsible for the imprinting?"

"The combination of the two, I think."

The rumble of an engine reached my ears as a truck turned onto the street, headlights piercing the rain. Rocket growled.

"He doesn't chase cars, does he?" I imagined him racing after a truck and tearing the bumper off for fun.

"No."

As the truck rumbled closer, I sensed that the driver had the aura of someone with magical blood. At first, I thought it might be my thief, but this felt like a shifter, not a half-dwarf.

Chain link rattled as an automatic opener activated the rolling gate in the fence of the property across the street. Rocket's growls grew noisier.

"He doesn't like that neighbor," Mom said. "He always growls when the man is out on his property. I don't know why. He seems like a decent man. I've met him a couple of times walking to the lake. He's a retired painter who used to have a modest instructional show on cable TV."

"Are you sure about that?" Now that the truck was right in front of us, slowing to turn, I could identify him as a werewolf. "A butchery and cooking-with-raw-meat show seems like a more likely choice."

Mom gave me a strange look as Rocket rose to his feet, hackles up. "I looked him up. His name is Liam Walsh. The show has been off the air for twenty years, and he never had the success of a Bob Ross, but he's still publishing books on painting wilderness and animals."

"He must have a hard time getting those animals to pose."

"Val?" Her tone was puzzled.

"He's a werewolf. That's why Rocket doesn't like him."

The truck's window rolled down and an arm lifted to wave. It was clad in plaid flannel, not fur, at least for the moment.

"Evening, Sigrid," the werewolf—Liam—called over the idling truck. "What are you doing out in such cold, dreary weather? Is that the daughter you mentioned?"

"You mentioned me? I'm touched."

"How can he tell we're over here?" Mom whispered. "All the lights are off."

"Because he's a werewolf. He can sense me, and he can probably see in the dark and smell whether or not you put deodorant on after getting out of the sauna. Wave back. He's smiling over at you. If you have a werewolf for a neighbor, it's good to stay in his good graces."

"I don't want to *encourage* him," she whispered.

What did that mean?

"I'm Val." I waved since Mom wouldn't. "And, yes, I'm the daughter. As native Washingtonians, we enjoy a dreary, rainy night."

On the off chance that my thief was out there listening, I decided not to mention our stake out.

"The rain doesn't make for good hunting. Coffee in the morning, Sigrid?"

Mom finally answered. "A visitor drank all of my good coffee."

"I'll bring some over and make you breakfast if you're willing. I hope the pottery wheel is working well now."

"Yes, it is. Thank you, but my daughter is staying over, so I don't think this is the appropriate time for coffee." She paused, glanced at me, then blurted, "Maybe this weekend."

I raised my eyebrows.

"I look forward to it. Are you wearing shoes?"

My eyebrows climbed further.

"Not currently. There's no snow on the ground yet."

"You're a hardy woman, Sigrid." He sounded like he approved. "Goodnight. Nice to meet you, Val. And always a pleasure, Rocket."

The dog rumbled, a growl, not a nicety.

The truck turned into the driveway, the gate clanked shut, and Liam parked beside the house. He went inside whistling. I got a glimpse of his face by the porch light, slate gray hair with a trimmed beard and mustache accentuating a strong jaw. He waved again before disappearing inside.

"Interesting," I said.

"What?" Mom asked warily.

"A werewolf is flirting with you."

"He's not a werewolf. That's ridiculous."

"Trust me, Mom. It's like the kid at the candy store at Lost Lake. I can tell."

"He *paints*. Deer and elk and other animals. What kind of werewolf would do that? Who paints what they're going to eat?"

"Food photography is a whole thing, Mom. Haven't you seen Amber's social-media page? She posts pictures of good-looking desserts she's about to chomp down."

"That's not the same. Besides, he does pottery too. He fixed my wheel. He's a fixer, not a killer. A nice, peaceful man."

"Are you sure? I bet he's got some sexy animal magnetism that oozes all over you and makes you horny."

She shot me a scathing look but didn't quash the notion, as I would have expected. Too bad there wasn't enough light for me to see if her cheeks were red.

"Besides, Rocket likes everyone," I said. "Except predators who might be a threat, right?"

"That's why I couldn't date him. If Rocket doesn't like a man, that means he's not right for me. I only made him coffee because he fixed the pottery wheel."

"This isn't an ordinary man. Rocket would growl at any shifter, I'm sure." I waved to the dog, though he'd settled back onto his stomach now that the werewolf had gone inside. He was back to listening to the critters scuttling around under the porch. "That doesn't mean he's someone you shouldn't date."

"I'm not dating anyone, Val. Just drop it." Her rocking chair creaked as she stood up. "I'm going to bed. Holler if you need any help with your thief." She patted the hip where her Glock was tucked under her jacket.

"I will," I said, even though I wouldn't.

Even though I doubted the thief would show up tonight—maybe she didn't even have an idea of where in the greater Seattle area I was—I would handle her myself if she came.

Rocket sat up but was looking out into the trees again and didn't rise to follow Mom inside.

"Bring him with you when you come in, please," she said. "He's an indoor dog."

"Yes, I've seen him sleeping on your bed."

"He hogs the pillows and the covers, but at least I don't have to worry about catching a chill on cold nights."

As she stepped inside, I thought about teasing her that a werewolf could keep her sufficiently warm in bed, but if she didn't want to date someone, that was none of my business. Even if a nature-loving painter who didn't find her shoeless tendencies strange seemed perfect for her. Besides, I wasn't an expert on dating or a talented matchmaker. Zav had fallen into my life unasked for. It was amazing he'd turned out to be such a good guy under the haughty dragonness.

Rocket growled softly. Nobody was visible in the yard, nor could I sense anyone, but the door to the Jeep opened.

CHAPTER 19

I ROSE TO MY FEET, PREPARED to spring over the railing and grab what had to be an invisible person opening my door. But I caught myself. It could be a trap. She could be using magic to open it from afar. "Sindari," I breathed, touching his charm.

Even though I hated using him as bait, if anyone was going to be trapped, someone who could turn to mist and disappear to another realm was a better bet than I was.

But as Sindari formed, Rocket's growls turned into raucous barking. He evaded my belated grasp and rushed down the porch steps and into the yard.

Our thief is here, Sindari, I telepathically told him, running after Rocket. The last thing I wanted was for Mom's pet to fall into some heinous trap.

I do not sense anyone. Sindari sprang over the railing and prowled, not toward the Jeep, but toward the trees bordering the yard. *I will hunt for her.*

Rocket rushed to the Jeep door, alternately snuffling the air and then the ground, but he didn't seem to find what he'd expected so he defaulted to barking at the open door. I approached warily, Fezzik in hand. Like Sindari, I didn't sense anyone. If she had a camouflage charm like mine, and she had opened the door, I ought to be close enough to see through the magic and glimpse her.

I swiped at the air with my pistol, in case she had an even greater invisibility charm, but I didn't contact anything except the tip of Rocket's tail as he swished it about, jumping in agitation.

The lights came on, both in Mom's cabin and in the house across the street.

A twang of magic plucked at my senses from the side of the property. *Forest* magic. It felt like one of Freysha's traps flaring to life.

I started to turn, but my sword in its scabbard rose up from my seat, levitated by invisible power.

"Oh, hell no." I lunged in to grab it, but something small and hard slammed into my back, startling me. It struck forcefully enough to send a sting of pain through me, even though I wore an armored vest. I stumbled forward a step before catching myself on the door, then spun to face the trees. That projectile had seemed to come from the same direction as the magic I'd sensed.

I dropped to one knee, pointing Fezzik into the shadows, searching for shaking branches or anything that would hint of the thief's exact location. Which tree had Freysha's trap been in? They all looked the same in the dark.

A faint *tink* sounded as something fell out of my pocket. No, not my pocket. From my back, where whatever had hit me had stuck in my leather duster.

I activated my night-vision charm, but it did little more than show me the empty air between the trees. My attacker was invisible; I was sure of it. The nearby lights caused the charm to flood my eyes with too much brightness, but I was able to spot a tiny dart that had fallen to the gravel. I grabbed it and stuffed it in my pocket.

Try the side of the house, Sindari, I suggested. *Someone fired at me, and I think it came from that—*

Another projectile struck me, slamming into my abdomen. I swore at the sharp stab of pain—and because not so much as a leaf out there had moved.

I whirled, intending to grab Chopper and run to the other side of the Jeep for cover, but the sword had continued to rise. It was outside of the vehicle now and rising higher into the air, already well above my head.

I saw where it came from that time, Sindari replied, springing through the brush from the rear of the house and toward the trees to the side.

Good. Get her! I sprang for Chopper—and just missed it. The sword floated several feet above my head as it drifted slowly toward the trees.

I scrambled atop the hood of the Jeep, to the roof, and leaped off as the sword floated farther away. The added height let me catch it, one hand wrapping around the scabbard like a vise, but to my surprise, my weight wasn't enough to pull it out of the air.

A branch moved as Sindari hunted through the trees, having as much trouble pinpointing my attacker as I was.

Try by Freysha's trap, I told him.

Hopefully, he could tell the trees apart better than I could in the dark.

I fired at the tree I *thought* the trap was in, then twice more to either side, hoping to get lucky. One of the branches shuddered, and was that someone's gasp?

Sindari charged in that direction.

"Val?" Mom called from the doorway as I floated across the yard, hanging from my sword, my feet dangling five feet off the ground.

"Stay inside!" I called.

"Sigrid?" the werewolf—Liam—called from the doorway of his own house.

The whole neighborhood had probably heard my gunshots.

"We're fine," I called to him, not wanting to endanger anyone else with my trouble.

Sindari and I could handle this.

Or so I thought. Then a chill breeze swept across me, raising the hair on my arms. The glow of ominous purple light came from farther back in the woods. Had she gotten that box *again*? How? Zav had taken it with him back to Dragon Land, hadn't he?

Branches rattled as Sindari ran all around the area where I'd fired, but he still hadn't found the thief.

Try up in the air. She may be caught in Freysha's trap. I imagined the half-dwarf dangling upside down from her ankle high in a tree.

Sindari sprang up onto a thick branch, the limb quivering under his weight. *Ah, yes. I caught a scent.*

Just don't fall. I wanted to rush over and help, but I dared not let go of Chopper. It kept floating away from the yard and toward the trees, but not the same tree Sindari was climbing. No, it was pulling me toward that purple glow.

I groaned and gripped Fezzik, not sure whether to fire at the glow or fire toward my invisible enemy. I didn't want to risk hitting Sindari, but I was getting desperate. My forearm muscles quivered from holding my body weight up by one hand. There was no way I would let go of Chopper and let her have it, but…

Skeletal fingers brushed at my cheek. I jerked my head away and tried again to yank Chopper off its trajectory. I needed the blade to attack the wraiths, if that was what I was dealing with again.

Gunshots fired, not mine. They had come from the direction of the house. Mom?

A crash sounded—Sindari's branch broke, and he plummeted to the ground. He twisted, landing on his feet, and snarled.

I injured her, but she shot me.

She's got a gun?

No, it was a dart. Maybe a tranquilizer. His snarl floated back to me.

"Val?" Mom called uncertainly. "Something's trying to get in the house. I felt…"

Damn it, were the wraiths molesting her? My gut clenched at the idea of her being dragged into that box.

"Stay there, Sigrid," the werewolf called. He was in Mom's front yard now. Maybe that was good. If there were further threats and he could help her…

Except that it was *my* job to help her. I couldn't even shoot toward Freysha's trap now if I wanted to. The sword kept pulling me deeper into the woods, and I couldn't see Sindari—or Mom and Liam. All I could see was the purple glow, and yes, now I could make out that big black box again. How did she keep getting it back? Or did she have an unlimited supply?

Something tugged at my braid. Not *again.*

I jerked my head away from the ghostly grip and tried to focus on using my magic. *Chopper*, I tried to will the sword, *free yourself!*

The scabbard shuddered in my hand, but it continued its inexorable aerial trek toward the box. Once again, its lid was open, and the darkness within seemed to be sucking me toward it. What had Zav done to close the lid and deactivate it?

I tried to send my power toward it, to use the wind to sweep the lid shut. No hint of a breeze stirred in the night. Unfortunately, Freysha hadn't taught me telekinesis yet, and when I created a mental fern frond to try to push the lid shut, nothing happened. Hopefully, it was only in my imagination that the box laughed at me.

Frustrated, I opened fire at its glowing purple sides. Not surprisingly, given that dragon magic had crafted the box, the bullets ricocheted off.

Since it wasn't helping, I holstered Fezzik. Maybe if I tried with both hands to yank Chopper out of the air…

Swinging my legs to create momentum, I lunged up and caught the hilt with my other hand. Chopper slid several inches out of the scabbard, almost startling me into losing my grip.

Wait, was the levitation magic acting on the *scabbard*, not the sword? I tugged myself up so I could create the space to pull Chopper farther out. It glided effortlessly free, leaving me dangling from one hand by the scabbard with the blade at my side.

Feeling victorious—if a little foolish—I let go and landed in the damp leaves. The scabbard continued toward the box, and even with solid earth under my feet, the pull of that magic was powerful. I stumbled several steps toward it before bracing myself against a tree and turning my back on the thing.

Invisible skeletal fingers gripped my braid again, as well as my duster. They tried to tug me toward the box. Something wrapped around my ankle, jerking my leg several inches off the ground.

"No, you *don't*." I whirled, slicing through the invisible fingers.

As before, Chopper met resistance as it passed through the air. In the morning, someone would find more finger bones on the ground out here.

Branches snapped in the direction of Freysha's trap, and Sindari snarled as someone shouted in surprise—and pain? The sound of a woman swearing in a language I didn't understand followed.

I've got her! Sindari said.

Good! I slashed my way free of the grasping fingers and rushed toward him.

The thief was still invisible, but Sindari had clearly pinned her under his legs.

Through the trees, the lights of the house were visible, as were Mom, Rocket, and a giant wolf three times Rocket's size. Rocket barked as the wolf—Liam—lunged and snapped at invisible enemies.

Worry for Mom charged through me. I had to get that lid closed and the box shut off, so the wraiths would leave them alone.

"Hold her, Sindari!" I shouted and veered back toward the box.

More fingers grasped at me, but I didn't slow down, only slashing at them as I ran. Twenty feet ahead of me, Chopper's scabbard, still floating through the air, tilted downward and was sucked into the box.

The pull grew stronger as I ran toward it, and fear made me want to turn the other way. But there was a tree next to it, and the magic wasn't doing anything to pull its branches into the box. If I could grab it and brace myself, then I could close the lid.

By the time I was five feet away, it felt like a black hole sucking me in. I angled my path, hooking one arm around the tree and anchoring myself to avoid being pulled in after my scabbard. My braid floated over my shoulder toward it.

I leaned out, reaching toward the lid with Chopper. The tip touched it, and I nudged it upward. Since I could barely reach it, I couldn't quite get the leverage to lift it.

"Just a little closer," I whispered, letting my grip on the tree slip slightly.

A skeletal hand grasped my shoulder. It yanked back harder than I expected, and Chopper slipped free of the lid.

Snarling, I twisted and slashed through the invisible grip with the blade. Something thunked to the ground.

I whirled back and levered Chopper under the lid. It rose slowly, my sword's blue glow mingling with the purple.

A boom and a white flash came from the trap.

Watch out, Val, Sindari warned. *She got away.*

I flicked the lid shut, and the purple light disappeared.

Movement off to my side made me jerk back. Something hurtled through the air toward me. A grenade.

I shoved myself away from the tree, but my foot caught on a root. I tottered backward, then twisted and threw myself into a roll away from the box—and the grenade. At the last second, I flung my arms over my head, almost lopping off my braid with my sword.

The grenade blew up with a boom and a flash that rattled my teeth, and the shockwave tossed me farther away. A tree snapped and went down. Branches slammed to the ground all around me, one cracking me on the back of the head hard enough to stun.

I struggled to recover, to push myself to my feet and brace for an attack.

Something thudded to the ground beside me. Another branch, I assumed, but then the purple glow of the box returned. It was open again and on its side only three feet away. Its power pulled me stumbling toward the swirling blackness inside, the purple light flaring even brighter around it, as if it was excited to swallow me whole.

I tried to plant my feet, but the pull was too strong. I flailed at the air, trying to find something else to grab. There was nothing. I lifted Chopper to swing at the box, but a blurry figure lunged out of the shadows and grabbed my sword arm. The thief?

Instinctively, I kicked at her. But with only one foot on the ground, that made it easier for the box to vacuum me up like a piece of lint.

I had the satisfaction of connecting with the thief's stomach, but it didn't matter. The power of the artifact swept us both into the box, and darkness enveloped me.

CHAPTER 20

I LANDED HARD ON MY BACK, the gray daylight sky and sulfur-laden air telling me that I wasn't on Earth anymore. I rolled to my knees, relieved Chopper was still in my hand, and got one foot under me before I saw her.

She'd also rolled into a crouch, a black helmet half-falling off her head, her dark hair slumping out of a ponytail and framing her dirty, bloody face as she glared at me. Since I'd seen Willard's photographs, I recognized her, though she looked to have had as bad a night as I had. One of her dark eyes was swollen halfway shut, her shirt was torn—slashed by tiger claws—in several spots, and her lip was cut open, blood dribbling down her chin.

"I can see you," I pointed out, keeping an eye on her but also surveying our surroundings.

Were we back on the dwarven world? The air smelled right. But maybe this was that haunted world. We were crouching on a rocky ledge near a cliff, a hint of greenery visible far below. The idea of having a battle up here wasn't appealing, but she gripped a magical dagger and what looked like a miniature crossbow. She hadn't aimed them at me—yet—but she squinted at me, as if she was considering it.

Fezzik's weight was reassuring in my thigh holster, and Chopper had deflected projectiles before, so hopefully, I could handle her now that she wasn't camouflaged. *Why* wasn't she camouflaged?

She reached toward her throat. I thought it was to check one of her injuries, but she stopped short of her bloody lip and instead tapped at her collarbones. Looking for something?

She scowled at me as if whatever she was missing was my fault. Maybe it was. If she had something similar to my charm thong, Sindari might have ripped it off. Wherever he was. He hadn't come through the box with us, the box that had apparently been left back in the woods by Mom's cabin. There was no equivalent of it on this side. Which meant I might not have a way back.

"You've got my sword," she said in accented English.

"It's *my* sword, thanks. I don't appreciate your attempts to steal it." I spotted Chopper's scabbard lying on the ground a few feet away and snatched it up.

"You are not the rightful owner. *You* originally stole it."

"No, I slew an enemy who had it and claimed it as mine."

Her eyes narrowed. "Then your *enemy* stole it. That is a dwarven dragon blade made by the master enchanter Dondethor Orehammer thousands of years ago here on Dun Kroth."

"Yeah, I've heard that. It's mine now." I smiled cheerfully as I studied her clothing, hoping that portal generator was the size of a TV remote and tucked into one of her pockets.

I wanted to go back and check on Mom. With luck, all the invisible wraiths had disappeared when we'd gone through that box, but I had no way to know that. Maybe it was still open and even now trying to suck her and her werewolf acquaintance through it. And what about Sindari? Based on my previous experiences with his charm, he should have poofed back to his realm as soon as I was out of range, but I'd never been sucked through a strange demonic portal while working with him.

Unfortunately, the photograph I'd seen of her portal generator had shown it as significantly larger than pocket-sized. She was wearing a backpack, one strap dangling off her shoulder as it slumped to one side, a compact crossbow attached to it, but it didn't look large enough to hold the generator. I could sense more magical items inside of her pack, but who knew what?

"I am Li, daughter of Dorrik Orehammer," she said, "the only remaining descendant of Dondethor Orehammer. The sword is mine by birthright."

"Uh huh. I'm going to need to see your driver's license."

"My dwarven lineage is not on my *driver's license*."

"No? Guess you're out of luck then."

Tension knotted my shoulders, and my chest tightened, making me glad I had my inhaler in my pocket. Not that I would use it in front of an enemy. No way would I show her that weakness.

"You will not return the blade to its rightful owner?" Li asked.

Uh. Would I? My fears that she could be presenting the truth returned to the forefront of my mind.

"How can you possibly know you're its rightful owner? You're a half-human mongrel from Earth, like me, right? Whoever your father was could have been lying about his heritage. Or your mother might have made it up."

Her dark eyes flared with indignation. "My father was a great dwarf enchanter, trained by the masters of this world. When I was young, he told me *personally* that he came to Earth to seek his ancestor's legendary sword. Only when he met my mother and fell in love was he distracted for a time. He always intended to return to his quest, but his death put an end to that prematurely." She scowled at me, as if *I'd* been responsible.

Not likely. I'd never been to China, if that was where all this had happened, and I probably wasn't much older than Li was. We might even be the same age. She only appeared to be about thirty, but so did I; we ought to have similar lifespans. Assuming she stopped bleeding. She was leaving droplets on the bare rock underneath her, but she didn't let go of her weapons to check her wounds. She still looked like she was contemplating shooting me.

"That's a nice story," I said. "You'll have to prove it to me though. No offense, but my boss says you're a thief who's taken all sorts of artifacts and treasures from our country in the past few months."

Her chin lifted. "Artifacts and treasures that were stolen from the Old World. I am not a thief. I am a relic hunter and, when necessary, a vigilante. I deal with criminals that others can't handle." Her eyes narrowed. "Like assassins with magical tigers and all manner of magical trinkets that make them hard to kill."

"Uh, like the magical trinkets that make *you* hard to find and kill? What happened to your invisibility charm? Did Sindari rip it off?"

"Sindari," she mouthed. "The tiger? Yes. It is good that you gave me his name. If you do not give me the sword that is rightfully mine, then I will slay you and take the items *you* have stolen, including that charm."

"You're welcome to try." I gave her another smile, though I mostly wanted to kick her again. I wouldn't since she was bleeding and hadn't tried to shoot me since we arrived here, but she was the reason I was stuck here, so the temptation was real.

"You will not do the honorable thing?"

"Not unless you prove to me that the sword is yours."

"*Yes.*" Her eyes glinted with triumph. "I can do that."

Uh oh. Had I walked into a trap?

"That is why I brought you here. I knew you would be difficult to kill, but I also believed that if you learned the truth, you *would* do the honorable thing." Her eyes narrowed again, and she looked me up and down in contemplation. "Your reputation is not one of dishonor."

This talk of honor disturbed me, bringing to mind my chat with Zav in the sauna. He would want me to do the honorable thing. He'd made that clear. But Li *had* to be lying. This all had to be some scheme. What were the odds that one of the handful of dwarf-human beings living on Earth would be the descendant of the dwarf who'd made my sword ten thousand years ago? That was way too much of a coincidence to be true.

But if this was all a ruse, why did Li believe that she could prove the sword was hers?

She must have a whole scheme set up. If that portal generator had brought her here previously, she would have had the opportunity to plant some fake evidence ahead of time.

"What are you going to do?" I asked. "Take me to some ancient dwarven shrine that lists all of Dondethor Orehammer's descendants? Including your father and you?"

"Something like that." Li pushed herself to her feet and pointed off to a huge black mountain in the distance. Smaller peaks framed it, all covered with snow, but the black peak was mysteriously free of a white cap. Was this Mount Crenel? "You will come?" she asked.

"It looks like a long walk. Why didn't you just bring us out there?"

"Portals may not take one into Mount Crenel. Great magic protects it."

"Oh, a dwarven security system. Won't that be fun to bypass?" As I was looking at the ominous mountain, a large bird flew into view.

Not, fortunately, one made from bones, but it pinged my senses as magical, and it was headed in our direction.

Li saw it too. "Stone roc. It may see us as food. Or it may be drawn to our magic."

It screeched, the primal sound echoing from the mountains. Its beady eyes focused on us, and it picked up speed, its beak parting in eagerness for a meal.

Li gripped her dagger and switched the dart weapon for her crossbow, then crouched, facing the creature as its great wings brought it closer. I drew Fezzik and, as soon as it was close enough, opened fire.

Lately, it had been rare for my pistol's bullets to pierce an enemy's defenses, but this time, my first round bit in with a satisfying thud. The bird shrieked and pulled up.

We ducked, and Li fired a bevy of crossbow bolts at the roc's belly as it sailed past above. The magical weapon proved to have a repeating feature, new rounds thunking automatically into place. Her quarrels and my bullets both struck true.

I fired twice more, not convinced the huge bird wouldn't turn around to try again, but it flapped its wings hard and flew away from us.

Only after I'd spent the bullets did I realize that I had a more limited supply than usual with me. All I had was what I'd been wearing when I'd been sucked through the portal, which meant no food and water and only the single spare magazine in my belt pouch.

"We should get off this ridge." Li slung her crossbow across her back and adjusted her pack. "There are many large predators on this world. The lich is not the only reason the dwarves spend much of their time inside the mountains."

"Did you say the *lich*?"

Li was studying the sky in all directions and didn't answer until she walked past me, heading down a slope that would take us to lower ground. "You are unaware of the dragon lich?"

"The *dragon* lich?"

Suddenly a dwarven security system seemed very innocuous.

I ran to catch up with Li. Though she was shorter than I was, she walked quickly.

"I assumed your mate would have informed you that one of his dragon kin had made a deal with the underworld on Nagnortha to give itself eternal life and great power to control the undead." Li spoke matter-of-factly, as if that didn't sound like something out of a fantasy novel.

"I've encountered zombies and vampires—and the crazy stuff that comes out of your black box—but as far as I'm aware, liches are…" I stopped myself before saying *make believe* or *something out of Dungeons & Dragons*. "Not something found on Earth," I finished.

Li gave me a look that reminded me of Amber's scathing-pitying expressions. "We are not on Earth."

"I know that, but... Zav didn't mention a lich. I'm positive he would have if he'd known about it." I thought about sharing that the dragon who was supposed to rule over this world had disappeared, but Li wasn't my ally. Telling her everything I knew wouldn't be a good idea. Better to find out what *she* knew without spilling my own guts. "What's this dragon, uh, lich's name? Did it tell you?"

"It did not. I do not know what it bellowed at me as I was fleeing through my portal back to Earth." Li scrambled down a slope more agilely than one would expect from a dwarf—or half-dwarf—keeping her balance as scree tumbled loose.

"Why were you here visiting a lich?"

"I did not expect it to be inside Mount Crenel. I was there to find proof that the sword you carry is rightfully mine." Li came to the bottom of the slope and slanted an indecipherable look back at me.

"Ah. And did the lich have that proof?"

Li snorted. "It is camped out on top of it. For some reason, it chose Mount Crenel as its base of operations. I did not learn this until I traveled here, found the entrance, and was halfway to the ancient dwarven tomb and knowledge repository before I sensed its presence. Soon after, I ran into its minions. I was still able to slay many of them and get close enough to take photographs of the Wall of Ancestry and Wall of Great Makers. But unwisely, I grabbed a couple of artifacts that I thought might be useful in dealing with *you*—" Li gave me another look over her shoulder, "—and that roused the lich from its ruminations. It sent more minions to chase me out and attacked me with its own power. Even though it was from afar, it almost killed me. The lich is even more powerful than a dragon, thanks to the deal it made with the underworld."

"Uh." I stopped and held up a finger. We'd reached a valley of the same squat evergreens I'd seen when visiting this world with Zav. "The lich's new lair is the place you want to take me?"

"Yes."

"How about you just show me the photos and then we go back to Earth?"

Li turned to regard me. She hadn't cleaned her wounds or even wiped the dried blood from her face. If I'd had my own pack, I would have offered her the contents of my first-aid kit. Maybe she had her own first-aid kit and simply couldn't be bothered to stop and tend to her wounds. Her eyes had the hard determination of a zealot on a mission.

"You would accept photographs as proof that I am the rightful owner of that sword?" Li touched a lump in her pocket that was probably a smartphone.

"No. You could easily have doctored photos."

"I assumed that would be your response. That is why I will take you and show you in person."

"While the lich is there?"

"It leaves sometimes."

"No pizza delivery to underground tombs?"

"I believe not." Li turned, as if we'd made our decision and were going.

"Look, I'm open to checking this place out—" hell, my entire reason for coming to this world originally had been to check it out, "—but not with only you for backup. No offense."

"Summon your *tiger* again then." Her voice had turned bitter, and she touched the claw marks on her face. "Only keep him off me."

"If you hadn't been trying to steal my sword, he wouldn't have jumped *on* you."

I touched Sindari's charm, tempted to do exactly what she suggested, but I didn't need him for a hike through the woods. If we came face-to-face with undead minions—or a *dragon* lich—I would need him then.

"I was thinking more of Zav," I called, though Li was speed walking away from me again, heading resolutely toward the dark, distant peak. "He knows there's a problem here, and he's in a meeting right now with his dragon kin about this very world. How about we go back to Earth, grab a hot apple cider, and wait to storm the tomb until *after* the dragons have handled the lich?"

That sounded like a reasonable request.

"We can't," Li said.

"Why?"

"Your trap and your tiger separated me from the belongings I brought. When I freed myself from his claws, there was no time to grab the rest of my gear. I saw you near the *Zhapahai* and had to act quickly."

Quickly or impulsively? I worried where she was going with this.

"I am without the portal generator that would have allowed us to return, and the *Zhapahai* was also left behind."

I stopped walking. "Meaning we're trapped here?"

"Yes."

I trusted Zav would realize I was missing and come to find me, but how long would *that* take? From what I'd seen, dragons didn't make decisions quickly. His meeting could involve days of deliberation. And until he returned to Earth to check on me, he wouldn't know I was missing. And even when he realized I was, would he know to check here? He hadn't known where that box would lead. He might first spend days scouring that haunted world in search of me.

Li had *not* stopped walking. I was tempted to fold my arms over my chest and refuse to continue with her, but I didn't have any supplies or gear for surviving on an alien world. She might not have her portal generator, but she had a pack that probably held food and water. I hoped. So far, I hadn't seen any water out here, and who knew if streams on dwarven worlds were safe for humans to drink from?

She must have realized I'd stopped, for she turned to look at me. "You will not come?"

"It's a bad idea. We should wait for the dragons."

To my surprise, she tilted her head and seemed to consider it. "When will they come?"

"I don't know. It might be a few days." Or weeks. I grimaced at the idea of trying to survive off the land here for that long.

She also grimaced. "That is too long."

"You got a hot date you need to get back for?"

"My people need me."

"They can't need you that badly, or you wouldn't have quested all the way to the US—and to *here*—to steal my sword."

Li hesitated. "It was at their request—at my mother's request—that I came. I have only recently become aware of you and that you have my father's sword. Recently, it was emitting a beacon that allowed me to sense it."

Her and everyone else. I sighed.

"I told my mother I knew where the sword was, and she insisted that I retrieve it. I must honor her request." Again, Li hesitated, as if reluctant to share any of this with a stranger. "I wish for my mother to see that I am successful before… She is dying."

"Sorry," I said automatically, though I didn't know yet if I cared. I was stuck here because of Li.

I also didn't trust that this wasn't an elaborate spiel that she was making up on the fly to win my sympathy. Admittedly, I *wanted* that to be the case, because if she proved to me that Chopper belonged to her… what then?

CHAPTER 21

THE SORENESS OF MY FEET suggested we'd walked at least ten miles before we came out of the rugged forest and onto a road built of pavers. Wide and gray and flawless, the uniformly shaped and fitted stones stretched through the trees, heading toward the black mountain that grew larger and larger as we traveled closer.

I hadn't decided yet if I would go inside with Li once we reached it. It seemed like a very bad idea. I'd spent the last five miles eyeing her backpack and contemplating beating her up to take it, then running off to camp in the woods until Zav came looking for me. But I hadn't seen Li fight yet. It was possible she could kick my ass, or at least injure me badly, and then what? I would not only be stuck here, but I'd be wounded.

It crossed my mind to shoot her in the back, but she'd stopped and shared her water and given me a granola bar. Bullets would be a poor way to pay her back. Besides, with all the magical items she carried, she might have armor that could deflect Fezzik's rounds. That simple black helmet surely wasn't there for decoration.

Earlier, I'd asked Li about her magical artifacts, and what kind of training she'd had, but she hadn't answered. I probably should have been more subtle, pretending I just wanted to chat and wasn't trying to get intel on her. But *subtle* wasn't one of my talents.

I touched Sindari's charm on its thong and considered summoning him for company. I'd called him forth earlier to make sure I still could. He'd been startled to find himself on the dwarven world, saying he'd been trying to catch Li, after she'd escaped from him back on Earth, when our bond had snapped. That had thrown him back to his realm without warning. Unfortunately, he'd seen no more than I about what happened with my mother.

Not sure how soon we would run into danger, I resisted the urge to summon him. I was positive I would need Sindari later.

I would also need to sneak off into the woods to use my inhaler again soon. The sulfur-tainted air of this place was bothering my lungs more than usual. I would pay a lot of money if some magical being could wave a hand over me and cure my overreactive body. In the meantime, I tried to think calm, meditative thoughts as we walked. It didn't help. Despite Mary's regular admonitions that I should practice more often, my meditation skills hadn't improved. If I could ever see *results* from my practice, I might be more inclined, but it always seemed futile.

"I have been considering your reluctance to enter the tomb," Li said over her shoulder, speaking for the first time in an hour.

"The tomb isn't the problem; this lich you've promised me is."

Furry animals that peeped like marmots commented on our passage as they skittered among the trees. Numerous birds chattered in the branches, though their markings were all alien to me. Once, I saw something parrot-sized with butterfly-like wings fly past.

"As I told you," Li said, "I was in there before. There are a great many artifacts inside. I am not certain if the dwarves placed them there to protect their dead or if the lich stole them to hoard."

"Did the lich not discuss his dreams and goals with you while he was chasing you out of his lair?"

"It did not." Li insisted on not giving the lich a sex. Maybe once you were undead, such things didn't matter. "It must have ambitions, or why would an already-powerful dragon consider giving up its breathing body in exchange for a little more power, but it's hard to imagine that hoarding artifacts is one of them. I believe it more likely that the dwarves put them there. My reason for telling you this is that it's possible we could find another portal generator. Will that motivate you to go inside?"

"I don't know. What are the odds that it would lead to Earth? Does yours go to more than one place?"

"Not that I was able to determine, but it returned me to Earth after I used it to come here. I originally found it in my homeland, near the camp my father and the other dwarves lived in before they were slain by the government. I believe my father made it to allow my mother to visit him once his people left." Her voice turned hard. "Unfortunately, they were not permitted to leave. They were deemed freaks and eradicated."

"Sorry," I mumbled, feeling like I was saying that a lot to her tales. "How old were you then?"

"Five. I remember my father and my uncles—they were not blood uncles, but my father called them thus—and how excited I was whenever they came to visit the village. They always knew it was dangerous to mingle with humans, but my father and my mother had a secret relationship and loved each other, I believe." She glanced back. "Your story is similar?"

"Yeah." Similar but without the eradication. "I didn't get to meet my father until recently though."

Li blinked. "He still lives?"

"In Veleshna Var, yes."

"His people escaped your government then." Her mouth twisted with bitterness, but she didn't say anything else, merely faced forward again and continued to walk.

But we'd only taken a few more steps when numerous creatures with familiar magical auras pinged my radar. At first, I thought they were more of those rocs, coming back to try again to turn us into lunch, but I groaned when I realized what they were. More of the winged skeletal creatures that had attacked me and Zav.

"Take cover." Li must have sensed them, too, for she darted into the trees, waving for me to follow her.

I ran into the trees on the other side of the road. If the creatures attacked, it would be better to be split up so we could divide their attention.

The wildlife that had been peeping in the woods fell silent. Even though they were mundane animals, maybe they could sense the magical flying skeletons approaching. There was a whole pack—or flock—of them again.

Last time, it had taken Zav battling seven of them while Sindari and I fought one. And he'd been gravely injured. There was no way Li and I could deal with all of them.

"It sure would be nice to have a portal generator right now," I muttered, though if Sindari had been the one to keep her from grabbing hers, it probably wasn't fair to gripe that she didn't have it. It was, however, *completely* fair to gripe that she'd dragged me here.

The foliage-dense branches kept me from seeing the undead creatures approaching, but I sensed the power of their magic and tapped my cloaking charm, hoping it would hide me. Li crouched behind a tree, brush partially camouflaging her from view, but since she'd lost her own such charm, I continued to sense her presence.

I drew Chopper and willed its magic to make her disappear, though I'd never used the sword to do such a thing and doubted it could. I added my own neophyte power to the mix, mentally envisioning fern fronds wrapping around her and hiding her from sight.

Maybe it was my imagination, but she seemed to fade into the foliage, blending in further.

The skeletal creatures reached us and circled above the trees. I should have used the camouflage charm earlier. At least they seemed to have trouble pinpointing us. They didn't shriek or screech or emit any other noises as they hunted for us, but as they flapped their bone-colored wings, their big avian shapes visible now and then through the leaves, the sound of the wingbeats drifted down to us.

One flew close enough that it scraped its rib cage on the top of my tree, making branches shake and sending leaves flitting down. My fist tightened around Chopper's hilt, though I dreaded the idea of fighting. If they got close enough to see through the magic of my charm… or if they sensed Li… we would be dead.

Mom would have no idea where I'd gone, have no idea what to tell Amber. Would my daughter miss me? Had we spent enough time together this year for her to develop feelings and care one way or another what happened to me?

I shook away the depressing thoughts. I had to focus on what seemed an inevitable battle, be ready to fight or run.

Across the road, one of the creatures landed in the tree that Li was hiding under. I stifled a groan and held my breath. From my spot, I could clearly see its hollow eye sockets scanning the road, as if it were a living bird.

It jerked its skull of a head up, and I was sure it had spotted me. But its head swiveled to the side, and it sprang out of the tree.

I sensed a dragon—a *living* dragon—at the edge of my range, though I was more confused than relieved. It was Xilneth. I hadn't seen him since he'd admitted to being forced to work for the Silverclaw dragon that had hired an assassin to come after me. What was *he* doing here?

Ruin Bringer! he blurted into my mind. *Are you in that forest? I sensed you before, but then you disappeared. And all these dreadful flying bone bags are coming toward me. What* are *these foul things?*

He wasn't speaking into my mind, I realized, but broadcasting telepathically to the whole forest. I hoped the undead creatures couldn't understand him.

I'm here, I risked replying, though I worried the undead creatures would hear my telepathic thoughts. I tried to pinpoint Xilneth with them.

What are you doing here? he asked at the same time that I sent the same question to him.

A half-dwarf thief who is trying to get my sword from me whooshed me to this world.

That is not the answer I expected. The stuffy and haughty Lord Zavryd'nokquetal said you were on your own planet. I did not think to find you—ah, they give chase!

I dropped my forehead into my hand. *Get out of here, Xilneth. Zav and I fought those guys the other day, and they're tough.*

I was sent here to scout. I did not know I would immediately be set upon.

Who sent you?

The Stormforge Clan queen. My role in obeying Mythrarion Silverclaw is now known to all, and even my own clan is ashamed of me. I heard about the big meeting and that there is a problem on the dwarven home world, and I volunteered to help. To redeem myself!

Xilneth had to be fleeing the creatures, for I no longer sensed him, but his words came through loud and clear. Hopefully, he could still hear mine. My telepathy was much weaker than a dragon's.

Zav already knew about the undead creatures. Why would the queen send you to scout?

We must know who is responsible for summoning them!

Do you know about the lich? As I asked the question, it occurred to me that I had only Li's word as to what we were dealing with, but it did make sense that someone—something—powerful and with a link to the undead was behind making the skeletal creatures.

The what? Xilneth asked.

I'm told there's a dragon lich.

A dragon would never allow himself to be made into such a creature!

Maybe you can take it up with the things chasing you.

Ah, they are driven. Why do they attack me? Ow!

Get out of here, Xilneth. You can't fight that many.

He didn't reply, and I frowned down at the moss under my feet. He wouldn't truly let them catch him when he could make a portal and leave any time, would he?

I wished he'd made it all the way to us, so he could make a portal so *I* could leave. Maybe it wasn't too late for that.

Xilneth? Are you still here?

Again, he didn't answer. Across the road, Li stepped warily out of the brush. I could no longer sense the creatures. They'd all flown after Xilneth.

They have wounded me! Xilneth told me just as I'd assumed he had already left. His voice didn't resonate as strongly in my mind, so he must have flown farther away. *I will be forced to make a portal and flee.*

I suppose there's no chance you can come open it near me so I can jump through too?

I am far from you now. They are trying to cut me out of the sky. I knocked one into a cliff and destroyed it, but there are so many more. I do not wish to fail again, Ruin Bringer!

If you were just sent to scout, and you found something, I don't think you've failed.

After a long moment, Xilneth quietly admitted, *The queen did not send me. She did not even acknowledge me when I came to the court.*

Then why are you here?

I thought I was crafty enough to figure out what's going on and to find Lord Braytokinor and solve the problem myself. This would show the others that I am not *an embarrassment to our kind.*

The way he said that made me think he was quoting someone. Not Zav, I hoped.

Just tell your people that there's a lich and that they need to get here pronto and en masse to deal with it, please. Oh, and let Zav know I'm here and that I wouldn't mind a ride back to Earth.

I could give you a ride if I weren't being harried like some weakling prey! Let me attempt to get to you.

No, just give my message to your people. Someone needs to know about the lich and do something about it. And Zav needed to know I was here, so I didn't get stuck going into some lich lair with a crazy half-dwarf on a mission.

I wish to be heroic! A proper dragon! Why are there so many of these foul things? I—

I rubbed my forehead again. Out of all the dragons who could have popped up on this world, I had to get the teenage hippy, as Zav called him.

But then, what other dragon, besides Zav himself, would have bothered communicating with me or even recognized me if they'd shown up here?

Get yourself out of trouble, Xilneth, and pass along my message. Please!

He didn't reply. I couldn't sense him, but after a few quiet moments, Li hustled back under cover. The creatures sailed into range of my senses, and my stomach sank.

Had they given up because Xilneth made a portal and fled this world? Or had they, when he'd been distracted talking to me about heroics, caught him and killed him?

My camouflage charm was still active, and I willed Chopper to hide Li again, in case it had helped before. Then I leaned my forehead against the tree, birch-like bark cool against my skin, and willed myself to blend into the trunk so they wouldn't notice me.

The creatures flew past overhead without stopping to search for us. Maybe they'd forgotten we were here.

Or maybe—I grimaced as I sensed them flying straight toward the black mountain—they were reporting back to their master that they'd killed Xilneth... and that we were out here somewhere.

CHAPTER 22

TWILIGHT SETTLED ON THE FOREST as I sat in the moss, leaning my back against a tree, Chopper in its scabbard at my side. Li paced in front of me, thumping her fist against her thigh and muttering to herself in Chinese.

She could mutter all she wanted. I wasn't continuing on. This was her quest. It wouldn't become my quest until the lich was cleared out from the mountain and it was safe to stroll inside to visit the repository of knowledge. I'd waited ten years to learn Chopper's secrets; I could wait ten more if need be. Though I trusted Zav's people would be along to deal with this problem sooner than that.

Li stopped, faced me, and jammed her fists against her hips. "We must continue to the mountain."

"I'm not going," I said for the tenth time.

After the near miss with the flying skeletons, I'd refused to go farther. I'd been sitting under this tree for the last hour.

"I am *positive* there will be a device in there that can create a portal to take us back to Earth," Li said.

"*I'm* positive that if there is, the lich will be sitting on it."

"You have your stealth charm." She pointed to my neck. "And you were able to help me hide even though I was not near you. The power of the dragon blade is great. We can sneak in without the lich knowing we are there."

"*Or* we can wait until Xilneth gets word back to his people and an army of dragons shows up to deal with the lich."

"You said yourself you don't know if that dragon survived to take the message to others of his kind."

Earlier, I'd shared the details of Xilneth's visit and the conversation we'd had. Maybe I shouldn't have been so honest.

"Even if he didn't, Zav knows there's a problem here. He'll lead his people here soon."

Li scowled. "You only want your powerful ally here so he can fly you and my sword away from me after I've proven to you that it does not belong to you. Do not think that I will not find a way home. If you flee, I *will* get it from you. I will return it and the other treasures I've reclaimed to my homeland, so that my people will be able to sell them and get out of poverty. And I will show my mother the sword that my father came to Earth to find so long ago. She will be proud of me for fulfilling his mission and reclaiming it for our family."

"How wonderful for you."

The scowl deepened, and her fingers twitched toward her dagger. I watched her, ready to spring to my feet to defend myself.

"I should have told you *nothing*." Li dropped her hand, spun, and stalked into the trees.

"Fine with me." I let my head clunk back against the trunk, hoping she would give up on me and continue to the mountain on her own. Though if the whole point of her going was to prove to me that Chopper was hers, there was little point in her going without me.

Li returned scant minutes later, her face more composed. Maybe she'd done some deep breathing or meditation—and was better at it than I was.

She sat cross-legged on the ground and pulled a few things out of her pack, including her canteen and an assortment of energy bars. My mouth watered. She'd given me one earlier, but we'd been here for a full day by now. My stomach was certain of it and growled pitifully. Li must have heard it for she glanced over, but she didn't comment, merely returning to her pack. A blanket and a tiny collapsible lantern followed the food. Setting up camp for the night.

"Zav wouldn't do what you think," I said. "He wouldn't fly me away with something stolen. He's honorable, and he encourages *me* to be honorable."

"Then why do you carry a stolen sword?"

"Because I don't have *proof* that it's stolen."

"You *know* it is. You should have returned it to the dwarven people long ago."

"They don't knock on my door very often."

"If you wished to find a way to them, you could have." Li splayed her fingers across her chest. "*I* found the portal generator so I could come to this world."

"Great. I'd award you a cookie if I had one, but you rudely sucked me off to another world without giving me time to raid my mom's cupboards."

Li gazed at me with a stony expression—or perhaps one lacking in understanding. So far, her English had proven good, but my sarcasm might be tough for a non-native speaker to decipher. Even Nin, who'd been in the country for years and was an excellent student of America, gave me puzzled looks from time to time.

"I will give you food," Li said, "if you promise to continue to the repository with me in the morning."

"Nope. I'll just gnaw on my own stomach lining until Zav shows up."

"It must be comforting to have a dragon at one's beck and call." She sounded bitter again.

I was beyond caring. I leaned my head back against the tree and said, "It is. If you want me to hook you up with one, let me know. Xilneth seems to be into mongrels."

She didn't respond to that. Good. I was done with the conversation.

I had no intention of sleeping while she was within a mile of me, but my feet and legs could use a rest after all that walking. In case she thought about trying something, I pulled Fezzik out of its holster and rested it in my lap. I shifted Chopper so that its scabbard was under my butt. It wasn't comfortable, but it would make it difficult for her to slip in and take it.

A few seconds later, something struck me in the chest, and I almost sprang to my feet and pointed my gun at her. But it was only one of the energy bars.

I eyed her suspiciously, but she was opening a bar of her own, the wrapper rustling in the growing darkness, and not looking in my direction. She'd also put her back to a tree, opting to face the road, and pulled her stuff close. Noshing noises floated over to me.

My stomach growled again, but the thought that she might want to poison me burbled up in my mind. Not until she'd finished hers and rolled onto her side to sleep did I touch mine.

I pulled out my phone, which I'd barely touched since arriving, knowing there was nowhere to charge a battery here, and shone the flashlight app onto her gift. Even though I'd eaten one of her bars earlier and suffered no ill effects, I examined the label and made sure it hadn't been opened before unwrapping it. As with the previous one, it was a familiar brand and had come from a grocery store, not some chemist's lab.

After another pitiful whine from my stomach, I opened the bar and took a bite. Like other energy bars I'd had, it had the familiar unpalatable tang of strange protein powders that made the faux chocolate barely palatable, but I was hungry enough not to care. Not so hungry that I didn't think fondly of my chocolate-covered caramels back home, but at the moment, I would have preferred a steak to either option.

After finishing, I stuck the wrapper in my pocket, not wanting to be the rude foreigner who littered on someone else's planet, and leaned back again. Even though I had no intention of falling asleep, drowsiness came far more quickly than I expected. The long day's hike, I supposed. The thought that I should summon Sindari to stand guard in case I fell asleep came to mind, but my arm was so heavy that I couldn't manage the effort to lift it to touch my charm.

An alarm bell rang in the back of my mind. I never fell asleep so quickly or completely. I tried to stir myself, to at least grab Fezzik in case I needed it, but my arms remained limp at my sides.

The soft crunch of someone walking across the undergrowth reached my ears. Li.

I was in trouble, but I couldn't do a thing about it. My body betrayed me, and I fell asleep.

CHAPTER 23

IT WAS FULL DARKNESS WHEN I woke with a start, heart pounding in my chest, hands and feet so numb they hurt. When I tried to push myself off the ground, my arms were almost as numb, and I pitched back down on my side.

Adrenaline surged through my veins as I feared I was having a heart attack or something equally bad. All by myself on an alien world. My lungs tightened, and I heard my own wheezing.

Damn it, how would Zav find me if I was dead?

I shook my hands and kicked my feet, willing the blood to return to them, so I could dig out my inhaler. Meanwhile, I tried not to panic at the thought that Li might have taken it. If she had, I was screwed. I didn't sense her nearby. She was probably long gone, leaving me to be eaten by some nocturnal predator.

As soon as a semblance of normalcy returned to my hands, I dug out my inhaler, relieved to find it in my pocket. I patted around for my weapons and found Fezzik right away. It had tipped out of my lap when I'd fallen asleep—when I'd been *drugged*. But Chopper was nowhere around.

Even though I knew I wouldn't find it, I couldn't keep from patting all around on hands and knees, as if I might get lucky. Maybe she'd dropped it as she fled.

"Yeah, right," I muttered, the words slurred.

Even my lips were numb. What had been in that bar, and how had she gotten it in there? I'd checked the wrapper so carefully.

"Thieves," I grumbled, the word a curse.

Maybe I hadn't been out for that long. Maybe it was still possible to catch her. Sindari could help.

If she hadn't taken my charms. Fresh fear lurched through me at the thought, but when I reached up, I found the reassuring feline shape of his charm. The others were all there too. Strange mercies from a thief.

"Sindari," I whispered to summon him. "I need your help."

I am always prepared to go into battle, he said as soon as he formed at my side.

"It's your nose that I need right now, though if we catch her, I'll let you kick her ass again."

Sindari gazed around, nostrils already sniffing, as I explained what had happened.

He padded over to the tree where Li had been sitting. *I can tell that she was here, but I believe it has been several hours since she left.*

I slumped against my own tree and rubbed my temple, a fledgling headache creeping into my skull. "I was hoping whatever she gave me hadn't knocked me out for that long."

After sniffing around the area, Sindari headed to the road and stood with his snout in the direction we'd been walking. Toward that damn mountain.

She went this way.

"Of course she did." I holstered Fezzik, looked around as if I might have other gear along to grab, but I had nothing, not even a bottle of water. "She could have left me a Gatorade."

Disgusted, I hobbled to the road, waving for Sindari to lead. A blister that had developed during the day's walk had proven impervious to my usually fast healing. Maybe that drug had affected my regenerative abilities. Lovely.

Would you have consumed a beverage given to you by the person who poisoned your meal?

"Depends how thirsty I was."

His green eyes gazed judgingly at me.

"She's already got my sword. It's not like she has another reason to drug me."

Your pace is slow. Are you still under the effects of the drug?

"Yeah." That sounded less wussy than admitting to a blister. I sucked up the discomfort and picked up my pace.

If I were not tethered to your charm by magic, I could race ahead and perhaps catch her.

"I really wish the magic worked that way, because I do *not* want to go where she's going." I summed up what she'd told me about the lich, since he hadn't been there for that discussion.

Sindari looked at me, this time with concern instead of judgment. *I do not want to go there either. Even a dwarven or elven lich would be difficult to battle. I cannot imagine how powerful a dragon lich is.*

"Powerful enough to make those skeletal minions that tried to kick our asses." I remembered Sindari flying over the trees after our winged nemesis flung him off. I also remembered the ghoulish gouges that would have killed him if not for the dragon healer.

The master is always significantly more powerful than the minions.

"Fact of life." I would have sighed, but I was too busy forcing my legs into a jog—and regretting that I'd let my cardio workouts slide of late. Willard would be ashamed of me. Sadly, my jog was barely a trot for Sindari.

I will run to the edge of my range and see if I can catch her. He sped off down the road.

Just come back to help me if minions show up.

Naturally.

The forest thinned, and the black mountain loomed larger and more ominously on the horizon. The only good thing was that I didn't see any volcanic smoke wafting from its peak. I had no desire to crawl through magma tubes or breathe any more toxic air this year.

Some of the winged creatures are leaving the mountain, Sindari told me from farther up the road.

I'm really starting to hate those guys. I activated my cloaking charm. *Hide yourself with your magic, and let's hope they don't notice us.*

As much as Sindari loved battle, I doubted he wanted to fight the undead creatures again. Especially when Zav wasn't here to transport him to a healer afterward.

I am, Sindari replied. *I thought I glimpsed someone climbing up the lower levels of the mountain a couple of miles ahead, but then the person glanced back and darted out of my view. The thief also has a cloaking charm, does she not?*

Actually, I think you broke it or ripped it off back at Mom's place. I grimaced, realizing Li would have a harder time hiding now. Unless she knew better than I how to use Chopper and could summon some magical camouflage from *it*.

Sindari did not respond. Eight creatures flew into view over the mountain, dark winged shapes against the starry night sky.

"Why can't this lich ever just send out one or two?" With my charm active, I remained on the road longer than I otherwise would have. I wanted to see which direction they flew.

I am making my way back to you in case we need to do battle, Sindari said. *Thank you.*

The creatures swept down the front of the mountain, their dark bodies blending into the dark terrain and growing difficult to see. But I sensed them now. They were flying around the foothills in a search pattern.

Is that where you saw Li? I spotted Sindari heading toward me, trotting through the trees alongside the road, our link making him visible to my eyes.

It is the approximate area where I saw someone, yes.

My first thought was that it would be better if they found Li than me, but what if they succeeded in killing her and took Chopper home as a gift for their master? Would a dragon lich care about a magical sword? Maybe not in general, but he might care about a magical sword that could harm *dragons*. He might prefer it be buried in a mountain where nobody could ever find it. Or was it possible that he would destroy it?

Maybe it was silly to feel so distraught at the idea of losing a possession, but fresh frustration bubbled up inside of me. Chopper made my job a lot more doable than it would be without it. Even now, I was keenly aware that I had nothing that would harm those creatures if they came after me. Sindari might do some damage, but I'd already seen that Fezzik was useless against them.

The winged creatures appeared again in the sky over the mountain, confusing me because my senses told me they were still searching the foothills. Then I realized it was *another* batch of them. That brought the total to sixteen.

I really hope they can't see us with our camouflage magic activated. I placed a hand on Sindari's back as he joined me.

He turned to watch them. *As do I.*

The second batch of creatures did not join the first. My gut knotted as they flew away from the mountain—and toward us.

Off the road, I urged, slipping silently into the trees.

Sindari selected a nearby hiding spot. With the branches overhead now, I could no longer see the creatures, but their auras grew stronger as they flew closer.

I willed my magic to further hide us, if possible, and resolved to spend more time learning from Freysha if I survived this week. Not having Chopper made me keenly aware of how nice it would be to have more powerful—and versatile—skills to draw upon.

As one, the creatures flew over the trees, drawing closer and closer. I held my breath. Earlier, the others hadn't seemed to see through the camouflage magic, but maybe they'd simply been distracted by Xilneth's approach.

This time was no different. This new batch didn't circle my area. They flew past without slowing down.

I let my breath out, relieved but still concerned. Where were they going? The others were still searching the mountainside.

A familiar aura brushed my senses.

Zav! I cried out telepathically before I could catch myself. I crossed my fingers that the creatures hadn't detected that, but they were flying... Crap. They were flying toward Zav. And was that Xilneth I sensed too? The two dragons were at the edge of my range.

My mate! Zav responded. *Are you well?*

I'm okay. I lost my sword, but I'm going to get it back. Watch out. Undead minions are coming your way.

I see them, he replied grimly. *I will battle my way to you, and Xilnethgarish will attempt to assist me instead of impeding me or fleeing in a cowardly manner.*

He wants to prove himself and be heroic.

We shall see. I must battle now. Be ready. I am attempting to reach you so I can create a portal and take us back to my world.

I hesitated, not wanting to leave until I got Chopper back—especially now that I worried the lich would get it and destroy it—but I didn't want to distract Zav. Not when the creatures were almost upon him. Also, maybe it was foolish to want to stay, to risk my life for a sword. It was a *valuable* sword, but still...

I'm ready. We could figure out the rest once we were together. Maybe we could plan a return from the safety of another world. *Be careful, Zav.*

They had *better be careful. I will utterly destroy them for daring to challenge the might of a dragon in his prime!*

Uh huh. I'll get out in the open where you can fly down to me and make a portal.

Do this. Yes.

Come on, Sindari. I waved for him to follow me back to the road. *Zav is going to try to pick us up.*

Lord Zavryd is being attacked by the creatures.

I know. He promises to destroy them utterly.

There are eight of them, and they are not easy to destroy.

I know, but he has backup. I hoped Xilneth was a better fighter than Zav believed. And that he wouldn't attempt to impress the undead creatures by singing to them.

As I jogged down the road, looking for a spot where Zav could easily reach me if he had to hurry—and where the sky might be open enough for me to see the battle—I worried for him. If he had been closer, I would have run *toward* him instead of away, and used my remaining bullets to distract his enemies. But he was two or three miles away and not near the road. I wouldn't be able to get there in time to help.

The road sloped upward, and Sindari and I came out of the trees into an area where only charred snags and logs remained, the victims of some past wildfire. The craggy black slopes and cliffs of the mountainside loomed ahead, blocking out half of the starry sky and casting deep shadows. I almost missed seeing several carcasses of animals similar to deer lying on the road. I hoped whatever had killed them wasn't crouching nearby.

After skirting them, I slowed down, aware that we'd drawn closer to the other group of creatures. They must not have found Li yet, or they wouldn't still be out there. I couldn't sense her *or* Chopper. That didn't mean they weren't there. When I'd worn Chopper, it had camouflaged itself from other people. Now, if it was on Li's back, it would camouflage itself from *me*. That gave me a twinge of betrayal, but it wasn't a pet, just a magical object.

When I spotted a rocky hill to one side, I veered off the road. The top was out in the open, which made my shoulder blades itch, but it would be easy for Zav to reach me.

I sensed him flying about behind me, and Xilneth as well. They'd managed to get closer, but the creatures were all around them, harrying them and keeping them from advancing toward the mountain. Toward *me*.

As soon as I reached the top of the hill, they came into view over the trees, the dragons lighting the night—and the undead creatures—with their fire. One of their enemies had crashed into the treetops and wasn't moving, but that left seven more in the sky with them.

I drew Fezzik, hoping they would come close enough that I could help. Even if all I could do was ping those skeletons with bullets that did no damage, maybe it would draw one or two away.

Xilneth broke away from the battle and flapped back the way they had come, his flight crooked, one of his wings damaged. Two of the creatures took off after him. The rest stayed near Zav.

He flung a wave of power at two, and they tumbled away, somersaulting through the air. Two other creatures he bathed with his fire. I hoped it blackened and incinerated their bones.

For a second, none of them were attacking him. He broke away and flew straight toward me.

I am coming for you, my mate. His telepathic voice sounded pained, and I winced, knowing he was risking his life to come get me.

Four of the creatures gave chase, flapping their wings hard enough to keep up. I hoped Zav would have time to form a portal. I'd seen him do it before, and it never seemed to take more than a few seconds, but it had never been when he was in the middle of battle and had enemies nipping at his heels—his talons.

A human scream came from the mountainside where the other creatures were hunting. Li.

"Shit." I turned, scanning the dark slope, but I still couldn't see or sense her.

Blue light flashed. *Chopper's* blue light.

I glanced toward Zav, torn between waiting for him and wanting to go help Li. This might be my last chance—my *only* chance—to get Chopper back.

Magic pulsed beside me, and I jumped. But it was a portal forming, not an enemy.

Leap through, Zav commanded me as he turned to snap at two minions that had caught up to him and were clawing at his backside.

Not without you.

They were in firing range now. I lifted Fezzik, aiming at one of the creatures but waiting for an opening. They were too close to Zav, and I couldn't risk hitting him.

Sindari, I thought as an opportunity came, and I fired at one of the minions' skulls, *can you try to get Li? It looks like she's less than a mile away.*

I will try. Do you wish me to assist her or only get your sword?

My bullet streaked away, its magic leaving a blue trail in the air, and it slammed into the creature's skull. It jerked its head and flapped away from Zav, momentarily distracted. Zav turned and threw his full power at one of the others, hurling a wave of magic that I sensed from hundreds of yards away.

He roared, the mighty sound echoing off the mountainside, and spewed fire at two more creatures.

Help her if you can, I told Sindari, not voicing the cold thought that popped into my head, that my problems about an ownership dispute with Chopper would be over if Li were dead, *but I don't want you fighting eight of those things.*

As Sindari sped down the hill and toward Li's position, one of Zav's enemies spiraled down in flames, crashing in the trees like a World War I biplane.

I fired at another creature that had caught up and was aiding its buddies against Zav. My bullet streaked away, flying into one of its empty eye sockets and—I hoped—cracking through its skull and out the other side.

The blow did little more than cause its flight to falter for a few seconds, but that gave Zav time to whirl on another foe, snapping his mighty jaw down on the vertebrae of its neck. He shook his head and tore through magic and bone. The creature's skull tumbled free, plummeting to the trees, and when Zav released the body, the rest of it followed.

Only two remained in the air with him.

You've got them, Zav, I whispered in my mind, though I didn't want to distract him.

As I raised Fezzik to fire at one of the remaining creatures, a new ominous aura came into my range. It was so dark and menacing that I almost dropped my gun, my instincts telling me to flee into the forest. Or better yet to flee into the portal floating scant feet away.

Another dragon came into view, climbing up from the back side of the mountain to stand near the peak and look down on the battle. Its aura stank of the grave even as it radiated power like a sun.

The dragon lich had arrived.

CHAPTER 24

THE GLOWING RED EYES OF the dragon lich locked on to Zav's battle, and a blast of raw energy struck him and the two skeletal minions fighting him. They flew backward as if they'd been struck by tidal waves. The bones of the minions blasted into a thousand pieces.

I gaped, startled that the lich had blasted his own team, but maybe he could make more minions any time he wished.

Flee through the portal, now! Zav ordered me as he struggled to right himself and raise his magical defenses against the lich. This time, there was magical compulsion in the words. He didn't want me to disobey.

But one of my charms helped me resist compulsions, and I only took a step toward the portal before stopping myself.

Not without you. I would shoot at that damn lich if he came close enough. *Hurry over here, and let's go together.*

I glanced back, but I couldn't see Sindari or the blue glow of Chopper's blade anymore. Since Sindari would be dismissed automatically if I went through the portal, he ought to be all right.

The lich blasted Zav with another wave of power, more intense than anything I'd ever sensed. Had it been directed at me, I knew I'd be dead.

Zav was ready this time, and didn't fly backward, but a roar of pain mingled with defiance came from him, and I sensed his defenses crumbling under the intense power.

Zav, the portal. Let's go. Don't stand there and take that.

He must have agreed, for as soon as he recovered, he flew straight toward me. The lich's red gaze swept toward me, and its startling power seeped the life from my muscles. I almost pitched to the ground. He was too far away for me to shoot at, but that would have been futile anyway. I had no doubt. Would even Chopper be able to damage that guy?

His eye sockets pulsed with red light, and the portal disappeared, winking out like a candle's flame. Two seconds too late, Zav landed next to me.

Magic flared, and another portal started to form, but once again, the lich snuffed it out.

We have to get away from him. Zav wrapped his power around me and levitated me onto his back.

I'm not arguing.

As he sprang into the air, I expected another attack, but the lich's gaze swept toward his other minions—and toward Sindari. And Li, if she was still down there.

Did you find her, Sindari? I still sensed him over there.

They have her, he replied grimly.

As Zav flew farther away, I made out several of the creatures, visible again as they were outlined against the starry night sky. A limp human form dangled from the talons of one. Unconscious? Dead? I couldn't tell. I also couldn't tell if Li was wearing my harness and had Chopper across her back, or if the blade lay abandoned among the rocks.

We flew beyond the range of Sindari's charm, and I sensed our link breaking as the magic propelled him back to his realm. At least he would be safe there. I assumed that the lich wouldn't follow him. He had what he wanted, though I had no idea why he wanted Li. Because of Chopper? Because she'd presumed to visit his lair before and had taken photos and swiped some of his loot?

Whatever the reason, I doubted I would see her alive again. Was there any chance I would see Chopper again? I didn't know.

As Zav flew farther from the mountain, I let my forehead thunk against his scales and spread my arms across his back. But my fingers encountered warm dampness—blood—and I jerked them back.

How badly are you injured, Zav? I wished I could hug him, but that didn't work well when he was in his native form. *And where the hell did Xilneth go?*

Indignation swept through me as I imagined him fleeing and leaving Zav to fend for himself.

I ordered him to try to lead some of them away, Zav replied, ignoring my first question. *And then make a portal when he could to return home and warn our people that we've confirmed the existence of a dragon lich.*

I patted his scales. *Are the rest of your people coming back soon to battle him?*

Her.

It's a female lich?

Yes. Unless I am mistaken, it is—it was—Peynar'dokla Silverclaw.

Ugh, I really hate those Silverclaws.

This proves that they truly will do anything in an attempt to gain more power over the Cosmic Realms. As to when my people will arrive... perhaps as soon as tomorrow, but this is a more problematic situation than we realized. It is likely Peynar'dokla has had time to amass a great many defenses inside of that mountain. Even with many dragons, she will not be easy to slay. Someone should sneak in and scout the mountain to ensure my people have the best intelligence possible.

Uh. It occurred to me that Zav was continuing to fly away, even though he could have stopped and created a portal to take us out of here by now. *Is that someone you?*

I am here. I am the logical choice.

Won't she be expecting you to come back? I peered back past Zav's tail streaming behind us and toward the black mountain. We'd already flown a dozen miles, so it was probably only my imagination that I could see red eyes watching us.

Perhaps. She may believe I will return home, as Xilnethgarish did, to report to the others. She might think she has time to further fortify her lair, but she also may wait to see if anyone else tries to sneak in tonight. Her minions will be alert and on guard.

Fun.

I will wait until daylight to return and hope she is resting then. Even the undead must rest to reenergize their powers. Besides, I must recuperate and heal my wounds first.

I eyed the bloody spot I'd touched and wondered how many more wounds he had. *Will you be able to? Or do you need to see the dragon who healed Sindari?*

And who happened to be related to this new lich. No conflict of interest there.

I convinced her to make me a potion that I could bring back with me in case of future injury. Hopefully, it is as efficacious as she promised.

Hopefully it's not poison.

I believe my magic would be able to detect that.

I hope so.

Tonight, I will apply the potion and heal to the best of my abilities. Tomorrow, I will be ready to risk facing her.

I hope your plan is for us to sneak in without being discovered and not face her at all. Not until we've got a horde of dragons to back us up.

That is *my plan,* Zav assured me, *but plans go awry. Also, I intend to create a portal as soon as I find a defensible resting place and send you home.*

You're not going in there without me. Funny how I hadn't been willing to go in there at all an hour ago, but now that Zav was determined to sneak in…

Admittedly, I didn't know how much help I could be without Chopper. I waited for him to point out that I would only get in the way.

You wish to stay so you can seek your sword and recover it? he guessed.

That would be nice, but I want to go so I can watch out for you. *I've still got a few bullets left. I can make a distraction if nothing else.*

Shooting your weapon in the tunnels of Mount Crenel would alert the lich to our presence.

I assume if I have to shoot something, she'll already know we're there. Look, I'm sure Sindari and I can sneak around as well as you can, and if we fail at sneaking, then we can be of some use. I stroked his scales. *Also, I don't want to go home and leave you here to face danger alone. I'll worry about you. It'll give me indigestion. You don't want that, do you?*

A puff of air that might have been a snort floated away from him. *Proper digestion is important.*

Especially with those all-protein diets dragons favor.

Yes. Very well. I will not send you home, but I ask a favor.

Wow, that sounded so polite and diffident. He'd never made a request like that.

What? I asked.

Do not attempt to vex the lich. She could slay you with a thought.

You know I have a hard time reining in my tongue. Can I at least taunt her and talk about how superior you are after you and your clan have defeated her?

I will allow this.

***

A cold breeze blew off the snowy peaks outside and into the mouth of the cave that Zav had located more than a hundred miles from Mount Crenel and—he promised—outside of the lich's range to detect us. When we entered, bats, or something like them, shifted and flapped about in the back, adjusting positions among stalactites before furling their wings tight for warmth. The nippy air made me wish for wings I could wrap around myself.

At least the air was clearer than it had been near Mount Crenel. For the moment, my lungs were content.

Zav shifted into his human form to accompany me inside, creating a soft yellow light to illuminate the area. It showed his elven robe slashed open in the back and on one side, revealing deep gouges in his flesh. The same eerie purple glow that had plagued Sindari's cuts hovered over these, almost an ominous mist that shifted and writhed just above the wounds.

I swallowed, trying to tamp down concern over their underworld taint and what it would mean if the potion he'd been given didn't work. Could we trust that Silverclaw healer? Especially when the lich was *also* from the Silverclaw Clan? Wasn't it likely that they were in cahoots?

"You said you have a potion I can rub on those for you?" I reminded myself that the healer had fixed up Sindari.

"Yes." Zav produced a slender tapered tube about a foot long with a cork in the top. "I will disrobe for you."

I accepted the strange holder. "That always excites me."

Zav gazed at me through his eyelashes. "I know this."

He floated his robe off and draped it over a boulder, using his magic to mend the rips in the fabric.

"Why does your clothing get torn when you're injured in your dragon form?" I'd seen it before and hadn't thought much of it, but it occurred to me to wonder since he could poof his clothes and other things into interdimensional storage cubbies.

"If I forget to put it away, it shifts along with me and is magically integrated into my scales. When I am in a hurry, I rarely worry about my human coverings."

"And when you're not in a hurry, you hang it in an interdimensional closet?" I imagined his robe on a hanger, floating inside one of those portable fabric closets.

"Yes. I strive to be a tidy dragon."

"That shouldn't be hard, given how few things you have."

"Some dragons hoard knickknacks and treasures."

"As the books tell me." I smiled and rested a hand on his bare shoulder. Normally, I would have appreciated the view and the excuse to run my hand along his muscular back, but the otherworldly wounds made me uneasy. "Do you have any water? Maybe I should clean these."

"There is a pool in the back of the cave." He pointed into the shadows.

"Under where the bats poo? I said clean, not infect."

"I will sterilize the water."

"And incinerate the guano?"

"A simple task. When I am done, you will enjoy drinking from it as much as the fizzy water in the cans of your world."

"I'm sure." I imagined a film of guano ash atop the water and wondered if I could survive not drinking again until we made it back home.

Zav reached into his magical cubby and drew out a bowl that reminded me of a dog dish. I didn't suggest he paint bones on the side, since I'd had enough of bones, skeletons, and all things death-related for the week.

He floated it back to the pool, filled it, then applied magic to boil the water. Another wave of magic washed over it, though I couldn't tell what it did. Maybe he was incinerating debris, or maybe it was UV light for sterilization. If he had the ability to produce UV light, I would hand him my toothbrush and other bathroom implements when we got home.

A cooling breeze whispered past, and the bubbling water ceased its boil by the time it came to rest at my feet. Next, he produced a couple of fuzzy squares of cloth. Or were those *furry* squares? I supposed dragons weren't big on textiles.

I dabbed water onto his wounds, trying to be gentle. Nobody had accused me of having a surgeon's hands, but Zav didn't complain. He let his chin droop to his chest as I worked on his back and side. Maybe I let myself work a few caresses in with my free hand. To help my patient relax, of course, not for my own pleasure.

"This is appealing," Zav said. "Henceforth, I will allow you to clean all of my wounds before I heal them."

"Is cleaning necessary? I haven't noticed you roaming around with infections from normal wounds."

"Usually, my magic is sufficient for sterilization, but healing my own wounds doesn't prompt you to rub my butt."

"I only brushed it; I didn't *rub* it."

"You may rub it."

"Thanks for your generosity."

He looked over his shoulder at me, his lashes lowered again.

"As much as I appreciate your smoldering bedroom eyes," I said, "we're not having sex on the lumpy rock-covered floor of a cave, especially not when there are enemies that could be searching for us."

"I can make the floor comfortable."

"And the enemies?"

"They will not find us."

"Cocky dragon."

"The term in your dictionary is self-assured."

"Cockily self-assured." I kissed his cheek, dropped the cloth, and uncorked the potion. A pungent odor that smelled like rotten eucalyptus wafted out. "This'll either cure you or kill you."

I tipped some of the goo into my palm, letting it rest there for a moment to make sure it didn't burn a hole through me or do anything else vile before I risked applying it to his wounds. A few of the bats made squeaky noises, probably protesting the scent.

The goo made my skin tingle but nothing worse, so I dabbed some on Zav's cuts. "Do you keep bandages in an interdimensional medicine cabinet?"

"No. I will heal the wounds once the taint has been extinguished."

My stomach growled as I was finishing up, reminding me that the last thing I'd eaten had been that drugged protein bar.

"I don't suppose you brought any food along." I hadn't ever seen Zav take a snack stash out of any of his invisible pockets.

"You require sustenance?" Zav floated his robe back over to him. "I will hunt for you."

"I'd settle for a packet of beef jerky."

"Remain here and settle in." He strode out of the cave, shifted into his dragon form, and launched into the night.

Since I had no camping gear, there wasn't much to *settle*. I found a dry guano-free spot against a wall and discovered that the cave floor was every bit as lumpy and unpleasant as I'd imagined. After fifteen minutes of sitting on it, I needed someone to rub *my* butt.

Zav returned, landing on a precipice outside of the cave, though he didn't come back inside right away. Orange light flared outside. Had he made a cook fire? I hoped so. Raw meat wasn't my thing.

I was about to go out and investigate when he walked in, holding something that looked like a large rotisserie chicken skewered on a branch, the outside crispy but not charred. The smells wafting from it were foreign, but I was hungry enough not to care.

"This is a dwarven delicacy." Zav sat beside me and held out the branch. "I lack seasonings and sauces, but salt is plentiful in these mountains."

I pulled off a wing and took a tentative bite. He'd salted it heavily, which was probably good because it had a pungent scent and taste that reminded me of liver. If this was a dwarven delicacy, I didn't want to attend any of their feasts. But I ate enough to sate my hunger, with Zav watching with approval. He waited until I'd had all I wanted to polish off the rest.

"You're also a considerate dragon." I wiped grease off his chin. "Thank you."

"Considerate, yes. Not cocky."

"Oh, you're still cocky." I smiled, scooted lower against the wall, and snuggled into his side.

"I will mend my wounds now." He closed his eyes. "Not cockily."

"That's good. Cocky wound-mending sounds problematic."

His body heat drove away the chill of the night. I rested an arm across his stomach, careful not to touch any of the wounds he was mending. They'd stopped glowing shortly after I'd applied the goo, which left me hopeful that he'd be fine in the morning.

His eyes remained closed as he healed himself, but he slid an arm around me. "I am thinking of softening the ground."

"Softening the ground? Like creating a mattress?"

"It is difficult to create something out of nothing, even with powerful dragon magic, but I could rearrange the molecules in the existing stone to make it less… lumpy."

"I didn't know dragons were bothered by lumps."

"As a dragon, I am not. My scales are armor that protect me from swords, bullets, magical attacks, and lumpy ground."

"Miracle scales."

"Indeed. I will do this for your comfort. One moment."

The ground snapped and shifted under me, and if he hadn't warned me, I would have leaped up, certain a fissure was opening up to swallow us. But there were no great cracks, only grinding noises along with the rising and lowering of patches of rock. A memory of being a kid in the ball pit at McDonald's came to mind.

When the shifting stopped, the ground was smoother and curved upward on either side of us to cup us in this new den. The slopes created enough of a hollow to keep the chilly breeze from reaching us.

"Have I mentioned lately that you're a handy dragon?" I asked.

"Not lately, but I know you know this is true."

"Even though you have trouble reading my mind?"

"I can tell by the way you beam appreciation at me and stroke my stomach."

I caught myself—I *was* stroking his stomach. Well, it was a nice stomach. Not my fault. But we shouldn't contemplate sex when we were on a strange world with enemies about that could harm Zav. Besides, he needed to use his energy to finish healing himself.

"I didn't know I was capable of beaming appreciation." None of my past boyfriends had mentioned it. Thad would have said I beamed sarcasm. Loudly.

"I have evoked this latent talent in you."

"You're skilled as well as handy."

"Yes." The hand he'd wrapped around my back slid under my shirt to do some stroking of its own.

Since we'd eaten, Zav was probably feeling randy. Maybe I was, too, because it crossed my mind to fling my leg over him and forget about the threat of enemies for a time. But even with our distance from the mountain, I doubted we were safe. Those skeletal creatures had to be out flying on patrols and maybe even looking for us specifically.

"My clan will see that we are good for each other," Zav said. "They will come to our wedding."

"You're still concerned about that? I don't mind if they don't come."

"That's because you do not like them," Zav said dryly.

I thought about denying that, but I didn't like to lie to him, and he knew me pretty well for a guy from another world who'd never read my mind.

"I don't mind your Uncle Ston," I offered, unfastening his robe so I could touch warm skin instead of fabric.

"He is affable for a dragon."

"That's why I don't mind him. Why do you want the others to come so badly? A few weeks ago, you scoffed at the idea of a human wedding, saying we were already mated in the dragon way and that's what counts."

Zav did not answer right away, though his fingers didn't pause in their perusal of my skin, trails of magic teasing my nerves even more than his physical touch. Little zings of pleasure ran through my body.

"The queen no longer objects to you as my mate, as she has seen your worth in battle and that you will fight at my side, but she does not believe our union will last many years. She believes you are reckless and have human blood, so you will die before long, and then I will take a dragon mate, and she need only be patient. She believes there is little reason to humor me by attending a meaningless human ceremony."

"Well, she may be right. Even if I don't get myself killed doing my job—or being hunted down by someone doing *his* job—humans don't live nearly as long as dragons. It sucks, but I won't be able to be your mate forever, or as long as you live. Aren't you all hundreds or thousands of years old?"

"Dragons live long lives, but it is also possible that I will get *myself* killed doing my job—or being hunted down by someone with a dragon-slaying sword." His tone had turned dry. "You do not have the only one, you must be aware."

"I assumed not, though with all the interest in it, I have wondered how many are left."

"There used to be more of them, perhaps a hundred. Many have been lost over the centuries. They *are* rare." His tone grew more serious again, his gaze shifting toward the dark stalactites above. "I wish for my family—especially my mother—to attend the wedding and show that they support me in this and realize that you are not a passing fancy. Always, I have supported my mother and my elders, often risking my life to obey their orders and be loyal to my clan. They could support me in this." As he spoke, distracted by his thoughts, his fingers had paused scant inches from my breasts.

I would prefer they continue to drift upward, but I tried to focus on his problem and think of a way I could help or at least commiserate. It was rare for Zav to set aside his dragon haughtiness and open up candidly about his family and his concerns, and I wanted him to feel he could do so with me.

"Parents are difficult for all races, I see."

"Yes," he said. "This is a universal truth."

"Have you *told* them you want their support? Told your mother?"

"We do not speak about such things."

"What things? Feelings?"

"Yes."

"You're speaking about them with me," I pointed out.

"That is because you're my mate and do not see such things as a weakness." His gaze returned to mine, his hand drifting upward to my breast. At some whisper of magic, my bra unfastened, and his warm fingers cupped me, thumb brushing sensitive skin. Hot tingles flushed my body, and I lost all resolve to avoid sex in favor of staying alert during the night. "You are aroused by me," he stated, his voice growing husky as I basked in his touches.

So cocky.

"I wouldn't marry you if I wasn't." I pushed his robe farther open, sliding my hand along the hard muscles of his chest, then dropping my mouth to his pecs to trace his warm skin with my tongue.

"You like it when we speak of feelings, and you take great pleasure in our mating." His other hand found the back of my head, his fingers threading through my hair and keeping me close to him. "That arouses *me*. This form should not appeal so much to me, but it is always so prepared to enjoy pleasure, not only the short bursts that dragons feel during mating season." His voice lowered to a growl. "There can be pleasure *all* the time."

"So you're saying that being human has its perks," I mumbled against his skin, shifting to lie atop him, feeling that he was indeed prepared for pleasure. I reached down and gripped him lightly, smiling as he gasped and shifted upward into my hand.

"Being with my *mate* has its perks. My family *will* come to see us wed. They will see that you are my mate and I am your dragon, and no others matter. They will respect this."

"I hope you're not suggesting something outré. You know I'm not an exhibitionist."

"You will perform only for me," he growled, his eyes flashing violet. His magic crackled around me and coursed along my nerves, this time making *me* gasp.

He guided my mouth toward his, but he didn't kiss me, instead gazing intently at my face as his hands roamed my body, peeling back my clothes, even as the caresses of his magic created desire all over. A part of me wanted to protest *performing* for him, but his heated gaze was avid as I squirmed under his touch, and such pleasure rocketed through me that I would have cursed if it stopped. I might have screamed as I reached my climax—something sure startled the bats into flying out of the cave—but I hardly cared. If Zav wanted to give me pleasure, I wanted to take it.

Before the pulsing waves faded, he pulled my head down to his, kissing me hard, his own need pulsing in my hand. He shifted me onto my back, and I ran my hands over him as he slid inside of me, wanting to give him the same ecstasy he gave me, willing my magic to light up *his* nerves.

He groaned against my mouth, movements full of urgency as he dove into me. I wrapped my legs around him, giving all that I could as his powerful body rocked against mine, heating me with his friction, bringing me toward another release.

The remaining bats grew bored of our moans and cries and settled down again long before we finished, before pleasure spilled over again, flooding me with love and gratitude for the most amazing lover I'd ever known. The most amazing mate. A dragon. Who would have thought?

My mate, Zav spoke telepathically to me, warmth radiating into my mind along with the words. He kept kissing me, even after he was sated, stroking me tenderly. *My mate forever.*

My love, I thought back to him, stroking his damp hair. *I'll try to help you figure out a way to get your clan to come to our wedding.*

I didn't know how yet, but if he wanted his mother there to support him, I would do my best to make it happen.

He lifted his mouth from mine, but only so he could gaze down into my eyes. *You will use your human wiles?*

I smiled. *Yeah, I will.*

This pleases me immensely. He stroked my cheek and brushed my lips with his thumb. *You know the nights are very long during dwarven winters?*

So, we'll get a lot of sleep?
No, very little sleep. His eyes narrowed and he kissed me.
It's a good thing you made the cave more comfortable.
I am a handy dragon.
Yes.

CHAPTER 25

THE NIGHT WAS AS LONG as Zav promised, but we still weren't ready to creep out of our cave until well after dawn. Because it was cold out there, and because Zav had been effusive after I'd promised to help him convince his family to come to our wedding. *Very* effusive.

When he stepped up beside me to face the wan sun rising over the peaks, I gave his butt a pat and was half-tempted to suggest we forget this quest, go back home, and spend the weekend in bed. But as much as Zav enjoyed pleasure, he never put it ahead of duty, and after giving me a long kiss, he walked out onto the precipice and shifted into his dragon form.

That made it easier to cool my jets and turn my mind back to this mission. I was still intensely aware of his aura when he was in his dragon form, but its power didn't make me think of sex. It made me think of flying into battle with him and slaying enemies. Though preferably not until his whole clan was here to back us up. I hoped Xilneth had made it back to warn everyone of the trouble and that a hundred dragons were already on the way. Though I knew Zav wanted to scout the area and gather helpful information for them, I worried about us being out there on our own. I'd only felt the barest touch of the lich's power, but it had been enough to scare the crap out of me.

Unfortunately, given how the rest of the dragons seemed to regard Xilneth, it was possible they would ignore any warning he gave. The idea of Zav and me having to deal with the lich on our own was terrifying.

He looked back expectantly at me—waiting for me to get on. I climbed onto his back, reminding myself that he'd offered to send me home to safety. Staying with him was my choice.

Without fear or hesitation, Zav sprang into the air and started flying back toward Mount Crenel.

I will do my best to camouflage both of us, Zav said telepathically, *but I suggest you also use your charm. A lich is very sensitive to magic and may see through my efforts.*

Let's hope she's napping.

Yes.

As the chilly wind tugged at my clothes and my braid, I mulled over the dragon-wedding problem. It was a more appealing problem to muse about than sneaking into that mountain and possibly finding Li's corpse hanging from a stalactite.

Have you invited Xilneth to the wedding? I asked.

Of course not.

Why not? You've invited everybody.

He is irritating, and he sang to you.

A criminal act.

It is inappropriate to attempt to woo the mate of a dragon.

I think he's done with that now. He knows we're meant to be. But maybe if you invite him and his clan, your clan will be more likely to come.

They would be less *likely to come.*

Not even to save you from embarrassment?

Zav didn't typically turn his neck and head back to look at me while he was flying, but his head tilted enough that I could see one violet eye looking at me out of his peripheral vision. *What do you mean?*

If I invited Xilneth and his clan—

You wish to invite the whole *clan? They are apolitical hippies. They cannot be tolerated.*

That's exactly why I want to invite them. You will then complain to your kin that they're coming and will embarrass you or act inappropriately at the wedding. Never mind that I had no idea what inappropriate dragon behavior would be—I was already concerned about the *appropriate* dragon activities Zav was planning. *Then your mother, who I am certain does not want her clan or her son to be embarrassed, will insist on coming with the rest of your family to keep an eye on the Starsinger Clan.*

You wish me to enact a ruse on my mother?

It's either that or tell her you're disappointed and hurt that she doesn't care enough to come. You seemed reluctant to do so.

I will enact the ruse.

I smirked. *Do you think it will work?*

Perhaps... I may need to modify what you suggest, but it is true that the Stormforge Clan never wishes to see its kin embarrassed. It is only because of your actions at the Crying Caverns that the queen no longer finds our relationship an embarrassment. She has told many of how you fought with me and risked yourself to free our kin.

She talks about me? I didn't know whether to feel mortified or pleased.

Yes. I do not believe she is truly enamored with you, but she wishes others to believe you are a worthy mate for her son.

I guess that'll do. I wasn't enamored with her either. *In-laws don't have to love each other, just refrain from throwing drumsticks at each other during Thanksgiving dinner.*

Drumsticks?

Yes. If we survive this—I paused to correct myself with some of the positive thinking that Mary recommended—*after we deal with the lich and return home victorious, I'll pick up a turkey. Thanksgiving is coming up. Make that ten turkeys. You'll need a few of your own, I trust.*

I am certain. Birds on your world are small.

Zav flew faster than I would have preferred, and the ominous black Mount Crenel soon grew visible on the horizon. I hoped he knew how to get in. The lich had appeared near the top, so maybe that meant an entrance was up there. I hadn't sensed her until she'd been outside, so she'd either activated some camouflage until she chose to reveal herself or the mountain had some inherent magic that hid its contents. That could make sense if the dwarves didn't want strangers finding their ancient tomb and repository.

Instead of flying straight to the top, Zav started his search over the foothills, sailing over the area where Li had been captured. I peered over his side, hoping vainly to spot Chopper lying down there, but the rocky slopes were empty of anything except a few sturdy tufts of vegetation growing up from cracks.

The road I'd been following the day before led to a vertical cliff on the side of the mountain, but if a doorway was there, it had been collapsed.

Stone columns lay tumbled to the ground and broken, reminding me of Roman ruin sites in Italy.

Several dead animals lay among the ruins, not only the deer-like creatures I'd seen before but large birds and something that looked like a scaly bear. This place didn't seem to be good for one's health.

It might be possible to clear that entrance and go in there, Zav told me as he circled the area, not commenting on the animal carcasses, *but I sense collapsed tunnels on the other side. They go back at least a quarter of a mile. That is as far as I can sense. The interior of the mountain is protected by obscuring magic.*

The creatures and the lich had to come out from somewhere that's open, right?

Yes. We will seek another entrance. Zav flew around the mountain and toward the peak. *I sense a hint of magic.*

A minion? I rested my hand on Fezzik.

An artifact. Perhaps a weapon.

I sat up straight. *Chopper?*

I do not believe so, but we will investigate.

With his powerful wings, it didn't take him long to fly up thousands of feet toward the peak. He didn't go all the way to the top but shifted his path to fly horizontally along the crown. I also sensed something magical and squinted toward the ground.

It could be a trap, he pointed out. *Something left outside to lure us down.*

Is it something that would entice a dragon?

No, but it might entice a human or dwarf.

Do you think the lich is worried about humans or dwarves?

Did she not capture the half-dwarf thief?

Yes, but we don't know why. It might have been a vendetta rather than worry.

After the talk of traps, I thought he might ignore the item, but he sailed closer to the ground.

This may be something useful, he said.

It *did* feel to my senses like a weapon. But why would a magical weapon be lying among the rocks? Unless it was being used as bait in a trap....

There was no road up this high on the craggy, uneven side of the mountain, nor even a path, but something glinted in the weak morning sun. Zav flew lower, gliding over what turned out to be a body, its armor reflecting the sunlight. There were *several* bodies, all armored, many with shields and great hammers or swords.

"Dwarves?" I wondered.

Zav surprised me by ignoring the potential danger and landing nearby.

One of the dwarves carried a magical sword. Zav's head turned on his long neck to look at me. *Perhaps you should borrow it in case you need it for a battle inside. It will be more effective against magic than your firearm. We can return the weapon to the dwarves when we are done.*

You don't sense any traps? I eyed the ground as if molten lava flowed over it, not wanting to be the one to trip an alarm and let the lich know we were here. *Something killed those dwarves.*

Admittedly, it had happened some time ago. Vermin had already chewed away their flesh and were working on the rest of the bodies. A grisly way to go.

I do not, but you are right that traps could exist. One moment. Rock and dust stirred as Zav trickled magic toward the bodies—there were six visible now, one decapitated and others appearing to have been crushed by boulders. I grimaced as his magic tugged a sword out of one of the dwarf's hands. The poor guy had died fighting. They all had.

The sword floated over to me, no dried blood on its blade. But why would there be? The lich's minions were undead and didn't bleed.

The hilt was cold in my hand, the weapon heavy compared to Chopper, but I would carry it and use it if need be.

A rock clattered farther up the mountain, and Zav's head jerked around. A stout skeletal humanoid creature between four and five feet tall stood up there, gripping a double-headed axe, his hollow eyes turned toward the bodies. I couldn't sense him, and Zav must not have either, but there he was. And even if he couldn't detect us through our camouflaging magic, he must have seen the sword float over to us.

Instead of coming down to investigate, the minion turned and stepped back between two boulders. An alcove he'd been assigned to stand guard from?

Zav sprang into the air and flapped up to it. But it wasn't an alcove. It was a hidden entrance, the tunnel opening not visible unless one stood—or flew—directly in front of it. It was only a few feet wide and seven or eight feet high. It was hard to imagine the lich being able to come out through the gap. Did that mean this wasn't the real entrance?

The skeleton went inside, Zav said, landing again on the rocks. *Likely to warn the lich that someone is out here.*

Are we going in?

Zav magically lifted me to the ground, then shifted into his human form. He continued to speak telepathically. *We must. I must gather as much intelligence as possible before my people arrive. If the lich has concocted some way to deal with numerous dragons coming for her… they must be warned.* He lifted his chin. *There is danger of traps. I will go first.*

Since he was far more powerful than I, I couldn't object. Since we would need all the help we could get, I rubbed Sindari's charm to summon him.

As Zav strode toward the tunnel, I noticed he wore the yellow Crocs. I would have thought elven slippers would be more appropriate for a quest, but maybe he thought he would need luck inside.

I had a feeling we both would.

CHAPTER 26

*Y*IS TARATHKA, A FEMALE VOICE rasped in my mind before we'd gone more than ten feet into the tunnel.

The lich? Not sure I wanted to know what she was saying, I tapped my translation charm.

Visitors? she continued. *A puny mongrel and one of the righteous Stormforge dragons.*

Zav continued on. If he answered, he didn't include me in the telepathic communication.

Thinking of his warning not to vex the lich, I also didn't answer. Sindari padded silently at my side, not commenting on the telepathic announcement.

I expected far more dragons than one, the lich continued. *And I am prepared. You will not survive if you continue farther into my abode. I have claimed this world for mine, and as soon as I have gathered the necessary forces, I will claim all of the Cosmic Realms.* After a pause, she purred an addition that seemed to be for me. *Including the wild worlds.*

I swallowed. That was Earth.

"There's no way she can do that, right?" I whispered.

Zav looked at me over his shoulder. *She will not defeat all the dragons and claim anything.*

I defeated one dragon already, she continued. *Once I made the change, the Stormforge dragon who ruled this world was no match for me. I slew him easily and allowed my minions to feast upon his bones.*

Sacrilege! Zav replied.

Some of my minions still retain enough mortal flesh that they grow hungry.

A dead dragon must be interred, not fed to scavengers. Zav's back was as stiff as a board as he picked up his pace, striding through the tunnel, no sign yet of the skeletal minion that had spotted us.

All Stormforge dragons will be treated thus. You have slain many Silverclaws, so I have been tasked to deal with your clan, to remove them from the Cosmic Realms. Permanently.

She had been tasked? Had the bitter Silverclaw dragons gotten together and drawn straws? Let's see who gets to turn themselves into an undead lich today…

It is the Silverclaws who will be dealt with permanently. Zav, maybe forgetting he wasn't in dragon form, growled.

"Don't let her vex you," I whispered, patting him on the shoulder. "Women like to play mind games with men. Don't give in."

I am regretting that I forbade you from vexing her, he replied.

You didn't forbid it. You only suggested I not vex her. Actually, you asked it as a favor. I can ignore your favor and vex her vociferously if I feel it's appropriate.

Do not.

Our tunnel slanted downward, growing darker as we traveled farther from the opening, and I activated my night-vision charm. The world turned a pale green, details more difficult to pick out and depth perception iffy. I almost missed a step when the flat ground turned into a staircase descending into the mountain.

So far, the walls, floor, and ceiling had been smooth, carved with magic or some stone-shaving tool. I ran my fingers along one wall as we descended. The stone felt more crystalline than porous, and the tunnel smelled clean and fresh instead of dank and musty, like most caves I'd been in, or acrid and sulfuric like the air outside. My sensitive lungs were grateful for this small boon, but it was confusing.

I brought a finger to my nose and sniffed.

It's salt, Sindari said.

Salt? Black salt? I'd seen black "lava" salt in the fancy grocery stores back home, but it was regular sea salt mixed with charcoal.

Black salt. The dwarven world is known for it. Some say it is as valuable a trade item as their enchanted weapons.

I'll gladly chip away a few barrels full to trade for my sword.
Does your new blade not satisfy you?
It's heavy, and it doesn't glow.
Perhaps it does, and you don't know how to activate its magic.

"Story of my life," I muttered, and Zav glanced back. "Sindari and I are discussing the dwarven salt trade," I explained, seeing little point in keeping my mouth shut since the lich knew we were here.

Zav didn't seem surprised. *They are known for it.*

After descending the equivalent of a couple of European cathedrals, we reached a wide tunnel at the bottom that stretched in two directions. A faint creaking came from the right, silence from the left. After coming upon the dead dwarves outside, my imagination had no problem conjuring bodies hanging from nooses, the creaking a result of them swaying on ropes buffeted by underground drafts.

Zav gazed in both directions but must not have had any better luck than I did sensing what was out there.

I am accustomed to striding straight into danger and trusting my prowess and power to be enough to win the day, but that is likely to be insufficient here. Zav faced me. *We must have a crafty plan and must not allow ourselves to walk into her trap.*

Is it my job to come up with that? I looked at Sindari, who ruffled his fur and shook his head. The tiger equivalent of a shrug.

As a less powerful being, you've had to be crafty before, Zav pointed out.

Yeah, but I'm not great at it. Can you sense anything down here?

Yes. I sense many, many undead minions in that direction. He nodded to the right, toward the distant creaking. *Anyone wishing to avoid a battle would choose the other direction.* He looked to the left. *This makes me believe that the trap is that way, perhaps some magical explosion that will bring down the mountain on us or kill us outright.*

I'd never seen Zav hesitate to face an opponent, and it scared me. How was I supposed to come up with something clever enough to best someone even *he* was worried about battling?

Can you read any of their minds and get the lay of the land? I asked. *If we had a map, that would be helpful. It would make it a lot easier to avoid her traps and sneak up on her.*

Or avoid her altogether until the others arrive. I seek only intelligence. A map would be excellent, but I also must know if she has found something that can defeat my people. She must know they are on the way, but she sounded confident. He arched his eyebrows toward me. *Cocky.*

Don't all dragons always sound confident and cocky?

Superior predators have that tendency, yes. As to the mind-reading, it cannot be done with undead minions. Their brains are gone, their skulls empty. That is why they are so easily led by their masters and so difficult to subvert by their masters' enemies.

A distant scream echoed up from the depths of the mountain, and I flinched. "That didn't sound undead."

Sindari cocked his head, listening. *It sounded like a human female. The thief?*

"Is Li still *alive*?" I'd been certain the creatures or the lich would have torn her apart, and my gut twisted at the idea of her being tortured. "Why would the lich keep her alive? To question her? What could she possibly know?"

Where you are? Sindari suggested.

"Why would the lich care about *me*? Besides, aren't we assuming she already knows where we are? She's been chatting with Zav and me."

A broad telepathic transmission. Zav held a finger to his lips. *I am certain she knows that we are inside the mountain, thanks to the error with the sword, but she shouldn't know our precise location if our cloaking magic is working sufficiently.*

Li wouldn't know our location either.

Zav frowned. *The lich may be torturing her for enjoyment. I can tell already from our brief conversation that she has been twisted by this deal she's made with the underworld. Peynar'dokla Silverclaw was never appealing, but now...*

She's evil.

Zav continued to frown, as if he objected to the idea of any dragon receiving such a descriptor.

Can you sense Li? I couldn't, but maybe with his range, he could. *Maybe you could read her mind and pluck a map out of it. Or at least her memories of the inside of this mountain.*

Mind reading is typically done at close range, but let me see if I can reach her without the lich sensing me.

I almost said that I didn't care if the lich sensed him, but that wasn't true. If she did, she might kill Li so she couldn't be a source of intel for us. Even if Li had only caused problems for me, I couldn't wish her dead. Not someone who was, whether I wanted it to be true or not, similar to me in a lot of ways.

You can do it. I swatted him on the butt.

Zav's eyebrows rose again. *Was that meant as encouragement?*

Yeah. It's a human thing. Like high fives. I smirked at him. *It's a low five.*

Sindari sighed, his tail swishing. *You are not engaging in foreplay here, are you?*

No. That was for encouragement. I swatted him on the rump. *Like that.*

I am not encouraged.

That's because you're a little stuffy and uptight.

I should gnaw off your foot for that comment.

I'm going to need it against the lich.

Perhaps a toe, then.

I bet people don't encourage you twice.

Zav, who might have been able to overhear our telepathic conversation, held up a hand. *I am able to sense her. She is gravely injured and not very coherent. Also, Peynar'dokla is near her, so I have to be careful, but I will attempt to extract useful information.*

Clacking sounds came from the tunnel, from what had been the direction of silence. I pulled Zav against the wall with me, wondering if there was any chance our camouflage magic would keep whoever—or whatever—was coming from noticing us. The tunnels weren't very wide.

Sindari also joined us, pressing one side to the wall but facing the tunnel, poised to strike.

Two dwarf skeletons marched into view, flaps of tendon and gristle still attached to their bones. They carried huge axes and shields as they strode toward us, walking side by side and taking up most of the width of the tunnel.

There was no way they would fail to see us. Unless we could scoot back and they turned to head up the steps.

Careful not to make a noise, I eased backward several steps, pulling Zav along with me. His eyes were closed. He had to be aware of the skeletons, but maybe he thought it was more important to try to get information from Li as quickly as he could. If she was dying—or in danger of being killed with a thought—he was probably right.

Sindari also scooted back, but he remained in front of us, determined to jump the skeletons first if we had to fight.

We may have to deal with them ourselves, I told Sindari.

I will handle it, he replied, his green eyes intent as the undead minions marched inexorably toward us, bones rattling as bare feet flapped down on the hard floor.

Mind if I help? I hefted the heavy dwarven sword.

The skeletons reached the stairs, and Sindari did not reply.

Zav still hadn't appeared to notice the skeletons. His brow was furrowed. Whatever he was finding in Li's mind must not be good.

The skeletons turned, as if to go up the stairs, but they halted, and their skulls swiveled on their neck vertebrae, empty eye sockets rotating toward us. We were ten feet away from them.

Sindari crouched to spring, but I put a hand on his back to stay him. If we attacked, there would be no more chance of hiding.

I started to creep farther back, but more clacking feet came from behind us. Another pair of minions being sent to join the first?

The skeletons in front of us stepped in our direction. Sindari sprang— only to be levitated straight up in the air with a whisper of magic. My feet left the ground right after his, Zav lifting all three of us to the ceiling. Sindari didn't make a noise, but his legs flailed in the air, claws extended.

Be still, Zav whispered into our minds.

The skeletons clacked past right under us, walking slowly. Their skulls swiveled left and right, as if they could see out of those empty sockets, but they didn't stop. They continued down the tunnel as we hung suspended ten feet above them. Two more skeletal minions walked into view from the opposite side.

They stopped when they reached each other, then both pairs turned and headed back the way they had come. The first two walked under us again without pausing, then headed up the stairs.

It will be better if we don't battle the minions, Zav told us. *I am certain they are only roaming about to search for us and that the lich doesn't know exactly where we are.*

I assumed so, but I didn't realize we had an alternative. I lifted my fingers to touch the black ceiling inches above my head.

Once Peynar'dokla pinpoints me, I believe she will attack. She does not fear me.

That'll be her downfall, right? I looked at Zav and gave him an encouraging smile.

He didn't smile back. *In her current state, she is more powerful than I am. And if my people appear in this world, I must send them away.*

What? Why?

That wasn't the plan. But his bleak expression suggested he'd learned something from Li. Something bad.

Peynar'dokla was inspired by the bacterial infection that was used to infect my kin, though she deemed it too slow-acting for her plans. She wanted to kill us much, much quicker. After doing a great deal of research, she found buried in this ancient dwarven repository a recipe for a poison that was concocted thousands of years ago, a poison designed to float in the air and kill our kind quickly.

A dwarven king from those distant times hired an outcast gnomish scientist to make it. The king wanted to rid the realms of dragons. All of them, forever. The poison turned out to be effective at killing dragons, but it also ended up killing a great many dwarves. The remaining dwarves rebelled against the king, and he was slain in battle, then entombed in this mountain along with the recipe for his concoction and the magical artifact the gnome made to disperse it into the air all around an area.

When Peynar'dokla learned of this, she searched relentlessly until she found both recipe and artifact. She has set it up, and at a touch, it will eject the poison in an aerosol that can be spewed out into the air around this mountain, should my people show up to attack her. As they plan to do. She's already tested it, and it killed all those animals we saw in the area. It is very virulent.

I grimaced. *We're lucky we didn't arrive during the testing phase.*

Yes.

Won't your people be able to raise their barriers and keep any poison in the air from reaching them?

We must breathe, so our barriers do not keep out air—or particles tiny enough to float in the air.

Wait, is Li your source for all this? How does she *know? I can't imagine a dragon lich would make a human a confidante.*

Back when she'd first come here, she intended to steal artifacts from the dwarven tombs. She was searching primarily for a dragon blade—having learned of you and yours. Peynar'dokla happened to be here testing the device, and Li saw everything.

Why had she come searching for a dragon blade if she was the rightful owner of Chopper? Had the story of her lineage and right to the sword been a fabrication to trick me into coming with her? Until she had an opportunity to steal Chopper from me? But if that had been her plan, why had she wanted to bring me to this awful place? Especially when she'd snagged Chopper back in the woods?

There was a dwarven engineer, Zav continued, *that Peynar'dokla brought with her to make the aerosol and ensure the artifact was operational, and she was speaking to him as they ran the tests. She killed him once she knew she had a working system and added him to her undead army. The thief heard and saw all of this.*

The skeletons hadn't returned, so Zav lowered us to the ground. Sindari spread his legs, claws managing to dig into the hard salt floors, and appeared relieved to be out of the air.

We will go that way. Zav pointed in the direction that creaks still whispered from and where an army of those skeletons might be waiting.

That's better than the other way? I asked.

The thief had a partner when she came into the mountain. The partner went that way and was incinerated by traps in the walls. It is possible that I could defend us from them, but it is also possible that if Peynar'dokla made them, they would be too powerful. Zav pointed again. *Besides, I must go that way. The artifact and the poison are that way.*

Is the lich that way too?

Yes. He strode into the lead again.

I trotted to keep up but said, *Maybe we should leave and warn your people instead.*

It takes time to transport to another world through a portal, and I fear they are already on the way. If they are coming while I am going... I would miss them and be too late to warn them. I must destroy the artifact before they arrive.

Am I right that it's heavily guarded?

It is guarded by many minions and the lich herself. She is waiting for us.

How fun.

CHAPTER 27

IMMENSE ENERGY RADIATED FROM THE dark tunnel somewhere up ahead. It rolled toward us in waves, buzzing my senses and making me feel like I was approaching a giant microwave oven without a door. My skin crawled, and I wanted to sprint in the opposite direction.

Were these the enemies Zav had said he sensed? Or some nefarious trap that didn't feel the need to hide itself?

Still insisting on leading, Zav strode toward the source of the energy without slowing down. He'd produced a magical sword I'd rarely seen him use from whatever interdimensional sheath he stored the thing in. Maybe he felt he needed all the help he could get, especially if he couldn't find enough room in these underground passages to shift into his dragon form.

When we rounded a bend and entered a straight stretch of tunnel, a lit expanse came into view ahead, a jumble of pale yellow and blue light making me wince and turn off my night-vision charm. The creaking we'd been hearing all along came from the lit area, though I couldn't see anyone—or anything—yet. The energy that buzzed at my senses grew stronger, almost painfully so. Oddly, the source seemed to be located just up ahead, *before* the opening of what appeared to be a deep cavern.

I sense many, many undead creatures in the chamber up ahead, Sindari said.

We were getting close enough that I could sense them, too, though something about this mountain muted my range a lot. *You wanted a fight, didn't you?*

Sindari looked gravely at me.

There is a barrier across the passage, Zav stated.

Is that what I'm sensing? With all that power, I was expecting something more epic.

It is an epic barrier. Zav stopped to regard an invisible field blocking the tunnel. *I believe I can break it, but then she will know where I am. That is most certainly the point.*

Any chance you can burrow a hole in the rock and go around it? I suggested.

Zav considered the walls thoughtfully, then turned an equally thoughtful gaze on me. *Perhaps I should alert her to my presence intentionally and see if I can get her to chase me out of the mountain. This would allow you to snoop around in her lair.*

I adore snooping in the lairs of uber enemies who can kill me with a thought.

She will attempt to kill me *with a thought.* Zav's eyes were fierce and defiant. *If she can catch me. Meanwhile, you can attempt to find your sword and the artifact set to poison the air. If you can destroy that, there would be no threat to my people when they arrive, besides the lich herself.*

The super powerful lich who's stronger than any dragon.

His eyes flared violet. *She is not stronger than two* dozen *dragons.*

I'd been hoping for a hundred, but I didn't say it. He was willing to nobly risk his life for me and his people. Not that I approved of that or planned to allow it, but I appreciated the gesture.

I patted his arm. *How about we sneak in together, don't let her know we're here, and bash the artifact to bits while she's looking the other way?*

She will not be looking the other way unless she's chasing me.

Zav... I frowned at him. *You're not trying to sacrifice yourself, right?*

I am not. I will only do what I must to keep her occupied and ideally get her away from the mountain so that my people, when they arrive, can attack her without flying close enough to be poisoned. He rested a hand on my shoulder. *But you must be careful not to unleash any poison or anything equally vile on yourself. Now that I think about it, there is no reason for you to go near the artifact if I succeed in leading her away from the mountain. Only retrieve your sword and then wait here for us to handle her.*

Us? You're so sure your people are on the way? Xilneth isn't the most reliable guy, you know.

They knew I was coming and were preparing when I left. They will come. He lowered his hand. *But I will first attempt to get around her barrier. I do not think it will be possible, but we will try your way.*

Good. My way is always excellent.

Zav strode toward the barrier and stopped a few feet from it. He stepped to the side and placed his hand on the wall, magic trickling from his fingers.

I came up behind him and peered down the tunnel, hoping to get a glimpse of what awaited us in the cavern. Intense power heated my skin, and the buzzing of my nerves increased until it was painful. My heart seemed to jitter in my chest.

One of the skeletal winged creatures flew across the opening at the end of the tunnel, startling me. I started to lift my sword before I remembered we were all camouflaged. Beside me, Sindari also tensed.

It looked like our tunnel ended well above the floor of the cavern. More of those winged creatures flew into view, circling the open area ahead, and I realized their wings were what was responsible for the creaking noises.

I rose on my tiptoes, not quite able to see to the ground below, but moving skulls came into view, the heads of more undead dwarven warriors stalking about down there. Depending on the size of the cavern, there could be hundreds. Tall stone statues of dwarves wearing helmets lined the far wall, and magic emanated from all over down there, artifacts of all kinds. Maybe information on Chopper was down there. Maybe *Chopper* was down there. I hoped so. It would do little good to finally get information about the sword if I never was able to recover it.

With so many magical artifacts, along with all the magical beings, I had no hope of picking out the blade. The possibility that the lich had destroyed it made my stomach hurt.

And what of Li? We hadn't heard another scream for a while. Was she still alive down there?

The aura of a living being was different from that of an undead creature or an artifact, and as I strained my senses, willing my magic to amplify my ability to pick out details, I thought I sensed someone alive somewhere along that far wall and off to one side. The barrier kept me from creeping to the end of the tunnel to look.

From my vantage point, I could just make out the top of another tunnel or maybe a dark alcove in that far wall. The power of the lich emanated from within it. Was she napping in there while waiting for her minions to find us?

Clacks came from the tunnel behind us. Sooner or later, those skeletons would walk this way on their patrol. The ceiling wasn't as high here as it had been by the stairs. There might not be room for Zav to lift us high enough that the minions wouldn't sense us.

For that matter, how would we get past all the minions in the cavern? If Zav left, there was no way Sindari and I would be able to deal with those guys. If we couldn't sneak past them, we would be screwed. Unless they also chased him out of the mountain, but I doubted the lich would take her entire army and leave her precious artifact unguarded. She might not even fall for Zav's attempt to lead her away from the mountain.

I have completed my examination of the barrier. Zav placed a hand on the wall. *It extends into the rock walls on either side, but not indefinitely. I will attempt to bore a tunnel parallel to it and then around the end. This will take time.*

Another creature flew across the opening into the cavern, the creaking of its wings floating on the air.

I hope you can do it quietly. As far as I'd seen, those things didn't have ears—not anymore—but I was sure they would sense disturbances somehow.

Quietly, yes, but not without using my power, which they may sense. Be prepared. If the lich comes, I will lead her away from the mountain. You will do what you can while she is distracted.

Yup. I hefted the heavy dwarven sword. *Got it.*

Smoke was already wafting from under Zav's hand, rock turning to pulverized ash as he created a hole. I'd envisioned him drilling into the rock, but it was more like he was burning it. Incinerating it, like breading on chicken strips.

I only felt the barest trickle of power from him as he did his best to hide it. Harder for him to hide was the scent of burning rock. It reminded me of the time I'd ended up battling werewolves in a foundry.

He created a tunnel just large enough for Sindari and me to crawl through—though it would be a tight and claustrophobic fit. The odor of burning rock floated into my nose, and my lungs grew tight. I backed away several steps, brushing against Sindari, and pulled out my inhaler. Since I'd told Zav about my weakness, I no longer tried to hide using it in front of him, but I still resented that I needed it.

One of the winged creatures appeared in front of our tunnel again. This time, it didn't fly past; it landed on a narrow ledge, thrusting its head inside and staring straight at us.

I barely kept from dropping my inhaler. Zav gazed back at the creature. He'd paused and wasn't using any magic, but it peered suspiciously into the tunnel. Trying to see us? Sense us? Could it go through its master's barrier?

It sprang backward from its perch, like a diver doing a backflip off the board, then sped toward the alcove.

It sensed my magic. Zav poured more magic into the tunnel, not bothering to be as subtle now. *I will finish the tunnel and attempt to camouflage it so they cannot see it here or where it comes out. You will use it.*

The power emanating from the alcove—the lich—grew stronger. Movement stirred back in those dark shadows.

Uh, maybe you should get out of here, Zav. I pointed my thumb back the way we'd come. *Sindari and I will be sneaky and try to avoid notice.*

Zav kept working. I expected creatures to fly into the tunnel at him at any second, but it was the lich who stirred. She strode out of the alcove in dragon form—how had she fit through the tunnels to get down there?—and spread her wings.

Tremendous power burst from her, and Zav whirled, pushing me down to the ground and wrapping his body and his protective barrier around both Sindari and me. Angry orange energy poured into the tunnel, tearing down the lich's own barrier and slamming into us. Even with Zav's barrier around me, the power clawed at my nerves and shocked my mind, making me feel like lightning bolts were striking me over and over.

I lay on my back stunned and unable to move. Zav sprawled atop me, his face straining as he struggled to keep his protective barrier up to keep her power from destroying us both.

I must change into my natural form, he told me, *to have a chance against this.*

I started to reply that it would be a tight fit in the tunnel, but he jumped up and ran toward the cavern. His barrier continued to fill the tunnel and protect Sindari and me, but it wouldn't once he rushed out there.

This way, Sindari. I leaped up as Zav flung himself out of the tunnel and changed forms in the air, and I dove into the side tunnel he'd made.

Sindari roared in pain, catching the tail end of the lich's power before it shifted away from the tunnel. Zav roared, and I knew she was targeting him as he dove for her.

Heat from the rock scorched my hands as I scrambled into the tunnel, with Sindari right behind, ducking his head in the low passage. We crawled and *kept* crawling. How far back had Zav had to drill to get around that damn barrier?

Finally, the tunnel turned a bend, and the yellow and blue light of the caverns came into view ahead. The orange of dragon fire flared somewhere out of sight, and through my link with Zav, I sensed pain from him.

Get out of there, Zav. Please! You can't fight her and all of her minions alone.

He didn't answer. I scrambled forward on hands and knees, the low ceiling bumping my head, the dwarven sword scraping on the rock. I knew I had to be quiet, but worry for Zav drove me forward as quickly as I could scramble. How I could help him, I had no idea, but I had to try.

A snap like thunder came from the cavern, and the earth shook. Boulders slammed down. Instinct made me pause as I feared my own tunnel would collapse, but I pushed on. Zav needed help.

As I reached the end of Zav's tunnel, and more of the cavern came into view, rocks kept raining down out there. Dust filled the voluminous space, the salty air stinging my nostrils, and I batted at the air, struggling to see what was happening. Which one of them had caused a rockfall? Or had it been accidental as they flung their magic around?

A cold draft came from somewhere, stirring the dust. At the edge, I made myself pause and peer around before jumping down. A good thing—I was more than twenty feet from the floor, a floor covered with rubble.

But most of the rubble was in a huge mound in the middle of the cavern, with numerous dwarf skeletons walking mindlessly around it. Some had been crushed, with leg or arm bones sticking out. A few of the flying creatures had been knocked out of the air and lay pinned by boulders. Others had landed and were peering toward the immense rubble pile.

The powerful aura of the lich emanated from under the largest concentration of rocks. Zav had dropped the ceiling on her.

Good work, Zav, I thought before realizing he wasn't in the cavern. *Where did you go?*

More rocks clattered down from above. A great hole in the ceiling led up a hundred feet and, judging by the chilly air trickling down, out of the mountain. Zav hung up there, somehow wedged with his legs and wings spread as he looked down at the rubble.

Our eyes met through the dust, but before he could respond or give any warning, the rubble stirred. I stifled a groan—barely.

Boulders flew away as if they'd been hurled from a hundred catapults.

I will lead her away now, Zav told me as the lich emerged, not appearing damaged at all. The power that she radiated hadn't diminished.

Zav twisted in the exit hole he'd made and used his magic to propel himself upward. The dragon lich snarled and sprang up after him like a missile.

Look out, Zav. She's coming fast, and I think she's mad.

Find your blade if you can. He had to also be flying fast; already his words were fainter in my mind. *I will attempt to lead her from the mountain and keep her busy until my people come.*

Maybe you should make a portal back home and get out of her reach.

Then she would return for you. And my people would have no warning of the poison.

I sure hoped his people weren't hanging out in their nests in their meeting place, noshing on popcorn. Or, given their carnivorous tendencies, small animals.

We are going down, Val? Sindari asked from behind me.

There wasn't room for both of us side by side in the tunnel, so he was stuck back there without a view.

Yeah. I'm going to find Chopper and whatever artifact is set up to poison dragons, so I can bash the crap out of it.

I peered down, looking for a spot where I could jump down and land without making noise. The lich was gone, but as I'd feared, she hadn't taken any of her minions with her. A dozen or two had been squished, but dozens more remained.

As I prepared to jump, they shambled and clacked toward the alcove. A groan came from within it, a human groan. Li?

I couldn't see into the shadows of the alcove, but with the lich and her overpowering aura gone, I thought I detected Li's aura. Her *faint* aura. She might not have long.

Can you hear me? I attempted to direct my telepathic words toward her.

Another groan floated out. The skeletons arranged themselves in squads in front of the alcove like a platoon of soldiers. The flying creatures returned to the air, patrolling from above.

Hey, Li. I'll help you if I can. Are you back in that alcove? Is the dragon-slaying artifact back there?

You came for the sword. Her telepathic voice came through as a whisper, weak and barely discernible.

Uh, yeah, but also whatever artifact is set up to poison the dragons.

Clacks drifted to my ears, not from the cavern but from the way we'd come. I peered along the wall to where the original tunnel came out—there were stairs leading from it down to the floor. Two dwarven skeletons came into view, looked down the stairs toward their buddies, and turned and went back into the tunnel.

They are searching for us, Sindari said.

Of course they are.

It is back here, Li replied.

The artifact? I asked.

She didn't reply again. I had no idea if she wanted to help me find it or wanted to lure me to my death. Nor did I know if she was talking about Chopper or the poison artifact.

We've got to get back into that alcove, Sindari. That alcove that had four rows of skeletal minions with axes guarding it. No way could I slip past them, even with my camouflage charm. They had the whole area blocked off.

And how will we do that?

I don't know.

CHAPTER 28

I STARED AT THE PLATOON OF skeletal warriors, trying to figure out how I could get past them. Too bad Zav's rockfall hadn't taken them *all* out. If Li was still conscious in that alcove, she was ignoring my attempts to communicate. Zav had flown out of my range. So had the lich. I hoped he was faster than she was.

If I had all of my gear, including a bunch of Nin's grenades, I would be lobbing explosives by now, I told Sindari, afraid I didn't have much time to figure this out.

What happened if the lich defeated Zav and came back? I had no way off this world without him. And without him, I had... nobody to marry. Nobody to buy ridiculous amounts of meat for. Nobody who knew all of my vulnerabilities and *still* thought I was a great warrior.

I swallowed a lump in my throat and willed myself to focus.

As soon as we reveal ourselves, Sindari said, *they will attack en masse.*
I know. I don't suppose you'd like to try to lure them off?
I am in the perfect position for foot gnawing.
Is that a no?

Sindari sighed into my mind. *I will attempt to do it.* He peered back into the darkness behind us. *It must be now. The ambulatory skeletons have discovered Lord Zavryd's side tunnel. Our side tunnel.*

Right. I swung down, holding on by my hand to get a little lower before dropping, then pushed off from the wall to avoid as much rubble as possible.

But I forgot to compensate for the heavier gravity. It brought me down sooner than I expected, and my foot brushed a rock as I landed in a jarring crouch. It clattered to the side, bumping another rock. Only then did I realize how quiet it had been in the cavern. The skulls of all the skeletal warriors swiveled toward me.

As one, the first rank in the platoon strode in my direction. Hell.

Sindari came down beside me, not making a noise. Not until he roared and charged across the rubble toward the advancing skeletons.

Thank you, I told him and ran along the wall, hoping to skirt the skeletons and find a way to slip behind the rest of the guards. I had no delusions about all of them taking off after Sindari.

He roared again, dropping his stealth so they could see him. They hefted their axes. He darted in but it was only a feint, and he didn't get close enough to be in danger of their swinging weapons.

Another squad of skeletons strode away from the alcove to help their buddies. They had no brains in those skulls, but whatever powered them gave them enough smarts to try to surround Sindari. Several of the winged creatures dove for him, talons outstretched.

Be careful, please, I thought as I reached the far wall and ran along it toward the alcove. I went as fast as I could without making noise, but the damn rocks were all over, impeding even agile half-elven feet.

Sindari was as fast as the apex predator he always reminded me he was, but there were far too many enemies for him to evade. As he sprang away from two of the axe-wielding skeletons, one of the winged creatures caught up with him, raking his back with its talons. Talons that created vile, tainted wounds that didn't heal on their own.

Regret surged into me. *Sindari, get out of here! Before they hurt you more.*

I had to slow as I reached the skeletons. There were still twenty in front of the alcove. They'd spread apart to ensure they could cover it—and would see through my camouflage if I got close. Their skulls were turned toward Sindari and his battle, but they were magical creatures and would doubtless sense me.

I crept closer and grabbed a rock. As Sindari ignored my order to get out, I threw it against the far wall, hoping the remaining skeletons would think I was over there and had tripped.

Sindari roared, taking a powerful swipe with his claws, and knocked the skull off one of the warriors. It clattered into a rubble pile and shattered.

But all of the flying creatures were above him now, more than a dozen filling the air around him like vultures. I drew Fezzik, intending to help him, even if it meant giving up my cover. I couldn't let him be torn apart.

Don't, Val, Sindari ordered a second before I fired. *Just get into the alcove. Get your sword and destroy the artifact. I'm fine. I'll leave this realm before they can kill me.*

I hesitated, torn and frustrated. I wanted to blow away as many of those bastards as I could.

Several of the skeletons in front of the alcove reacted to the sound of my rock hitting the side wall. They turned and marched off.

That left only ten in front of the alcove, and they weren't looking in my direction. I grabbed another rock. This was the best shot I would get.

Hugging the wall, I ran for the corner. I sucked in my belly as I eased around it. The two closest skeletons turned toward me as I slid into the alcove. I lobbed the rock over their heads. It clattered to the ground, but this time, none of them turned to look.

They had sensed me.

Sindari roared again, broke away from his fight, and charged toward the alcove. Blood dripped from dozens of gashes on his flanks. That didn't keep him from springing at the skeletons that were stepping toward me. They were forced to turn, swinging their axes to keep him from tearing their skulls off.

Again, I had to fight the urge to leap into battle with him. As he'd said, he could disappear into another realm. I could not.

I backed into the dark alcove, the light outside contrasting with the deep shadows and making it hard to see what was inside of it. The faint outline of a cage dangling from the ceiling was just visible. Li lay crumpled on the bottom.

A door at the back of the alcove stood open, more magic emanating from somewhere beyond it. Damn, did the tunnel system continue back there?

Two of the skeletons evaded Sindari and strode toward me, their axes hefted over their heads. I tried to call upon the magic Freysha had taught me, forming a barrier across the alcove between them and me.

They bumped against it. One swung its axe at it. Even though he was several feet from me, somehow the barrier was like an extension of me, and I gasped as the magical blade bit into it. The pain resonated in my skull, and I barely managed to keep the barrier up.

Sindari roared, knocking one of the skeletons into the side of the alcove. Another bumped against my barrier and lurched back, startled by it.

I ran to Li's cage, struggling to concentrate on keeping my magical defenses up as I tried to figure out how to free her. I didn't see the sword *or* any artifacts, not in the alcove, and I worried I would need her to direct me to them.

I'm going to try to get you out. I hefted my sword, hoping I could reach the cage, and that it was breakable. *Get off the floor of that thing if you can.*

One of the skeletons swung its magical axe at my barrier again. Again, the blow drove pain into my skull. They knew I was back here, and there was no way I would be able to keep my meager barrier up much longer, not when their blades could hurt it—and hurt *me* through it.

Sindari lunged in and grabbed the offending skeleton by the leg bone, flinging it into others that were trying to surround him. One of the winged creatures got close enough to rake him again.

Val, I cannot last much longer.

Save yourself, I ordered as I swung my borrowed dwarven sword at the bottom of the cage. *I'll figure something out.*

Whatever the cage was made of, it cracked under my assault, and a piece of it gave. A shard tumbled down, clattering at my feet. Bone. Of course.

Inside, Li finally stirred. She found the energy to climb up the side bars. I swung again, no finesse in the movement, only hoping I could damage the cage enough that she could rip her way out. Or that I could leap up and rip it apart. She might be too weak to do anything but hang on.

My foot slipped on something wet as I swung again. Blood. Li's? I couldn't see her well in the shadows but had no trouble sensing her pain and weakness.

Why did she capture you and torture you? I connected solidly with the corner, and more bone splintered and cracked.

Because I sneaked in here to get a dragon blade... before I knew the lich was here. Li, clinging to the side bars, thumped her foot against the bottom of the cage, trying to help me break it. *Remember how I said I got in, stumbled across the lich, and escaped before it caught me?*

Yeah.

I didn't. It caught me and scoured my mind for everything I knew. Dragon blades were on my mind—like I said before, I'd just become aware of you and yours—and the lich found out what I knew about your weapon. It commanded me to go back to Earth and get your sword. It didn't want any weapons with the power to hurt it unaccounted for in the realms. The lich is crazy. Li stomped again, and the bottom of the cage fell free. I sprang back, the heavy piece barely missing me.

It thinks it's going to kill all the other dragons and take over everything, Li added, letting herself drop down.

When she landed, her legs gave way, and she would have pitched over, but I rushed back in to catch her. She took a shaky breath and visibly braced herself.

I didn't want to be a slave to a lich. I thought that once I got back to Earth, it wouldn't have any sway over me, but it had put a magical compulsion on me.

Yeah, I know about those.

I had to obey the lich. Had to get that sword and bring it back here. It said it would free me if I succeeded, but I knew all along it was a lie. Li shook her head, gripping my arms for support. *I couldn't keep from obeying it though. It's too powerful.*

Outside of the alcove, Sindari ducked under another attack from above. He spun, leaving blood of his own on the floor, and raced toward the stairs and the tunnel out of here.

Some of the skeletons and flying creatures chased him, but most didn't. They turned to focus on Li and me, axes raised to strike at the barrier I was barely maintaining. I had no idea how their magic was attacking me through the barrier, but the worst migraine was building behind my eyes. It felt like my brain was swelling in my skull.

"Do you know where that artifact is?" I panted, giving up on telepathy—it wasn't like they didn't know we were here—and fighting to concentrate enough to keep the skeletal warriors from getting to us. "The one that can kill the dragons?"

Several of those axes struck my barrier simultaneously, and the collective pain stabbed into my brain from all sides. I gasped and dropped to my knee. I couldn't maintain the barrier.

"I don't give a damn about the dragons." Li pulled away from me and ran to the doorway in the back of the alcove, disappearing into the tunnel.

"I *helped* you!" I yelled after her, intending to ask that she help me, but another axe struck my barrier, bringing another blast of pain.

My barrier shattered in my mind. The skeletons rushed into the alcove.

I lurched to my feet, fury at being abandoned propelling me after Li. The skeletons clattered after me, their axes swinging.

If I caught up with Li, I would brain her. But she was probably sprinting for some hidden exit out of the mountain. I wished I could, but if I didn't find and destroy that artifact first, I might lose Zav forever.

CHAPTER 29

FAR AHEAD, ORANGE LIGHT CAME into view, promising another chamber. I sprinted down the long dark tunnel toward it, dozens of skeletal warriors chasing after me. Even though I'd let my barrier fall, my head still pulsed with pain. The idea of trying to stop and conjure another barrier, one they would once again attack, sounded less appealing than driving nails into my eyes. I would rather fight them with my borrowed blade if I had to.

As I pumped my arms and legs, Sindari disappeared from my awareness. He'd either reached the end of his one-mile magical tether, or he'd been so injured that he had no choice but to flee this world. I didn't want to think about another possibility—that he'd refused to leave and they'd managed to kill him.

A dragon came within range of my senses, flying about outside of the mountain. It wasn't Zav, and it wasn't the lich.

It was Zav's sister, Zondia.

A second dragon came within my range. They weren't flying into it, I realized as I kept running toward that light, skeletons chasing after me. The dragons were coming out of a portal right above Mount Crenel.

The cavalry had finally arrived. For an instant, relief washed over me—they could help Zav against the lich—but then I remembered. They didn't know about the poison.

What if that artifact was set to go off automatically as soon as a bunch of dragons flew close to the mountain? Or what if the lich sensed when they arrived and could use her magic to flip a switch from afar?

That second scenario seemed so likely that I feared it was already oozing poison into the air from wherever it was. I ran faster, reaching out telepathically to Zondia.

Talk to Zav! I urged. *There's an artifact in this mountain somewhere that can poison dragons. In the air. Outside, right where you are!*

Something grabbed my braid, jerking my head back. Pain lanced down my spine, and I pitched against the wall, shoulder ramming hard. One of the blasted skeletons had caught me. It raised an axe with its other hand, aiming for my head.

Furious, I spun, trying to tear my braid out of its bony grip as I sliced my sword through the haft of its weapon, breaking it in half. As the axe head slammed to the floor, I kicked my attacker in the torso. More skeletons crowded up right behind it.

Anger and frustration gave me power, and my kick sent it reeling back into the others. I swung my sword and cleaved through its rib cage to its spine. It lost its grip on my hair and I sprang free, then whirled and ran again. If I could reach that chamber up there, maybe there was something I could use to block the tunnel. I imagined a giant dwarven statue that I could shove in front of it.

But the skeletons ran as fast as I did and were right behind me. Even if there was a conveniently placed statue, I would never have time to push it into place.

Hoping for a miracle, I sprinted out into the orange light, almost tripping as movement to the side made me spring out of the way. I hefted the sword, bracing for another attack.

Li stood by the wall, and she flipped a lever. A huge stone slab of a door swung shut an instant before the first skeletons would have poured into the room. Thuds sounded as they ran into it.

"Took you long enough," she said.

"They grabbed my hair."

"That's what you get for having long hair." Li rushed into the room, another chamber ringed with statues of dwarves marking tombs. Something like sarcophagi rested at the feet of the statues.

In the back of the chamber stood racks of weapons, shields, and suits of armor all oozing magic. Li sprinted toward a rack of swords, the orange light showing her clothing torn in a dozen places, one of her shoes missing, and blood staining everything she wore.

With that many injuries, she shouldn't have been able to run. Pure adrenaline.

"My boss calls it my vanity braid." I spun, looking for an exit as the thuds grew louder at the door. But there weren't any other exits, not in plain sight. Maybe not at all. I groaned amid even more thuds. I didn't need my magical senses to know the skeletal warriors were battering at the door with their axes. "Will that hold?"

"I doubt it." Li grabbed a sword from the rack, not a random sword but *Chopper*.

I thought she might give it to me, but she rushed to the door and hefted it, clearly intending to use it herself.

"I'll hold them off. Find your artifact." Li glanced upward, no doubt sensing the dragons.

More had come through the portal. There had to be a dozen up there by now. If that poison worked, Zav might lose his whole clan.

Zondia hadn't responded to me. I thought about reaching out to her again, but Zav flew into my range, with the lich right behind him.

I swore and ran around the room, scouring the artifacts with my eyes. "You have any idea what it looks like?"

"A dragon."

"Is that a joke?"

"No. I don't know where she stuck it, but I saw it. A gray stone dragon. It's magic."

"Everything in here is magic."

"No shit. Find it."

The door shuddered under the assault from the skeletons. How many were out there in the tunnel now? It sounded like *all* of them.

At least the winged creatures shouldn't have fit into the tunnel. Not that it mattered. One on one, I was sure I could handle the skeletons, but *forty* on one? No way.

I rushed around, hunting for anything that looked like a dragon. Li, bloody but determined, faced the door. With *my* sword. If we both survived the next fifteen minutes, we would discuss that.

A rumble of power came from one of the side walls, followed by a faint hissing sound. My heart almost stopped. Was that it? The artifact releasing its poison into the air?

Zav, get out of here. I think I'm too late. Get your family out of here.

I followed the noise toward a wall full of sarcophagi, statues, urns, and piles of magical junk I couldn't identify. There was even a wood stove. Did the lich get chilly on winter nights?

My ears led me closer to the wall. The hissing was coming from...

The door flew open, slamming against the wall. Noise assailed the room as the skeletal warriors tried to storm the chamber. Li lunged forward, Chopper's blue blade flaring, and blocked the way. The noise of their battle rang out, drowning out the hiss.

"Damn it." I ran along the junk piles and clambered over the sarcophagi. She'd said it *looked* like a dragon. I couldn't possibly miss a dragon.

"I can't—" Li ducked a swipe toward her head, then kicked a skeleton before following up with Chopper "—hold them long," she finished. "Hurry!"

"Trying!"

If I couldn't find the artifact, I would have to run and fight with Li. But if I stopped searching now, every dragon up there, including Zav, might be killed.

Li summoned magic from within herself and said a word I hadn't heard before. Flames burst from Chopper, and an inferno roared, driving the skeletons back into the tunnel. At least for a moment.

"Make sure you teach me that one," I yelled across the room as I climbed over another sarcophagus, patting things, trying to sense magic beyond the dormant energy levels of all the artifacts. I almost tripped over the stupid wood stove. "Why *is* that in here?"

I almost rushed past it, but it was as magical as everything else, and that made me pause. My gaze snagged on the vent pipe running up the wall and disappearing into the ceiling.

"Shit." There weren't any other vents in the place. That *had* to be how the air would be pushed out of the mountain.

I grabbed the firebox door to tug it open, but a blast of electricity ran up my arms and knocked me back, almost to my ass. I flailed, recovered, and ran back in, lifting the dwarven sword. It crossed my mind to bash at the hinges to break the door, but first, I slid the blade under the handle, hoping its magic would protect me from the stove's defenses.

It buzzed faintly as it touched the metal, but I didn't get zapped again. The door squeaked as I levered it open.

Behind me, Li gasped in pain.

SECRETS OF THE SWORD II

"Hold on," I called without looking away from my task. "I'll get this and then join you."

We are battling, my mate, came Zav's telepathic voice as I hacked at the second hinge. *The lich has flown to a cave in the mountainside and is throwing her power at us. My kin and I must kill her and avenge Braytokinor. They are frenzied and not worried about poisonous air. Can you look for that artifact? I fear she will activate it.*

Working on it. And I think she already has, so have everyone hold their breath. Pale red light came out of the firebox, the open door revealing a dragon-shaped artifact that looked like a giant tea kettle. It rested on the bottom, pulsing with intense energy and probably poisoning the air and my lungs right now. A faint red mist trickled from its spout and wafted up the vent pipe in the back.

I fumbled for the leather thong around my neck and rubbed the charm that Zoltan had made for me that summer. It had protected me before against toxic stuff in the air. Whether it would do so here, I had no idea, but just in case…

After activating the charm, I tapped the artifact with my borrowed sword. Images of breaking it filled my mind, but raw power jolted me backward again. Cursing, I stumbled away. That time, the sword hadn't insulated me.

"Can't touch it, so how do I turn it off?" That urge to break the artifact came over me again, but all that would do was release all the poison at once. Li and I would be dead. "Gotta cut it off."

Using the sword, I shut the firebox door again, then eyed the pipe. If I could tie it in a knot… Or *melt* it closed.

I almost ran back to Li to grab Chopper, since one of its commands was *krundark—heat.* But the elf who'd told me about those commands had said they were commonly used when enchanting dwarven swords. Maybe my borrowed blade had the ability too.

Careful not to touch the stove again, I leaned the flat of the sword against the pipe. "*Krundark!*"

The blade turned cherry red. Palpable heat radiated from it, but nothing happened to the pipe. The stove was magical too. Maybe heat wouldn't melt the metal.

Li grunted as she continued to fight, Chopper slamming into skeletons and breaking bones. Several foes had fallen to the floor around her, but she'd been injured before she started, and I doubted she could hold out much longer. I was about to try something else—maybe I could cut the pipe in half and shove a sock in it—but then the metal gave way, sagging inward.

"Yes," I breathed and shifted to another spot, hoping to melt the sides together and seal the pipe without letting any poison out into our air. "C'mon, sword."

More metal melted. Then a gap appeared.

"Hold your breath!" I yelled.

I swung the sword hard, hoping to slice through the pipe above the melt spot. It cleaved through, the blade clanging off the wall behind it. I forced the crumpling sides of the pipe inward, then laid the hot blade on top, shaping the sagging metal to form a cap. Just in case my own magic helped, I willed the warped pipe to create a hard seal.

The hissing disappeared. I hoped that meant I'd done enough, especially since the artifact was still pulsing inside.

As I drew back, my elbow brushed the stove. White light flashed, and it blasted me with angry energy far stronger than before. It was as if it knew I'd destroyed its pipe, and it was *pissed*.

The power knocked me back twenty feet, the sword flying from my hand. I struck the ground hard, painful energy buzzing my nerves like a chainsaw.

On my hands and knees, I scrambled farther away, terrified the magic of the stove would allow it to destroy my seal, that the toxic air would spew into the chamber, and that I'd condemned Li and myself to death. But when I glanced back, the pipe was still melted closed.

A scream came from across the chamber. The skeletons rushed in, trampling Li, who had fallen to the ground.

"No!" I yelled, lunging to my feet.

A dozen skeletal warriors rushed at me, running over Li. She wasn't moving and didn't react.

I'd lost the dwarven sword, but I yanked out Fezzik and fired. The bullets broke through skulls and ribs, shattering bone on the warriors, but they pressed on toward me. Even more of them flowed in from the tunnel. I backed away, but there was nowhere for me to run.

Fezzik clicked, empty. And I had no more ammo.

I scrambled back, glancing left and right. Where had that sword gone?

My back struck the wall, and the skeletons advanced, far too many to fight. I lifted my arm to throw Fezzik, but that would be pointless. I gripped it like a club to defend myself as they hefted their axes.

And then they froze.

I stared at them, my back to the wall, my heart pounding in my chest.

Val! Zav's voice rang in my mind, startling me.

I'd been too afraid for my life to pay attention to what the dragons were doing outside of the mountain.

I hope you're on the way to help, I replied.

We have slain the lich. His telepathic voice turned smug. *I got in the killing blow.*

Good for you. I could still use—

One of the skeletons toppled over backward. The magic of their auras faded, and the others pitched to the floor, one by one, axes clattering atop their lifeless bones.

Never mind. I dropped to my hands and knees and pressed my forehead to the cool floor.

Hopefully, I'd destroyed the pipe in time. Hopefully, Zav would come find me and take me home. I'd had far more of this place than I'd ever wanted.

CHAPTER 30

AFTER I FOUND THE STRENGTH to pick myself up off the floor and navigate around the inactivated—hopefully *permanently* inactivated—skeletal warriors, I checked to see if Li had survived and might yet be helped. But she was dead, her sightless eyes staring up at the black ceiling.

A tangle of emotions twisted inside of me. She'd lied to me, tricked me, and stolen my sword, but she hadn't killed me when she'd had the opportunity, and in the end, she'd bought me the time I needed to find the artifact. Maybe she had come here to steal ancient dwarven goodies, but nobody deserved to cross paths with a lich. And I believed what she'd said—that she hadn't had any choice but to do the lich's bidding. Having been the victim of magical compulsions before, I had no trouble imagining the scenario.

Gently, I pried Chopper's hilt out of Li's dead fingers and saluted her with the blade, a silent thank-you for the help. I tried not to feel like I'd failed her, but it was hard.

Worried for Sindari, I pulled his charm out from under my shirt. I wasn't positive that he had made it back to his realm, and I needed to know. The thought of his mangled body lying dead in a tunnel made me sick.

My trepidation increased after I rubbed the charm and called for him and nothing happened. A long minute passed before the silver mist formed.

Sindari formed even more slowly, his silver fur matted with blood, huge gashes in his flanks and back.

"I'm sorry," I blurted, falling to my knees beside him. "I shouldn't have called you until Zav got here. I just had to make sure you weren't dead."

You may be assured that I will always return to my realm before my enemies deliver a death blow. As you know, I am wise as well as regal.

I snorted, glad he could muster the energy for humor, and wrapped my arms around his neck, being careful to avoid his wounds. "What I know is that you like to battle things, and you're noble enough to sacrifice yourself for someone else's sake."

I am noble, he agreed, *but if I sacrificed myself, I would never again be able to enjoy the invigoration of the hunt or feast on the flesh of the sleek and delicious* yavarra *of my home realm.*

"And you'd never get petted by Dimitri again." I patted his head, even though he'd insinuated that my hands weren't as good for petting as Dimitri's. What could I say? Nobody had accused me of having a gentle touch.

That would also be unfortunate. Sindari looked around without pulling away from my ministrations. Maybe my hands weren't that bad, after all. *You defeated all of those skeletons? Your skills as a warrior and sorceress have improved vastly in the time I've known you.*

"Actually, I ran out of bullets, lost the dwarven sword, and was about to get my ass kicked by those guys. Fortunately, Zav and his dragon army killed the lich at an *extremely* timely moment, and the skeletons collapsed."

You at least slew the thief who's plagued you so and retrieved your sword.

For a second, I was tempted to let him believe that, so he wouldn't think less of my warrior skills, but Li didn't deserve to have her sacrifice hidden. "The skeletons got her. She helped keep them off my back while I was dealing with the artifact." I brushed the sleeve of my jacket, grunting at a hole the stove had zapped in it. "I'm afraid I didn't defeat much of anyone."

I thought about explaining my mixed feelings on Li, and how I regretted not being able to save her, but it would be too much effort to articulate now. Maybe I would tell Zav later. He understood honor and trying to do the right thing and all that jazz.

"You're stuck working with a mediocre warrior and sorceress," I added.

You are not mediocre. Sindari sat down and started licking his wounds.

"Thanks." I released him and stood up. "Can you hang out here for a while? Zav has a potion now that can cure those tainted wounds. We just need to wait for him to get done dancing on the body of the lich, or whatever dragons do to celebrate after they slay enemies. And I'm hoping he has a more permanent solution to that artifact too." I eyed the stove, wary that the red mist would find a way to escape into the chamber.

Yes. I will wait and stand guard until he arrives. There may be other dangers here.

"True." I would be careful looking around in case there were booby traps. I held Chopper out, the hilt comfortable and familiar in my hand. "I guess I should do what I originally came here for and try to find out all about you."

It and the three others here, Sindari said.

"Three other... swords?"

Yes. I sense them over here. He rose stiffly and padded past tombs, amphoras, weapons racks, and artifacts of all kinds to a wall where scroll cases rested in rows of circular niches hollowed out forty or fifty high.

More weapons racks stood in front of the wall of scrolls. The entire area radiated magic, so I didn't know how Sindari could pick out anything in particular, but he stopped in front of an ornate rack of swords with the golden bust of a bearded dwarf looking down upon them. The blacksmith or enchanter—or both—who had crafted them long ago?

Chopper flared a brighter blue in my hand as I approached the rack. More than that, a humming sensation ran up my arm from the hilt. It didn't seem to hint of danger. If anything, my sword seemed... pleased.

Sindari sat in front of the rack. There were slots for four swords, but only three were in use. *To my senses, they are similar to your Chopper.*

I also sensed strong magic emanating from them, magic that *was* similar to that of my blade, but I didn't know if that meant they were all dragon blades. They could be some other kind of magical sword. But...

"Li *did* say that the lich sent her to get Chopper because she wanted to get rid of all the blades capable of hurting her. Maybe she also dug up these and put them here for safe keeping."

That is possible, Sindari said. *Or they may have always been here. There is a great deal of powerful and rare magic in here. It is not surprising that a thief would be drawn to this place, though it is surprising that she could get in. Maybe the lich destroyed whatever traps and deterrents were in place.*

"Probably. Anyone who can beat up Zav is badass." I eyed all the relics. "The dwarves should be happy to get the place back... whenever they come out of their underground cities and realize it's theirs again."

Perhaps someone should inform them that the lich is gone. They may be grateful to those who did the deed.

"I'll let Zav or one of the other dragons chat them up. I don't need credit for helping."

They may be more inclined to assist you in your quest to better understand your sword if they feel grateful to you.

Or they might demand Chopper back if they knew I had it.

"I'm hoping I can just find the right scroll, take photos of it, show Freysha, and she can translate its wisdom—and hopefully a long list of command words—for me." I'd turned off my phone as soon as I'd arrived here, hoping to save the battery in case I needed it. With luck, there would be enough juice for a photo op with a scroll.

Which scroll? Sindari tilted his head back to look at the rows and rows of circular slots in the wall. *There must be thousands.*

"You don't have to stay while I look."

I said I would guard you, and I will. He kept eyeing the rows and rows of scroll cases. *Though searching them appears... boring.*

"Boring? I thought apex predators were known for their patience. Don't you stand unmoving in a thicket for days, preparing to ambush whatever innocent antelope ambles through?"

I have no wish to ambush scrolls.

I didn't want to either. Or look at hundreds of them. Especially since I didn't read dwarven. How would I know when I found the right one?

I am coming for you, my mate, Zav's voice rang in my mind. *The lich has been disposed of in such a way as to ensure she cannot be reanimated.*

Uh, good. Was that a possibility? I didn't want to think about it. *I need you.*

When I am once again in human form, I will also be filled with ardor for you. The battle was magnificent, and I know how crucial a role you played in helping us.

I'm glad, but what I meant is that I need you to translate some dwarven scrolls and help me find one that pertains to Chopper.

That thought does not fill me with ardor.

Sorry.

I am coming.

"Zav isn't excited about ambushing scrolls either," I said, sensing him arriving in the tunnels.

The other dragons were having a powwow on top of the mountain. Since Zondia hadn't acknowledged me earlier, I felt no need to say hi to any of them. The idea of all of them showing up at my wedding was still moderately terrifying.

"Hey, Chopper," I whispered to the sword, assuming it would take Zav a while to make his way down here. "Any chance you can help me find your secrets? Is there anything in here that explains your history and... *you*?"

You believe it will answer? Sindari asked, a polite way of suggesting I might be crazy for talking to my sword.

"We have a developing relationship."

Chopper had responded to me, sort of, before, but other than its glowing interest in what might be fellow dragon blades, it didn't point me toward a particular scroll.

I closed my eyes, lifted the blade, envisioned it as a divining rod, and willed it to point me in the right direction. Was it nudging me ever so slightly to the right? Not sure if it was my imagination or not, I let my arms and the sword swing in that direction and walked slowly along the banks of scrolls.

Direct me, Chopper, I said silently, not wanting more commentary from Sindari.

But I couldn't tell if it was directing me anywhere. I took a few more steps, tilting the tip upward at a row of scrolls, and—

"What is she doing?" a gruff male voice asked in a language my still-active charm translated for me.

"I do not know," Zav replied. "She is a half-elf. That makes her quirky."

"Fortunately, dragons are into quirky," I said instead of explaining myself.

I lowered Chopper's point to the ground and faced the entrance.

Zav, back in his human form, had walked in with a red-bearded dwarf who could have been Gimli's brother. He wore a mashup of chain mail and plate armor and carried a battle-ax on his back. All of his gear radiated magic. Maybe he'd been on the way to challenge the lich himself.

"This is Lord Chasmmoor," Zav said, "an enchanter and blacksmith descended from the great dwarven masters. He is also a representative sent by the dwarven king to come and speak with the dragons and express their gratitude toward our kind for vanquishing the loathed enemy that took over this world and had designs on the entire Cosmic Realms."

The dwarf looked frankly at him, not intimidated by his powerful dragon aura. "The king just told me to see if the lich is dead."

"Your gratitude is assumed."

The dwarf grunted and strode toward me, eyeing Chopper. I couldn't hide a frown. What if he recognized the sword as belonging to his people and wanted me to leave it in the rack with the others when I left? Why had Zav brought him down here? If I'd found my scroll and taken a portal back to Earth without ever encountering a dwarf, I could have gone on pretending I was the rightful owner of Chopper—or at least one carrying it justly and deservingly, since the rightful owner was presumably long dead.

Sindari, I may need you to gnaw off this guy's foot if he tries to take Chopper.
He's wearing metal boots. That's a deterrent to foot gnawing.
Is it? Had I known, I would have gotten some steel-toed boots years ago.
That would have protected only your toes.
Modern Earth cobblers are short-sighted.
Obviously.

Zav must have sensed the artifact, for he turned toward the stove and scrutinized it. He lifted a hand, and power flowed from his fingers, wrapping around the stove. Orange light flared all around it, and I sensed the magic of the artifact inside fading and finally disappearing. Zav's power continued to flow, and the walls of the stove melted inward as the orange light grew so bright I had to look away.

Chasmmoor watched impassively. Apparently, the stove wasn't some beloved and priceless artifact, for he didn't object to its destruction.

When the light diminished, nothing but a lump of melted metal remained.

"That would be the more *thorough* way to stop an artifact," I murmured.

"Dragons are thorough," Zav said, looking pleased with himself.

Chasmmoor turned back to me, studying me almost as thoroughly as he had Chopper. "I have heard of you, Ruin Bringer. The dwarf traveler Belohk came here with stories of you a moon before the lich arrived and forced us underground."

"I've heard he's been chatty about me. Not sure that's a good thing. I may stick to rescuing taciturn dwarves in the future."

Chasmmoor didn't exactly smile, but his eyes crinkled at the corners. "That describes most of my people. How did you come by that sword?"

I told him about the battle with the zombie lord and that I had no idea how *he'd* gotten it.

"It is one of Dondethor Orehammer's ancient blades and was in use until a few generations ago, when its owner was slain and it disappeared." How long were dwarven generations? He didn't say. "It likely passed through a number of hands before ending up on one of the wild worlds. Your Earth. It may even have been taken there to hide it from our people, who would have looked for it. There are no direct descendants of the Orehammer remaining, so there is not a proper owner that it should fall to, but we as a people like to keep an eye on our historically significant works."

"By leaving them to collect dust in racks under mountains?" I waved to the others, prepared to argue that I should be allowed to keep Chopper.

"It was at the behest of our dragon rulers—" Chasmmoor slanted Zav a long look, "—that we sealed the remaining dragon blades inside this mountain. As I recall, they wanted any weapons capable of piercing dragon scales to be destroyed. We refused to let these masterpieces be treated thus. This was a compromise. They were stored here, along with the information on their powers and history." He looked toward the scrolls.

"Any chance you want to let me borrow the one that explains Chopper's powers?" I asked.

Zav stood back, his arms folded over his chest.

"Chopper?" Chasmmoor's mouth drooped open. "That is what you have named this great blade?"

"Yeah. The zombie lord neglected to tell me its real name. Or anything about it. I've learned a couple of command words, but some of my enemies have suggested it can do more than turning hot and cold."

It took Chasmmoor several long seconds to remember to close his mouth. Had I stunned him?

"You do not know the commands to activate its powers?" he asked.

"Just *keyk* and *krundark*." Chopper turned icy white and red hot in succession, hopefully not confused by me using them back to back. "Oh, and *eravekt*." The blade flared brighter blue. "I had it for ten years before I learned those. Like I said, no instruction manual was included."

"And you have slain dragons?" Chasmmoor looked to Zav. For confirmation?

"Not by myself and generally only after Zav sufficiently mangled them. I'm just your average half-elf." Admittedly, I'd only met a handful of half-elves and never chatted long with them, so I didn't know how average I was.

"She is not average," Zav stated. "She has slain dragons, even though this is not acceptable, and there are many who would like to see her punished and rehabilitated for such abhorrent behavior."

"Many *dragons*." Chasmmoor's tone suggested that no other species would find this behavior abhorrent.

"Many dragons." *Zav's* tone suggested that no other species mattered, though at least he didn't haughtily lift his chin and ooze arrogance. Maybe he was too tired after his battle to bother.

The response didn't faze Chasmmoor. He even looked amused. "The king is grateful that you've helped our people—we all are—so I am here to offer my services in helping your mate further learn the powers of the dragon blade. It is our wish that when she is dead, or no longer able to fight, she will have the blade returned to our people. But for now, we believe that it is proper that it rest in the hands of someone who is battling dragons who would prefer to enslave the other intelligent races rather than live in harmony in the realms with them."

I raised my eyebrows hopefully. They were going to let me keep Chopper? It sounded like I would have to stipulate in my will that Amber, or whoever survived me, take it back to the dwarves—maybe they would give me a portal generator to take home and keep in the closet for the trip—but I could live with that.

"It is better to rule reasonably over races for their own good and the good of dragons and the realm," Zav said.

"Our own good, yes," Chasmmoor said, proving that dwarves could be as dry and sarcastic as humans. But he didn't object further.

The dwarves, like most of the elves, probably saw the Stormforge Clan as the lesser of two evils, when it came to possible leaders. If they *had* to live under dragon rule, better Zav's family than the Silverclaw Clan.

"Politics," I murmured.

"The king informed me that you will return to Earth with us and instruct my mate in the ways of her blade," Zav stated, and I realized he'd known the outcome before he'd walked in here with Chasmmoor.

He could have mentioned it to me…

"Yes." Chasmmoor's tone was dry again. "He informed me thus as well."

"She will make you smoked ribs, a human delicacy. She is an excellent cooker of meat." Zav's tone grew proud, or maybe sly. "I gave her a ring that enhances her talent in this area."

My mother wouldn't believe it if she ever heard Zav praise my cooking abilities. When I'd been a kid, her attempts at teaching me to follow recipes and bake hadn't gone well. Never mind that the tiny avocado-colored oven in Mom's converted school bus hadn't exactly been Food Network-approved.

I held up my hand and wiggled my ring finger. "Accidentally, he says, but I have doubts."

"Dwarves enjoy smoked meat," Chasmmoor said. "I must check in with my king and my family before returning with you, but I will find the scrolls related to the dragon blades, so that you can copy them and start your learning immediately." He looked me up and down again. "Did you bring ink, a quill, and numerous blank parchments?"

Oh, sure. I never went on adventures without a quill.

"This should do the job." I held up my phone.

"Interesting," Chasmmoor said. "I'd heard that humans have learned to create technological gewgaws with similar functions as magical artifacts."

"Necessity is the mother of invention, as we say."

"I will retrieve the scrolls."

Zav came to my side and wrapped his arm around my shoulders. *Now you will know the true powers of your sword and have the confidence to vex our enemies even further.*

You know I don't need to be confident to vex people. Vexations fall right off my tongue.

Perhaps it is more accurate to say that you will soon be more able to defend yourself after you vex our enemies.

That sounds good.

The dwarf whistled as he selected scroll after scroll from the library. After he'd rested thirty or forty on the floor, I started to grow concerned.

"Are all those related to Chopper?" I asked. "Or are you selecting some bathtub reading to bring with you to Earth?"

"They are all related to *Thrallendakh yen Hyrek de Horak.*" Chasmmoor cocked a bushy red eyebrow at me. Was that the sword's real name? My charm hadn't translated it. "It means Lightning Harnessed from the Most Ferocious Storm."

"What does *Hyrek* mean?"

"Storm."

"I might be able to remember that."

The dwarf's other eyebrow rose, and he looked at Zav.

"My mate has a tongue impediment and has difficulty with names," he said.

"My tongue isn't impeded." I swatted him in the chest, not wanting Chasmmoor to think I was too dull to learn Chopper's powers. *Hyrek's* powers. "It's just saving itself for vexing enemies."

"And those with names of more than two syllables," Zav said.

"Are you teasing me?" I asked him.

"Yes. You informed me that mates in your culture do this."

"I guess I did." I couldn't keep from smiling fondly at him. Later, when we were back home and had nothing more substantial to worry about than the wedding, I would show him just how unimpeded my tongue was.

Chasmmoor's gaze shifted from Zav to Sindari, and my tiger nodded. I squinted suspiciously at him. What was he telling the dwarf?

Sindari gazed blandly over at me. I had a feeling I would never know.

"Chasmmoor, would your people be able to arrange a funeral or whatever is appropriate for a fallen warrior?" I pointed in the direction of Li's body. "I don't know if she has any human family or how I would even arrange for the body to be taken back to them for a burial, but since she's half-dwarf, maybe it would be appropriate for her to be buried here." I glanced at the tombs. "Or whatever you do."

"She died bravely?" Chasmmoor asked.

"Fighting the lich's minions and buying me the time I needed, yes." I almost shared the name of the dwarven father that Li had given me, the one supposedly descended from Chopper's maker, but realized that must have also been a lie. Had any of that story been true? Had she ever met her dwarven father? I might never know.

Chasmmoor nodded. "We can inter the body. Perhaps we can find out with blood magic who her ancestors among our kind were and where to situate the remains."

I nodded, relieved that he hadn't said a mongrel couldn't be buried among their kind. The elves seemed too uppity to consider that, but I didn't plan to request that in my will.

"Thanks."

It was possible Li hadn't been lying about *everything* when she'd told me about her family, and I would try to find out more when I got home, but this was more practical than lugging the body back and foisting it on Willard to try to get through channels back to China. Given how little our governments cared for each other, that might not even be a possibility.

Zav sighed and looked toward the tunnel. "Xilnethgarish comes with news."

"He couldn't deliver his news from the mountaintop?" I touched my temple to indicate telepathy.

"It is for you, and he wished to deliver it in person." Zav's eyes narrowed. "If he attempts to woo you, I will obliterate him."

I thought of all his talk about how it was forbidden to slay other dragons outside of duels and how criminals were always punished and rehabilitated. "That's allowed?"

"No. I will do it anyway."

"Don't get arrested before our wedding. Having your spouse in jail puts a big damper on a marriage."

"Hm."

Xilneth strolled into the cavern in elven form, handsome, blond, and green-eyed. I could envision him carrying a surfboard on a California beach.

He stopped in front of me, barely acknowledging the still squinting Zav, and bowed deeply. "The dragons have learned of the poison that was flowing into the air and might have slain us had you not stopped it. I cannot speak for the haughty Stormforge Clan, but the Starsinger Clan is deeply grateful for your assistance, Ruin Bringer."

"My clan is also grateful," Zav said. "I will *ensure* they are."

I patted him on the stomach. "Thanks." I added telepathically to Zav, *Invite him to the wedding.*

I thought you would invite him, he responded without taking his glower from Xilneth.

Dragons should invite other dragons. Don't forget to extend the invitation to the rest of his clan. Thus to further the possibility of embarrassment at the wedding. That's our plan to get your mother to come, remember?

I have not forgotten. Funny how he could manage to growl his words telepathically. You'd think vocal cords would be required for that.

"Xilnethgarish," Zav said, "you are invited to our wedding."

"Excellent. I, and my entire clan, agree to come." No hesitation there. Had he been planning to show up anyway? "We look forward to attending your union on Earth and to hunting the small but fleet creatures in the forests there. I intend to show my cousin Lynethdaron that shifting into this form and having sex with the natives is an enjoyable experience. He does not believe me!"

So far, Zondia was the only shape-shifted dragon that I'd seen roll her eyes, but Zav came close whenever Xilneth was around.

"Just not the natives at our wedding, please," I said.

"There will not be available females there?" Xilneth asked.

"Uh, not that you should have sex with. Unless Willard is game. She joked about being hooked up with one of Zav's brothers once."

Zav stared at me.

"Dragons are sexy," I told him.

"I know this."

"I think Dr. Walker would be a better match for her though. I'm still trying to hook them up. If my mom can get a werewolf, Willard should be able to get a lion shifter."

"And I should have many humans to mate with at your wedding." Xilneth nodded, following his own special brand of logic. "You may also mate with me during your bachelorette party, Ruin Bringer. Is this not a human custom?"

"*What?*" Zav roared.

"I don't think many humans mate with other people during their bachelor and bachelorette parties, despite rumors of promiscuity happening during them. I'm not planning to."

"Promiscuity? Mating?" Zav radiated displeasure. "What is this *bachelorette* party?"

"A get-together a month or so before the wedding, but it's very tame. Or at least mine will be. I'll probably just have some sparkling water at the coffee shop with Willard, Freysha, and Amber. There's a bachelor party for the groom too. It should also be tame."

"Tame?" Xilneth said. "Water-drinking? This is not at all what I have heard described by humans. I was looking forward to a raucous event with much sex."

"You're a horny dragon, Xilneth," I said.

"He is young." Zav curled a lip in disgust. "And has been rejected by all available female dragons."

"That's not true." Xilneth raised his chin. "I rejected some of *them*."

"Lies are dishonorable." Zav frowned at him.

"It is not a lie. Zondia'qareshi has complimented my magnificent wingspan and appealing musculature more than once."

"My *sister*!" Zav was roaring again. "You propositioned my sister?"

"She is interested in *me*."

"She is *not*. I will punish you for your impudence!"

Zav sprang for him, but Xilneth sprinted back to the tunnel. Zav raced after him, leaving me alone with Chasmmoor and Sindari.

"You are brave to wed a dragon," Chasmmoor said.

I concur, Sindari told me. *And not at all mediocre.*

"Thanks, guys." I had a feeling my wedding was going to be very memorable. I hoped I survived it.

EPILOGUE

AFTER MAKING ARRANGEMENTS WITH Chasmmoor to pick him up in a couple of days, Zav brought us back to Earth at my mother's house so I could check on her. It turned out to be five in the morning Seattle time, but she was awake and at the kitchen table, drinking coffee and sharing a newspaper… with Liam.

They were both dressed, so I didn't assume they'd been bed frolicking—though I supposed that was a possibility. Neither appeared flustered or embarrassed when I strolled in with Zav, not that many things embarrassed my mom. I wasn't sure she was capable of the emotion.

She stood and hugged me—a rare gesture from her and a testament that she'd been worried.

"There is a werewolf in your food preparation area," Zav stated.

"That's my neighbor," Mom said. "He's been sticking around in case more of those weird *creatures* come."

Zav eyed Liam. As far as I'd seen, Zav didn't have an aversion toward werewolves or other shifters unless they were on his criminals list, but maybe he was concerned for my mother? So far, he hadn't openly cozied up to any of my family members, but he *had* been willing to defend Amber from trouble.

"He has lustful thoughts," Zav stated.

Liam blinked. So did Mom.

Good grief, was *that* what Zav had been checking?

"Not toward me, right?" I also eyed Liam, who had, at first, faced Zav's scrutiny with equilibrium but now appeared flustered.

"Toward your mother," Zav stated.

Mom set down her paper slowly, her mouth dangling open and her cheeks growing pink. Huh. It turned out she *could* be embarrassed.

"I think that's allowed," I said.

"I am unfamiliar with human-werewolf rules of propriety, but if he mates with your mother, he should be invited to the wedding."

"Everyone else is coming," I said. "He might as well. Though I trust the mating won't be done *at* the wedding. After all, Mom has a sauna for that."

"Nobody is *mating*," Mom whispered harshly, her cheeks even pinker now. "We're just having coffee."

"The sauna..." Zav mused, brows rising as he peered out the window at it. Three minutes back in the damp November air, and he was already thinking of shedding his robe and going inside.

My phone buzzed, surprising me. Even though I'd avoided using it for much on Dun Kroth, I was surprised the battery wasn't dead.

Have you returned from your adventures yet? Nin texted. *We must have a meeting at the coffee shop this morning.*

Adventures, right. A near-death experience was more like it. Maybe Mom hadn't told Dimitri that I'd been slurped into a box alongside a dastardly enemy. Or maybe she had, and Dimitri hadn't thought much of it and only told Nin that I'd been out of town.

I'm out at my mom's place, I texted her. *I can be there in an hour or two.*
Good. It is important.

"We need to go to the coffee shop," I told Zav.

"I require food."

"We can find a drive-through on the way." I glanced at the clock. "One that opens early. How do you feel about breakfast burritos?"

When we had our morning meals together at home, Zav usually had more of what he'd had for dinner. Ribs, hamburgers, and other types of meat. Since cereal, toast, and oatmeal were of no interest to him, I hadn't bothered taking him out for breakfast before.

"What are breakfast burritos?" he asked.

"After you're done incinerating the burrito part and the non-appealing interior bits... eggs."

"Eggs are acceptable but small. I will need a great many."

"I have no doubt. It's hard work killing a lich."

Mom's and Liam's eyebrows lifted.

"Also satisfying my mate in the nest. Great vigor is required."

The eyebrows climbed higher.

"It was a cave, not a nest," I muttered, my own cheeks heating.

"Next time it will be our nest." Zav wrapped an arm around my shoulders.

"Here on Earth, we call it a bed." I decided I wouldn't bring up Zav's tendency to add blankets around the edges and turn the bed *into* something like a nest. Changing the subject, I nodded to Mom and Liam and said, "You two are welcome to join us at the coffee shop. I trust your one cup hasn't suitably caffeinated you for the day." I waved to the pair of mugs on the table.

Liam started to shake his head—most werewolves tended toward being reclusive, and his remote home on this dead-end street suggested he was that type—but Mom said, "I'll come."

"As will I," Liam said.

"You owe me a bag of beans," Mom told me.

"I do?"

"Your goblin ate mine."

"He's not my goblin. And he installed magical yard art for you. I saw the gargoyles on either side of the driveway."

"I'm your retired mom, Val. You're supposed to give me gifts."

"Oh, okay. Will you wear shoes?"

"No."

"You're not like other moms, you know."

"You're not like other daughters."

My phone buzzed, another early bird. It was Willard wanting an update on Li. When Willard said *update,* she meant a thorough report of no fewer than ten pages.

"How did everyone hear so soon that I was back on Earth?" I muttered.

Zav rested a hand on his chest. "I have been informing people that we vanquished our enemies, that you will soon have a tutor to instruct you about your sword, and that the wedding can proceed soon."

I looked at Zav. "So *you're* the reason I have to write a report this morning?"

"I do not know about reports, but I require eggs now."

"Of course you do." I patted his stomach. "Mom, know what you're getting into if you date someone who isn't fully human."

"A werewolf isn't quite the same as a dragon," Liam murmured.

"You better measure your kitchen and see how many commercial appliances you can fit in," I told her. "Have you ever used a smoker?"

"We're just having coffee," she insisted, though her cheeks were pink again.

Better hers than mine.

***

It was light out by the time we made it to Fremont and found parking a block away from the coffee shop. Liam and I, like normal if slightly magical people, were wearing boots. Mom was barefoot, despite the chilly autumn puddles proliferating the sidewalks, and Zav wore his Crocs, though they were scuffed and charred after his dealings with the lich.

Maybe they would fall apart, irreparable even by dragon magic, and he would be forced to select new footwear. I still had the fantasy of having some shoes made for him, but I hadn't had any time to shop, nor did I know where to go for custom footwear. Maybe Amber would.

When we stepped inside, the coffee shop was as busy as usual, but the two police officers standing with Nin and Dimitri in the back were not usual. With a surge of guilt, I realized I'd forgotten all about Dimitri, the door knockers, and the murder investigation.

Nin spotted us, hurried over, and patted my arm. "You must do something, Val. I have explained to the detectives what I believe *really* happened, corroborated by accounts provided by the neighbors, but they insist on arresting Dimitri. Our business cannot run without the CEO and majority shareholder here to supervise."

"Dimitri is the CEO? Did we have a meeting to decide that? Because I have concerns."

"Val, you must be serious."

The detective handcuffed Dimitri. This was further along than I'd realized.

"Zav?" I touched his arm. "Can you help? Dimitri is in trouble."

"You wish me to scare away those uniformed men who wish to incarcerate him?"

"They'll only come back if that's all we do."

"I cannot incinerate members of a sentient species, and if these are not criminals, I cannot take them to the Justice Court for punishment and rehabilitation."

"Uh, no, that's not what I want. Probably." Was it wrong to fantasize about the detectives being dragged off to face Zav's huge, angry, scaled mother? "Convincing them to listen to and *believe* Nin would be best. Can you do that?" I looked hopefully at him.

He'd once nearly convinced *me* to do things on his behalf, when we'd first met and before I'd informed him how annoying that was. Surely, he could mentally nudge the officers into deciding Dimitri was innocent... and ideally into forgetting this coffee shop existed.

Zav studied the men thoughtfully. "Their minds *are* simple, as with all humans on this world."

"So simple you could gently convince them to leave Dimitri and the shop alone without putting up a fight?"

"Hm."

Did that mean he didn't know if he could, or he didn't know if he cared enough to try?

The police had succeeded in cuffing Dimitri—his shoulders were slumped, and he didn't protest until they were ushering him toward the door, and he saw me.

"Val!" he blurted. "Can you do something about this? Please? Convince them I didn't have anything to do with that guy's death." He looked toward Chopper's hilt poking over my shoulder, and I had a feeling he wanted me to convince them with force rather than words.

"Val?" Nin looked imploringly at me and then more hesitantly toward Zav. She didn't presume to ask him for a favor.

"The coffee shop *is* named after you," I murmured to Zav. "It would be unseemly if you let the owner be arrested."

"It is named after a *weasel*."

"Only the color. The dragon part is definitely you. There aren't any other dragons who come here."

"They would not *dare*. I have magically marked this establishment and claimed it."

Nin blinked at this revelation. I'd assumed the magic that kept most mundane people from wandering in had been Dimitri's enchantment, but maybe not entirely.

"Good." I pushed Zav into the path of the policemen. "Protect Dimitri, please. I need him for the wedding. He plays an important role."

"Oh? Very well." Zav lifted his hands, magic ebbing from his fingers, and the policemen lurched to a halt.

"I should have started with that," I muttered.

"I am Lord Zavryd'nokquetal." He put his fists on his hips and blocked the exit while facing the men. "You will not remove this human from the premises."

I thought they might scoff at him, but he radiated power, and people at nearby tables picked up their coffees and got out of the way.

"Explain his innocence," Zav told Nin without looking away from the officers. They were gazing at him, their jaws slack, their eyes unblinking.

Nin hurried forward and spoke, sharing everything she'd learned from the baker's neighbors and even more information that I hadn't heard yet. She zipped through how she'd researched the dead man, found he had a history of abusing women, and believed it was very likely that the distraught baker had arranged for his death, since he refused to leave her alone.

"If you question her, you will get the answers you need, and learn that Dimitri had nothing to do with the death," Nin told them. "*She* was the one to modify the door knocker. Search in the basement. You will see that she has tools that she used."

"We will question the baker and search in the basement," the officers mumbled in unison, their eyes still glazed.

"That's a little creepy," Liam whispered to my mom.

"You get used to it," Mom surprised me by saying.

"You will leave now and not return to this structure." Zav lifted a hand, and the bracelet that I'd suspected allowed one of the detectives to sense this place floated off his wrist. It plopped down into someone's coffee mug.

The two policemen marched toward the door with the stiffness of robots, Zav stepping aside so they could exit. Their stiff gaits continued as they walked down the street to their car, got in, and drove off.

"*Thank* you." Dimitri slumped in relief, then lifted his hands. "But, uhm, they forgot to unlock these. Do you think you can…?"

Zav incinerated the handcuffs with a puff of smoke. Impressive since they were made of metal. I would have guessed metal had to be melted instead of incinerated, but dragon magic *was* amazing.

"Thank you," Dimitri repeated, though he winced as he rubbed his wrists, which were perhaps now lacking in arm hair. "I owe you a big favor. Is there anything I can make for you? Or do for the wedding?" He looked at Zav and me.

I started to say no, but a familiar voice spoke from the doorway. "He needs a bachelor party."

Willard stood there and smirked when I looked over at her.

"What are you doing here?" I asked, though I could guess.

From Mom's house, I'd texted Willard to let her know I was back, the thief was dead, and the lich controlling the dwarven world was no more. As I'd suspected, she had asked for a thorough report for her records, and I'd made the mistake of saying I hadn't been on assignment for her and therefore wasn't required to write up a report. I suspected she'd come to get that report in person.

"Bachelor party?" Zav frowned. "This is the event you discussed with Xilnethgarish? With promiscuous mating?"

"No, no." I lifted my hands. "Like I told him, it'll be a sedate gathering of friends at the coffee shop."

"I do not like coffee."

"You can have sparkling mineral water."

"That is sufficient."

"That's not quite the description of bachelor parties I've heard." Dimitri scratched the side of his head.

"Dragons are special and need special gatherings." I made a cutting motion with my hand, hoping he wouldn't go into more details about bachelor parties.

"That's a given. I guess I can figure something out."

"It doesn't have to be as sedate as Thorvald suggested." Willard stepped up to my side. "Her bachelorette party won't be sedate."

"I was thinking I wouldn't have one of those." I was too old for raucous parties, wasn't I? And what did I need male strippers for when I had a sexy dragon?

"Think again." Willard's eyes were still twinkling. Wedding planning sure brought out her light side. "I have ideas. I'll tell you about them after you give me your report."

"Won't that be fun?" I muttered as she headed to a table.

Zav touched my arm and pointed to Dimitri. "What role does he play?"

"What?"

"You said he has a role to play in our wedding."

"Oh, he'll probably be your best man, unless you're able to convince a male dragon friend to do the job." I hoped not. Everything would be confusing enough without any more non-humans playing important roles in the wedding. "Xilneth, perhaps?"

"I do not know what a best man is, but Xilnethgarish will not be it."

"Dimitri will be tickled to know he has the job."

Dimitri arched his eyebrows but didn't protest, given that Zav had just saved him from being arrested.

"Hm." Zav didn't yet appear convinced.

"Maybe we should start with the party." Dimitri grabbed a pen and notepad off a counter. "What kind of mineral water do you want? And do you care if other people drink? I have a feeling the party will go over better with the guests if they're drunk. Should we invite the goblins?"

"I'll leave you two to figure out the details." I patted Zav on the shoulder and headed over to join Willard.

Before I reached her table, my phone rang.

"Hey, Amber. Everything okay?"

"You didn't show up for the second dress fitting."

"Uh, was that yesterday?" I didn't know what day it was or how long I'd been on the dwarven world. The days and nights there had been *long*.

"It was. There's a twenty-dollar charge if you miss your appointments. Do you need me to take you down there personally?"

"That's not necessary." I imagined Amber riding her bike all the way down here to get me. "I won't need to leave Earth to battle liches and retrieve my sword from dwarven thieves again anytime soon. I hope."

"I don't think that excuse is going to save you from the no-show fee."

"No? Should I say I was sick?"

"You should have *called. Before* leaving the planet. I can't believe I have to tell you these things."

"I was sucked through an interstellar portal with no time to make phone calls before I left. Will *that* get me out of the no-show fee?"

"Ugh, Val. *I'll* pay the twenty dollars if you *don't* say any of that stuff to the bridal people."

"Deal." I set my hand on the back of a chair at Willard's table and casually asked, "How are things going at school?"

"Fine."

"Any decoy-boyfriend news?"

"I gotta go." Amber hung up.

Willard raised her eyebrows as I lowered the phone.

"Amber is opening up to me more these days."

"It sounded like she was lecturing you."

"That's how she opens up."

"Being a parent must be interesting," Willard said.

"So my mother tells me." I slid into the seat to give an oral report—hopefully, that would suffice—to Willard.

While I spoke, Gondo and several of his goblin buddies came in. They joined Dimitri and Zav, with Gondo jumping up and down and pointing at Dimitri's notepad as he spewed what might be ideas for the bachelor party.

"I think my second wedding is going to be a lot different from my first," I observed.

"You're just now realizing that?" Willard asked.

"I realize it anew every day."

"I was hoping to make it proper and respectable for you. Now, after speaking with Zav several times, I'm just hoping we can avoid goblins, ogres, and dragons burning down the city."

"That seems like a good goal to have."

"Hopefully, not a naively ambitious one."

"We'll find out."

THE END

"Any decoy-boyfriend news?"

"I gotta go." Amber hung up.

Willard raised her eyebrows as I lowered the phone.

"Amber is opening up to me more these days."

"It sounded like she was lecturing you."

"That's how she opens up."

"Being a parent must be interesting," Willard said.

"So my mother tells me." I slid into the seat to give an oral report—hopefully, that would suffice—to Willard.

While I spoke, Gondo and several of his goblin buddies came in. They joined Dimitri and Zav, with Gondo jumping up and down and pointing at Dimitri's notepad as he spewed what might be ideas for the bachelor party.

"I think my second wedding is going to be a lot different from my first," I observed.

"You're just now realizing that?" Willard asked.

"I realize it anew every day."

"I was hoping to make it proper and respectable for you. Now, after speaking with Zav several times, I'm just hoping we can avoid goblins, ogres, and dragons burning down the city."

"That seems like a good goal to have."

"Hopefully, not a naively ambitious one."

"We'll find out."

THE END

Made in United States
Orlando, FL
30 November 2023